Written in Blood

Rebecca Deel

ISBN: 1979733465
ISBN-13: 978-1979733465

DEDICATION

To my amazing husband.

ACKNOWLEDGMENTS

Cover design by Melody Simmons.

CHAPTER ONE

Megan Cahill turned and froze. Prickles of fear crawled down her spine as a chill December wind rattled bare branches and scattered leaves along a trail that disappeared into shifting shadows.

Her friend, Sherri, tugged on her arm. "Let's go. Now."

Meg nodded and matched Sherri's quick pace, wishing she had not agreed to meet her friend in such a deserted area at four o'clock in the morning. Meg's suggestion for an early morning coffee shop meeting appealed even more at the moment. Twigs cracked in the semi-darkness on Churchill Trail. A deer?

"Don't stop." Sherri's voice quivered.

Footsteps thudded behind them, footsteps too heavy for a deer. Too fast for an early morning jog, too dark to wait and see if she was wrong. Meg's adrenaline spiked. "Move it, Sherri!" She broke into a run.

"I'm sorry, Meg. I shouldn't have involved you."

A shot rang out. The bullet skimmed bark from a tree to her left. Meg flinched and swerved right. Evasions might throw off the shooter's aim.

Sherri screamed and ducked, stumbling. She righted herself and plunged ahead.

Meg dropped back a step. Just one look. She wanted a name or description to give the police. "Hurry, Sherri!" She glanced over her shoulder. Gloom and tree limbs concealed the shooter's identity.

Footsteps drummed closer. Meg slowed as much as she dared. Every second gave Sherri, a slower runner, a better chance to reach the car. Hair rose on the nape of her neck. The runner was gaining ground. Meg sprinted for the car.

Legs and lungs burning, she hurried toward the parking area. As Meg approached the trail entrance, Sherri jammed her key into the door lock. Hope surged. A few more feet to safety.

Footsteps hammered behind Meg, edging closer, until a hand shoved her headlong into the stone wall at the entrance. Stunned, she lay motionless on the dirt, the scent of molded leaves assaulting her nose.

Sherri's scream shattered the silence.

Gritting her teeth, Meg told herself to get up, but her hands moved an inch instead of pushing her to a sitting position. "Move, move," Meg whispered. She must help Sherri. A shot splintered the stillness. Meg forced weight onto her hands and knees. The ground tilted.

Footsteps again. Coming closer. Not Sherri. Meg's jaw clenched. If death awaited her, she wanted to face her killer. She turned her head in time to see a sneaker-clad foot arch toward her.

Meg twisted away from the attack. Pain exploded from her back as she collapsed once more against the stones.

Lights flashed. Someone cocked a gun and pressed it to the back of her head. Pine fragrance merged with the scent of decaying leaves. As blackness closed in, she wondered if her sisters would lay pine wreaths on her grave.

Rod Kelter's hand fumbled around the nightstand, searching for the ringing phone. He located the handset and, without opening his eyes, punched the talk button. "Yeah. Kelter."

"Dead body and an assault victim on Churchill Trail."

He squinted at the clock. 4:30 a.m. "Santana's tied up?"

"Robbery at the bar."

Busy night in Otter Creek. "I'll roll in ten." He flung aside the covers and stumbled into the bathroom. After a hasty shower, he dressed in warm clothes and slipped his badge and holstered weapon onto his belt.

Rod swung into the parking lot at 4:47, stopped beside the ambulance and moved to the officer waiting by his cruiser. "Run it down."

"Looks like a robbery gone bad." The patrol officer inclined his head toward the Mercedes coupe to his right. "DB's on the other side of the car. No ID."

Rod studied the vehicle, frowning. It looked familiar. Not surprising, he supposed. Otter Creek was a small Tennessee town, after all. He knew most of the citizens by sight if not by name. "What about the assault vic?"

"In the ambulance. EMTs arrived same time I did."

"ID?"

"Megan Cahill."

Rod spun around, concern knotting his stomach. "Did you call Blackhawk?"

"She wouldn't let me. Said her brother-in-law hovers too much, and she only needed a couple of band-aids." The officer cleared his throat. "She threatened to follow me around for weeks with her camera if I called the chief."

Rod scowled at the patrol officer and ran to the ambulance. How badly was she hurt? His lips curled. Meg had probably been chasing a story. The *Gazette's* editor may have uncovered a lead someone preferred buried. He jerked open the door and climbed into the back.

An EMT glanced at him and nodded in greeting.

"How is she?" Rod asked, assessing her obvious injuries.

"Forehead laceration, bruising, scratches, maybe cracked ribs."

Megan stirred. Blue eyes opened. "Tell this goober to let me sit up. I'm fine."

Relief swept aside his concern. For once, he appreciated her sassy response. "You're supposed to cover news, Cahill, not make it. Want to avoid an ambulance ride? Get up and climb out under your own steam."

Determination morphed into a grimace and groans as Meg strained to rise. Rod shook his head. "Enough. You need medical attention." He eased her back against the stretcher.

The EMT maneuvered passed Rod. "We should get her to the hospital."

"Hold on a sec." He refocused on Meg. "What happened?"

"Met a friend at the half-mile bench. Somebody chased us, shot at us." Her gaze latched onto his face. "Nobody will tell me about Sherri. Is she okay?"

Dread pooled in Rod's stomach. Now he remembered who owned the Mercedes. "Sherri Drake?"

"Is she all right?" Meg gripped his arm with surprising strength. "Tell me the truth, Rod."

He patted Meg's hand, maintaining a bland expression. "I haven't checked on her yet."

"Tell me as soon as you know. Please."

"Want me to call your family?"

She jerked her hand away. "When I'm ready to leave the hospital."

He grinned. "Tough reporters can handle overzealous family members, Cahill."

"Not when my head feels like a nuclear explosion in progress." She eyed his pocket. "Hey, I need a couple sheets of paper from your notepad." She yanked a blue pen from her jacket. "Your cop cohort confiscated my notebook and I need to write all this down."

He rolled his eyes, but did as she asked. "No interviews with reporters or other *Gazette* personnel until I talk to you at the hospital."

A half snarl formed on her lips. Rod squeezed her hand and climbed from the ambulance. After the vehicle left, he moved toward the Mercedes, motioning to the patrolman. "Set up a barrier at least 500 feet away. I don't want civvies breathing down my neck. No press either, not until we make a positive ID and notify the family."

"Yes, sir."

Rod retrieved his crime scene case from the SUV and approached the body with a growing sense of reluctance. He aimed his flashlight at the body and knelt to examine the woman's face. His stomach clenched. Rod dreaded telling Ty Drake his wife had been murdered.

The patrolman returned. "Can you ID the vic?"

Rod stood. "It's Sherri Drake."

"Drake?" He gaped. "She related to Senator Drake?"

"His daughter-in-law."

"Oh, man, it'll be a media circus around here."

"We need to keep a lid on this for a couple of hours. Otherwise, we'll have reporters crawling through the woods, trampling clues."

"Yes, sir."

He tossed his keys to the patrolman. "Park my SUV behind Meg's Corvette. Her parents live near here."

Rod grabbed his cell phone. He needed help locking down the crime scene, fast. He flipped open the phone and punched his speed dial.

A deep growl answered his ring. "Ethan, I need you at Churchill Trail. Don't say anything to Serena yet, but someone assaulted Megan. We found another woman murdered."

One word came over the line. "Who?"

"Sherri Drake."

"Fifteen minutes."

Rod's mouth curved. Before Blackhawk married Meg's sister, he arrived at crime scenes within ten minutes. Marriage had slowed him down.

Ignoring the ache in his heart, he scrolled through his phone list and punched the number for Otter Creek PD's other detective, Nick Santana, Megan Cahill's other brother-in-law. Rod's crime scene extended half a mile down the trail, too large to process in an expedited manner without assistance.

"Santana."

"I need another pair of hands."

"Where?"

"Churchill Trail. Nick, Meg's in route to the hospital."

"What happened?" Cold fury seeped from Santana's voice.

"Somebody attacked her and killed Sherri Drake. Meg didn't want your wife or the rest of the Cahill family to know yet, but I need help processing this crime scene before the media descends."

"I'll be there in two minutes."

Rod tugged on latex gloves and returned to the body. One shot in the back, center mass, the white wool coat soaked with blood. Sherri had been running away. He hoped the coroner could retrieve the bullet intact.

Tires squealed as Nick Santana's SUV swung into the parking lot. He climbed from the vehicle, cell phone pressed to his ear. "A few more hours, baby. I'll bring you breakfast at the knitting shop. Love you, Madison." He ended the call and shoved the phone into his carrier. "What have you cleared, Rod?"

"Right side. The path is marked."

Santana approached the body, stepping between the markers. "Did you talk to Meg?"

"Briefly. She met Sherri. Shooter fired and chased them down."

"Robbery?"

"Meg didn't say."

The other detective stared at Sherri's back. "One shot. A .38?"

"Possible."

Backing away from the body, Santana said, "How can I help?"

"Meg met Sherri at the half-mile bench. Take a patrol officer and work your way to the bench."

Santana retrieved his crime scene case, waved over one of the rookies, and walked down the path, flashlight in hand.

Rod searched the parking lot in a grid pattern, bagging items which didn't belong, working toward Sherri. A few feet from her body, the flashlight beam illuminated a round, metal object. He bent closer. A button with an initial "D" engraved in script.

He recognized the distinctive Drake monogram. Did the button come from Sherri's coat? Maybe she lost the button while struggling with the shooter.

Headlights bounced across the tree line. The police chief's SUV slid to a stop behind Rod's. Ethan climbed out and zipped his jacket. "Talk to me."

Rod gave him a brief run down, ending with the bagged button in his hand. While he talked, Ethan scanned the crime scene, a grim expression on his face.

"Show me where the EMTs found Meg."

Rod walked with him to the stone entrance and pointed to the disturbed earth and blood-stained leaves. "Found her unconscious, head against the base of that wall."

Ethan crouched and studied the ground. "She fell or was pushed off the path right here. Looks like she tried to get up." He pointed at the depression and scuff marks in the dirt. "Overlapping shoe prints." Ethan glanced up. "Did you check the EMTs for print patterns?"

Rod shook his head. "No time. They were in a hurry to leave with Megan."

"How bad is she?"

"Cut on her forehead might need stitches. Otherwise, the injuries look minor. Possible internal injuries, though."

"You're positive about the vic's ID?"

"Yeah. I was an usher at Ty and Sherri's wedding."

Ethan stood. "You okay on this or should I give this one to Nick?"

"I'm fine. If it becomes a problem, I'll step aside." He owed it to Ty to track down his wife's killer.

"I'll notify the family, then, and return to help."

Megan frowned at the nurse checking her blood pressure for the millionth time. "Can't you copy the last reading on the chart and skip the rest? I'm all right. When can I get out of here?"

The nurse cocked an eyebrow. "You're free to leave after the doctor releases you, Ms. Cahill."

"And when will that be? Christmas?"

"Early afternoon if he doesn't keep you for overnight observation."

Meg glowered. Spend the night here? Not with an immovable deadline looming in 36 hours—press time. "Why?"

The nurse smirked. "High blood pressure."

Meg settled against the raised mattress, eyes narrowed. The *Gazette* went to press tomorrow night, and she still had four articles to write or farm out and edit. J.J. was holding the front page for Meg's story, but learning Sherri's condition ranked first on her priority list. Second was sending Madison or Serena for her laptop.

A light tap sounded on the door. Rod Kelter flashed his badge at the nurse who nodded, removed the blood pressure cuff, and left.

The red-haired detective paused beside the bed, watching her. "How do you feel?"

She touched the white bandage on her forehead. "Like Frankenstein's wife, thanks." Her gaze scoured his face. "How's Sherri? The medical staff wouldn't tell me anything."

Something flashed in Rod's eyes. Sympathy? Meg's heart sank. "Rod?"

"I'm sorry, Megan. Sherri didn't make it."

Sharp anguish struck deep. Meg closed her pooling eyes, not wanting to lose it in front of a man who had suffered so much sorrow himself. Tears trickled down her cheeks. A warm hand rested on her shoulder. Who hurt Sherri? What about her husband? How would he stand the loss of his wife? She swiped at the tears. "Does Ty know?"

"Ethan told him." Rod shoved his hand into his pocket. "Tell me what happened this morning, in detail."

"I know. Every minute counts in murder investigations." Meg sighed and shifted her weight off the bruised ribs. "Sherri called around midnight and asked me to meet her."

"Why?"

She lifted one shoulder. "Said she didn't want anyone to overhear." Had Sherri been afraid of a family member? What scared her enough for a meeting away from the house after dark? "We agreed to meet at 4:00 a.m."

"Why the trail? Of all people, you should have known better than to meet in an unsecure location at night. Why didn't you suggest a restaurant?"

She scowled. "Just because both brothers-in-law are cops doesn't make me immune from mistakes. Besides, I suggested the coffee shop, but Sherri refused." Meg blinked away more tears. "I don't need grief from you, Rod. I know

9

if I'd pushed harder for a populated meeting place, Sherri might be alive."

"Don't go there, Cahill." Rod's sharp tone brought her gaze to his. "Decisions come with consequences. We live with them because nobody gets do-overs." He waited a beat, then said, "Why did she insist on meeting at the trail?"

"She didn't want anybody to know she talked to me. We didn't have much time before . . . ." Her voice cracked. She cleared her throat and tried again. "Before the shooter arrived."

"How did she seem? Upset, worried, afraid?"

Meg thought through those few minutes with her friend. "Agitated, afraid. Sherri started to tell me about overhearing the Senator's phone conversation."

"Do you know the name of the person talking to the Senator?"

Meg shook her head, cringing when pain increased with the movement. "It always took Sherri forever to tell a story or a joke. Before she gave details on the content, we heard noises behind us."

Rod's hand patted hers. "You're doing great, Cahill. What happened next?"

Meg drew in a deep breath, teeth clenched against her body's protest. "We walked toward the parking lot, but someone started chasing us." She looked away. "I told Sherri to run. He shot at us."

"He?"

"The footsteps were too heavy for a woman. Sherri screamed and stumbled. I dropped back and told her to run."

Rod stared at Megan's pale face, her hand trembling under his. He fought an urge to gather her close. The sassy editor would probably slug him for thinking she was weak or offering sympathy. "You dropped back? Why?"

"Sherri wasn't a fast runner."

His blood ran cold. "What did you plan to do, Cahill? Face down an armed, unknown assailant in the woods with no weapon?"

"Don't go all macho cop on me, Kelter." She jerked her hand away from his. "The shooter was after her, not me."

"You sure about that? You're not exactly everybody's favorite person." She irritated hundreds of people some weeks with her editorials, him included.

Her eyes narrowed. "No death threats this week. Look, I hoped to outrun him, but hamper his aim. His first shot peeled tree bark."

Jaw clenched, he nodded, not trusting himself to speak. Yet. Santana had found the marked tree and the bullet lodged in a nearby oak. He motioned for her to continue.

"When I reached the trail entrance, Sherri jammed her key in the door lock." She covered her face with scratched hands. "I thought she would escape, but the footsteps kept coming closer. He shoved me into the stone wall." She fell silent, dropping her hands to her lap.

Rod sat on the edge of her bed. "Take your time."

"The fall stunned me so much I couldn't move. Sherri screamed and I heard a shot. Then nothing."

He stiffened. "Nothing? Do you mean the shooter ran from the lot, followed by silence?"

"No. I can't remember anything else."

"Planning to expose the murderer yourself?" His face burned. "Don't hold out on me, Cahill."

"One of my best friends is dead and you're accusing me of impeding your investigation?" Meg's voice rose. "Why would I do that?"

"Circulation."

"That's cold, Kelter. We report news. Period."

"Right. Talk me through it again." Rod yanked a notebook from his pocket. "Start at the bench. You heard a noise. What was it?"

Meg closed her eyes, for a moment visualized decking a certain aggravating detective, then replayed the morning's events in her mind. "A cracking sound, like a twig or branch breaking."

"What did you do?"

"Headed for the cars. Then we heard footsteps."

"Running or walking?"

"Running." She shuddered. "Long, ground-eating strides." Strides she knew would haunt her dreams for years to come.

"Did you see anyone?"

"Too dark." Her heartbeat soared as she remembered dense, oppressive darkness, the isolation from people and safety.

By the time she finished reliving the incident with Rod, her headache scaled new heights while her energy level sagged.

Rod stood, tucking his notepad into his pocket. "Look, Meg, I know you believe in freedom of the press. Because you're involved in this case, you're privy to information I wouldn't release to reporters."

Meg crossed her arms. "Every major news team in the country will be here when they find out the Senator's daughter-in-law was murdered."

He scowled. "Don't you want us to collar Sherri's killer?"

"Of course I do."

His face flushed a deep crimson. "So you won't help me?"

"I didn't say that. I promise what goes into print will be discreet. If you ask me to leave something out, I'll do my best to see that it doesn't make the *Gazette*. But I will keep Otter Creek's citizens informed. They deserve the truth."

"I'm not sure Ethan will agree to that arrangement."

"He doesn't have a choice and neither do you."

CHAPTER TWO

A knock at the door brought Meg awake again. She turned her head carefully and waved into the room the blond mirror-image peeking around the door frame. "Hey, Maddie."

Madison engulfed her in an embrace. "Are you all right?"

"I'm fine." At her sister's doubtful glance, she added, "Really. A few bruises." She smiled and pushed her hair away from the bandage. "Look. I'm trying to make it harder for people to tell us apart. Now I'll have a scar, too."

Her sister frowned. "Not funny, Meg."

"I know, but if I don't joke about something connected to this nightmare, I'll end up in tears. Again."

"What did you do to Rod?"

"Nothing, why?"

"Ha. Try again."

"I refused to fall in line with his idea of reporting."

Madison chuckled. "He was pretty steamed walking down the hallway a minute ago. Serena cornered him."

"Wish I could have seen that." With a camera in her hand. Meg envisioned the lifestyle section headline, "Detective Cowed by Chief's Wife."

Serena slipped into the room behind Madison and closed the door. "It was interesting. I'd say Ethan will get an earful before noon." She sat on one side of the bed and tilted her head, speculation in her eyes. "Planning to spill your guts on the front page of the *Gazette*?"

"It would be the scoop of the year in Otter Creek. Who better to report on the crime than a witness." Meg sighed. "I can't, though. I don't remember everything." She wanted to tell Sherri's story. Maybe a series of in-depth articles? But Meg couldn't do that until she knew what was bothering Sherri. Her hands fisted. "And Sherri didn't have the chance to tell me anything before some lowlife pond scum killed her."

Madison sat on the other side of the bed, and the three sisters joined hands, forming a circle. "We're grateful you're safe, Meg."

Megan squeezed their hands. "I don't understand why someone killed Sherri. She wasn't a celebrity attracting a stalker, didn't run with a rough crowd. She didn't take drugs." A wry smile crossed her lips. "She hated taking any drugs, even over-the-counter pain relievers. So no illegal activity which might lead to retaliation."

"Was this just a random act of violence, a crime of opportunity?" Serena asked.

Meg shook her head. "No chance. He shoved me aside to reach her. This guy wanted Sherri dead. I just don't know why." But she would find out, no matter the cost.

"Tell Sherri's story," Madison said. "All of it, not only the murder. Don't let that be the story people remember, Meg."

"People expect the *Gazette* to share information about the investigation. I won't have enough space to do justice to her life story in a few column inches."

"Think bigger than the newspaper," Serena said. "Finish her book."

Meg sat in silence a moment, turning over the idea in her mind. What purpose would it serve? Sherri had asked Meg to write the book and planned to use it as a fund-raiser for The Haven. What would happen to Sherri's dream now? "You really think I should finish the book?"

"I do. At least think about it."

Meg knew it was good advice. But if she followed this story to its conclusion, she was bound to cross paths and swords with Rod Kelter, and interfere with his investigation as he'd accused her earlier. "I'll get in Rod's way. You know that, right?"

Serena laughed. "You're already in his way. What are a few more roadblocks?"

Meg glowered. "He wouldn't dare arrest you for interfering in an investigation. You're married to his boss. If I so much as look at him cross-eyed, he goes into battle mode."

Madison's eyebrow rose. "Battle mode?" She looked at Serena and grinned. "He's never shown that side to me. How about you?"

Serena shook her head. "Nope. Must be reserved for only you, Meg."

Meg sank deeper under the sheet. "Great. How did I rate such special treatment?"

Speculation gleamed in Madison's eyes. "I'd say you matter to him. You get under his skin."

"Yeah, like a rash."

"How can she be so callous? Sherri Drake was her friend." Rod paced in front of Ethan's desk, jerky hand motions punctuating emotions. Anger boiled inside him. "If she interferes in my investigation, I'll toss her in jail. I don't care if she is your sister–in–law."

"Why so much animosity?" Ethan sipped his coffee and set the mug on his desk. "Meg has a strong sense of responsibility to the public, but she has worked with us in the past to control information flow. I find it hard to believe she wouldn't cooperate now when the stakes are so high. What exactly did she tell you?"

Rod relayed the conversation, still pacing.

"Sit down, Rod. Watching you prowl around my office makes me tired." He sat back in his chair. "Look, you're burning a lot of energy better utilized elsewhere. Meg has integrity. You can trust her to do what's right. If she promised to be discreet, she'll do it. The *Gazette* is not going to be our problem. Those media hounds from the major networks are the ones we need to watch."

Ethan tore a sheet from his yellow legal pad, set it aside, and grabbed a pen. "Talk to me about the Drakes. How well do you know this family?"

Rod drew in a deep breath and replaced emotions stirred by the gorgeous, but aggravating Megan Cahill with memories from his past. "Growing up, Kyle Drake and I were best friends until high school. Ty, Sherri's husband, is Kyle's younger brother."

"Were friends? What happened?"

"Warren Drake was elected to the Senate. Kyle and I moved in different circles until college, where we roomed together." He grimaced. "I found out during those four years how much we had changed. I went to UT on scholarship. I spent every free moment studying. Had to maintain the grades. Kyle, on the other hand, spent every free moment rolling from one party or bed to the next."

"Did he graduate?"

"Oh, yeah. He graduated." Rod laughed, some of the bitterness he felt through those hard years surfacing. "Senator Drake would have made sure of it if necessary, but he didn't need strong-arm tactics or a large donation. Kyle has a photographic memory. He majored in political science with a 4.0 grade point average."

"What's the story with Sherri and Ty? Any marital problems?"

"Don't know of any, but I haven't spent much time with Ty in recent years. He always seemed to fall under Kyle's shadow. Where Kyle was outgoing and popular, Ty kept to himself. He was bookish, read everything that fell into his hands."

Ethan jotted notes on his pad. "That's probably what made him a good teacher."

Rod nodded. Ty had taught computer science at Otter Creek Community College for ten years. "He and Sherri seemed happy, but marriages aren't always how they appear on the surface."

Meg dashed into the *Gazette* office in the early afternoon. The headache still throbbed in her brain and her stomach burned, but deadlines were unyielding taskmasters. The paper went to press in twenty-four hours. She still had a feature article to write about the town's proposed water system improvements and the front-page story about Sherri's murder. First stop, her desk drawer and the bottle of antacid tablets.

"Boss, what are you doing here? You look terrible!"

She scowled at the bald and chubby part-time photographer who also ran the press. His mechanical genius kept the equipment running. No easy task on their shoestring budget. "Thanks a lot, J.J."

"Think you might have a black eye by tomorrow? It would make a great front-page picture to go along with the headline."

"Forget it. No battered editor pictures. Too many people might enjoy them." She glanced around the empty office. "Where's Zoe?" Her part-time reporter, part-time receptionist usually sat at the front desk which J.J. now occupied.

"Chasing down the mayor for an interview."

Meg frowned. "I assigned that interview to Amanda."

J.J. shrugged. "She bailed. Said she was moving to Knoxville. She stopped by on her way out of town with the moving truck."

Great. Another vacancy. She'd been working short-staffed since the spring. Now she had only one part-time reporter and J.J.

"What are we going to do, boss?"

"A good question to which I have no answer. Reporters aren't beating down our doors." Meg trudged into her office and sank into her leather chair, the one luxury she allowed herself to purchase when she started the paper. The rest of the furniture and computers were donated or bought at a large discount. Her biggest expense had been the used press.

She grabbed the large bottle in the desk's bottom drawer and popped a couple of antacids in her mouth. She chewed, wrinkling her nose at the chalky cherry taste, and leaned back, closing her eyes. Who could she con into pitching in for a few weeks until she hired another reporter? Somebody able to handle pressure-cooker deadlines. Someone with writing skills whose articles didn't need a total rewrite before they were fit for public consumption.

She toyed with toughing it out for a few weeks, but she couldn't write seventy-five percent of the news stories and expect the paper to remain objective.

Meg rubbed her face with her hands, flinching as she brushed against the bandage covering stitches in her forehead. How could she write an objective front-page article when her anger raged at the killer for running her and Sherri to ground like foxes chased by hounds? As much as she hated to admit it, Rod was right about her knowing too much. She needed someone from the outside to follow the investigation. So who could she hire?

Her eyelids flew up and a grin crossed her face. Of course. The perfect solution. The perfect person. Wonder what Ethan and Rod would say?

"You want me to do what?" Ruth Rollins's eyes widened, her voice pitched high.

"Work for me a few weeks, Ruth. I need somebody to pinch hit as a reporter and you're perfect for the job." Meg pushed the Starbuck's coffee cup across Ruth's dining room table. "Consider this your first cup of coffee as an official journalist."

"But, Meg, I write cozy murder mysteries. I don't know the first thing about being a reporter."

"Sure you do. You meet deadlines. You write a beginning, middle and an end to stories. You structure sentences properly and you can spell."

"I know that's not all there is to reporting." Ruth lifted the cup to her lips and sipped.

"You write murder mysteries for a living, Ruth, and the hottest story going is Sherri's murder. This is your chance to dog Ethan and Rod about their work. Think of it as an extended research opportunity."

Ruth tilted her head. "Well, it would give me a legitimate excuse to watch my nephew work. But, dear, I'm 72 years old. I can't go traipsing around the county at all hours of the night in search of a killer or another breaking news story. I guarantee Ethan would protest."

Protest? A mild word for how Ethan would react if he thought she'd coaxed Ruth into tracking a murderer. "I don't need you to be an investigative reporter. Just attend the news conferences and see what you can learn from the guys at the station about Sherri's case. You look like a kindly grandmother, someone in whom to confide."

The novelist's white eyebrows shot upward. A spark of amusement zipped through Meg. Yeah, that description had been a bit much. Ruth was well known for being the police chief's nosy aunt.

Meg leaned forward, hands clasped on top of the table. "The truth is I can't be objective about this story since I'm involved. I don't want to blow Rod's case by leaking too much information. I'll track down whatever information you want, conduct the interviews, give you my notes." She slid a piece of paper from her jacket pocket and handed it to Ruth. "This is a friend's number. He's in town and with the *Knoxville Sentinel*. Compare what you have to the regular media so we're sure not to leak important information before Ethan and Rod want it out there."

"What about other stories? Can I write other things as well?"

Meg maintained a blank expression. She knew Ruth well enough by now to realize her novelist friend was hooked. "You can write about anything you want or I can assign you stories like I would a real reporter. Which would you prefer?"

Ruth considered her options for a minute. "I want real assignments." She narrowed her eyes. "What about you? You aren't planning to sit on the sidelines. Will you work on Sherri's murder?"

"In a way. I don't want Otter Creek to forget who Sherri was as a person. I have to write about her, Ruth. She was my friend and someone stole her future. I'm going to write a series of articles on Sherri, but not about the murder. I want people to know how special she was. Maybe her story will inspire others to overcome adversity like she did."

"So, when's my first deadline?"

"Tomorrow afternoon at 4:00. That will be enough time to get your copy in the system, edit it, proof it, and get it into the mid-week edition." Barely.

Ruth laughed. "No pressure. Any words of advice before I begin this new venture?"

"Just answer the questions who, what, when, where, why, and how."

"Well, then, let me find some paper and we'll begin. I have a deadline to meet. You're my first assignment and I hear my boss is a tyrant."

Rod drove by Megan's house for the third time, checked the rearview mirror, completed a U-turn and pulled into the driveway behind a department SUV. He couldn't tell whether the vehicle belonged to Meg's brother Josh or Nick Santana. It wouldn't be unusual for either of them to stop after work and check on her.

Just like he was doing, though he couldn't figure out why.

Megan Cahill wasn't a close friend. She made him angry more often than not and seemed to enjoy it too much. He scowled and shoved open his door. He was here to check on a witness, see if she remembered anything else that might help their investigation. Nothing else.

Right. So what was the panic he'd experienced this morning when he learned Megan was the assault victim? Simply worry for an annoying friend and his boss's sister-in-law, he assured himself.

He needed to talk to her again about articles in the paper concerning the case. Despite Ethan's assurances, he wanted more of a commitment from the newspaper's editor not to compromise his investigation.

He climbed the porch stairs, rang the bell and waited. When the door opened, he nodded at Josh. "How is Meg?"

The six-foot Army special forces soldier motioned him inside. "Stubborn as ever. She needs medicine and sleep, but says she can't stop working yet."

Rod glanced around the living room, curious what made Megan Cahill tick, though not surprised by what greeted him. Books stacked three rows deep on floor-to-ceiling bookcases, towers of books on the floor, mini-mounds on coffee tables and the television. A leather couch and love-seat hosted a couple of paperbacks each.

Since his reading consisted of law enforcement journals and the occasional murder mystery, Meg's love affair with the written word intrigued him. Rod stepped closer to one of the stacks and read the titles. His lips curled at the corners. Otter Creek harbored a criminal in training. Bookmarks held Meg's place in reading about cracking safes, picking locks and counterfeiting money. "She has an eclectic taste in reading, doesn't she?"

Josh chuckled. "Meg is always reading weird stuff. I prefer a good Robert B. Parker book."

"I hear you." Rod shifted his gaze from Meg's book stash to her brother. "I need to talk to Meg again if she's up to it."

"If I can get her attention away from the computer, I'll tell her you're here."

Rod surveyed the room again. Megan needed a few more bookcases. A nice oak stain would fit well in her living room. He inspected the overflowing bookcases and guesstimated on the height and width.

Josh re-entered the room. "Meg needs to finish a paragraph before she loses her train of thought. Want a Coke while you wait?"

"Thanks."

Josh shot him a knowing look. "Had dinner yet?"

"No time."

"Sit." Josh nodded at the bar stools near the counter. "Do you like roast beef?"

Rod's mouth watered at the mere thought. "Sure."

"Good. I'll make both of us a sandwich. Meg's not a domestic diva. If I depended on her to feed me, I'd starve."

Josh slid a can of Coke across the counter to him and returned to the refrigerator for bread, meat, mayonnaise and mustard. Rod popped the tab on the cold Coke and took a long drink. The sugar rush lifted his flagging energy.

"How's the investigation going?"

"About like you'd expect with a media circus. Reporters are on my heels the second I step outside the station. I had to duck out the back door when I left tonight so I wouldn't lead them straight to Meg's door."

"I appreciate that," Meg said, walking into the kitchen. She sniffed. "Roast beef?"

"Want a sandwich?" Josh asked.

"I'm not really hungry."

"When did you last eat?" Rod asked.

She shrugged. "I can't remember."

"Then it's been too long. Make her a sandwich, too, Josh."

Meg eased onto a stool across from Rod. "Make it half of one, Bro. And could you turn off the overhead light?"

Rod studied her face, noting the pallor and careful movements. "Pain still bad?"

"Getting worse by the hour."

"When can you shut it down for the night?"

"As soon as I eat and take pain medicine."

Rod frowned at her. "Why didn't you take something sooner?" She looked almost fragile, something he never thought he'd connect with the gritty editor.

Meg's mouth curved. "The paper goes to press tomorrow night, with or without articles. I'd prefer something in those columns besides a string of Zs. Prescription pain meds knock me out."

His lips twitched. He couldn't imagine Meg Cahill surrendering easily to medicine-induced sleep.

She palmed the Coke and medicine Josh handed her. She swallowed the pill and faced Rod. "What do you need, Detective? Did you think of something else to ask me?"

Josh placed a plate with two sandwiches in front of Rod and one with half a sandwich for Meg on the counter. "Eat before that medicine kicks in."

She made a face at him. "Yes, Mother."

Josh snorted. "You're just lucky Mom and Dad left town last night. Otherwise, Mom would be camped out in your extra bedroom instead of me."

"You're not staying with me."

"Want to try kicking me out?"

She glared at him, grabbed her sandwich and took a bite.

Josh grinned and walked out of the kitchen.

Neither Rod nor Meg talked for a while. As he ate, Rod watched Meg tear apart her sandwich and eat tiny bites off one piece. He figured she was having a hard time dealing with the aftermath of the murder, something that would affect her appetite for a while.

He ate most meals on autopilot. He also knew from experience he'd skip more meals than he should while investigating Sherri's death. He buried himself in cases and forgot to eat. Erin used to make sure he ate at least once a day. Now, no one cared if he ate.

He chewed the last bite of his second sandwich and rose. Rod placed his bare plate in the dishwasher and noticed her empty glass. He opened the refrigerator and brought another Coke to the counter.

"Thanks."

"Have you remembered anything else since I talked to you at the hospital?" Rod seated himself next to Meg.

She gave him an almost imperceptible shake of her head.

He pulled one of his business cards from his pocket, grabbed a pen and scribbled his cell phone number on the back. He slid the card beside her plate. "Call me if you remember something during the night."

Meg quirked an eyebrow. "A writer's muse strikes at odd hours of the night. What if it's 2:00 a.m.?"

His lips twitched, knowing she meant the comment as a joke. "Cops keep weird hours too. Call no matter what time it is." He would probably be awake anyway. He hadn't slept through a whole night since his wife and daughter died. "Even if you don't remember anything but can't sleep, call me."

Suspicion gleamed in her eyes. "Why the generous offer, Detective?"

"When the medicine wears off, your mind will replay this morning's events. You'll analyze every minute you remember, do what-if scenarios." He shrugged. "It's how people work through the shock, the disbelief, the grief."

Meg dropped her gaze and reached for her glass, hand trembling. "I'm familiar with the process."

Rod stilled, his gaze focused on her face. The echo of haunting memories played across her features. "What happened?"

"I lost a cousin in a bank heist in Las Vegas two years ago. A robber shot her when she didn't move fast enough to suit him. She died in my arms."

He covered her hand with his, squeezed. "I'm sorry." A close look at her grim features sparked another question. "Think you could walk through the crime scene with me tomorrow?"

Meg's gaze shot to his face. "Why?"

"Any information you offer will be a great help."

"You don't have any leads." Her voice rose, outrage evident.

He frowned. "I didn't say that."

"You don't have to."

"Look, Cahill, you're our best witness. Will you cooperate or not?"

"After the paper's put to bed."

Irritation flared inside Rod. "What time will that be?"

"If nothing goes wrong with the press, around nine o'clock tomorrow night."

"You can't get around to helping me any sooner?"

"Look, Kelter, I'm short on staff and money and loaded with assignments for which I have no writer." She leaned close, her eyes glittering. "If you keep nagging me about this, I'm desperate enough to draft you as a guest writer."

He opened his mouth to protest, then closed it again. He had interviews scheduled for tomorrow anyway. And retracing Meg's steps at night might bring more details to the surface of her memory. "9:00 p.m., then."

Rod stood. "Get some rest." He strode through the living room and motioned for Josh to follow him outside. "You're staying with her?"

"Yeah. I'll keep an eye on her whether she likes it or not." Josh surveyed the street. "You think the shooter might come after her?"

Rod stared at the closed door a moment. "I think if those two joggers hadn't shown up when they did, Meg would be lying on a slab at the morgue beside Sherri Drake."

The Watcher cruised slowly up the street, noting the SUV still parked in Megan Cahill's driveway. His lips curled. Which cop was staying with her? Probably Josh, the former special forces soldier. He didn't want to tangle with Josh Cahill unless it was unavoidable.

The Watcher slammed his fist against the steering wheel, vaguely registering the pain in his hand. He'd have to plan another way to dispose of the nosy editor.

CHAPTER THREE

Tuesday morning, Meg stumbled into the kitchen, eyes bleary, body sore, but grateful the headache had moderated to a dull roar. Without saying anything, Josh poured coffee into a mug and handed it to her.

After the second cup, she turned to her brother with a sigh. "Okay. It's safe now."

He approached her, wariness in his gaze. "Hungry?"

She rolled her eyes and made a fist.

"Guess not. How do you feel?"

"Like somebody stomped all over me, then beaned me over the head with a baseball bat."

"Taken anything yet?"

Meg eyed him.

"Okay, okay." He held up his hands, backing off. "How about some over-the-counter pain medicine with a side of fresh homemade biscuit covered in orange marmalade?"

Her stomach growled. She had forced herself to eat yesterday, but the biscuit with marmalade sounded like it would settle well on her stomach. "You cooked?"

"Ha." Josh grabbed a plate from the cabinet and dropped a couple biscuits on it. "Serena stopped to check on you earlier. She thought you might like something easy on your stomach today."

God bless her sister for taking such good care of her. Then again, Serena did all of Meg's cooking. She had hired Serena through her personal chef business, Home Runs, Inc., to keep her pantry, freezer and refrigerator stocked with food so Meg wouldn't have to be concerned with cooking healthy. Her lip curled. Right, like she cooked anything, healthy or not.

"So, what's on your schedule today?"

Meg swallowed a mouthful of biscuit covered with the spiced preserve. "Interviews for articles."

"Any dealing with Sherri Drake?"

Her eyes narrowed. "You spying for somebody, bro?"

"Just keeping tabs on my snoopy sister who has a tendency to land in thorny bushes."

"Did you have to bring that up again?" Her face flamed. "I was ten years old and a bee was chasing me. Why won't you let me forget that incident?"

Josh leaned across the counter and dropped his voice to a low rumble. "Because that's still typical of you. You leap into the unknown, hoping there aren't any rose bushes when you land. Not all the choices you've made are good ones. Bad choices have consequences like that leap into Mom's rose bush."

Meg swallowed the last bite of biscuit around a suspicious lump in her throat. "I love you, too, Josh."

"So, are you pursuing leads on Sherri's murder?"

"I'm conducting whatever interviews Ruth has lined up for me until lunchtime. Then I'll be back at the *Gazette* office to polish the last articles and check layouts for tonight's press run."

Josh stared, mouth gaping. "You convinced Ruth Rollins to write an article?"

"Not just any article, dear brother, but the lead article on the murder." She carried her plate to the dishwasher.

"Rod was right about one thing. I can't report on Sherri objectively. Despite what he thinks, I don't want to jeopardize his case." She shrugged. "I thought it best to hand over that story to someone not involved."

"Does Ethan know?"

"Did I hear you right?"

"I imagine you did unless you've lost your hearing since you married Serena."

Conversations in the squad room dropped to a whisper. Ruth's tart tone brought a smile to Rod's face as he watched the exchange between Ethan and his aunt. He had to admit, Meg pulled a fast one on him. He figured she would bulldoze her way through the article about Sherri's murder and, if he was lucky, let him or Ethan read it before it went to press.

"I don't want you involved in this murder investigation." Ethan's voice rose. "Don't you have a book to write?"

"Settle down, Ethan. I told Megan you wouldn't let me run around the countryside stalking a killer. All I'm going to do is write the articles."

Wait a minute. Rod's smile faded. Ruth couldn't create facts like she did for those Olivia Tutweiler murder mysteries. "Won't you have to do research or interviews for your story?"

Ruth shook her head. "I'm simply the writer. Someone else will do the interviews and research."

Oh, man. He knew what was coming and it wasn't good. "Who's doing the leg work for you?" His voice rumbled out of his chest.

Ruth smiled. "Megan."

Great. Rod scrubbed his face with his hands. His key witness planned to interview anybody she cornered about the murder. And since most murders were committed by people in the victim's circle of family, friends, or acquaintances, she'd most likely put herself back in the path of the killer.

"Aunt Ruth, you're . . ." Ethan paused, seeming at a loss for words.

She pointed her finger at his face. "You don't want to tell me I'm too old, Ethan Blackhawk. You may complete that sentence with stubborn, creative, determined, even incredible, but not old."

Ethan laughed, tugging her into his embrace. "No, ma'am. I love you too much to say that, but please be discreet. Don't blow our case out of the water by leaking too much information. This isn't the time to show off your ability to pry secrets from unsuspecting rookie cops."

"Since the rookies are off limits and you don't appear busy, how about an interview?"

"Rod's the lead detective on the Drake case." Ethan released his aunt. "Talk to him."

Rod grinned at his boss. "Sorry, Ethan, but I have an interview in fifteen minutes. You'll have to update Miss Rollins." He gulped the last of his coffee and strode from the squad room before the police chief found a way to hogtie him with a press interview.

Megan accelerated down the main road, glad none of the Otter Creek police were in sight. Since Ethan became police chief, she could paper her bathroom wall with speeding tickets. Her irritating brother-in-law had come down so hard on Officer Henderson for letting her slide out of earlier tickets that the rookie wrote her up for every tiny infraction now.

She pressed the gas pedal harder. What good did it do to have a 1990 Corvette if she couldn't drive faster than 35 miles per hour? The speedometer needle nudged 60 when her cell phone rang.

She dug her phone from her purse. "Cahill."

"How fast are you driving?"

Meg's foot eased up on the accelerator. "Hey, Tony. You don't want to know."

"The engine sounds good."

"I finally nailed the tune-up this time."

"Will you come by the store today?"

Tony owned the only auto parts store and repair shop in town. "The boots came in?" Meg had noticed a crack in the boots last week when she changed the oil in her car.

"Arrived on the truck this morning."

"I'll be there in five minutes." She ended the call and pressed down on the accelerator again. Her fingers itched to tear into the boxes and change out the parts. Her 'Vette was a fine piece of craftsmanship, one that deserved dealership parts in perfect working order. She could almost feel the grease on her fingers.

She'd have to wait until Saturday afternoon, though. The weekend edition of the *Gazette* went to press that morning.

She pulled into the parking lot of Tony's shop, making a mental note to check the rotors and brakes on Serena's Volkswagen Beetle. And she probably needed to order a couple cases of synthetic oil for her parents' cars while she was here.

Tony's parking lot in front of the store wasn't large and he already had enough customers to force Meg to park near the road. Looked like the ad in the *Gazette* was working for him.

She climbed from the car and started toward the building, stopped and retraced her steps. Meg grabbed her laptop and relocked her car. Zoe had put together a new ad for Tony. Now was as good a time as any to show it to him. The bell rang overhead as Meg opened the door.

The burly, bearded mechanic glanced up from the cash register. "Hey, Meg. I'll be with you in a minute."

"No hurry, Tony." She lifted her laptop. "Where can I set up? Zoe designed a new ad for you."

He rang up another sale, grinning. "If it brings in more customers than the one we're already running, I'll have to expand the parking lot."

Meg smiled. "Can I quote you on that?"

After the last of Tony's customers left the store, Meg showed him the new design for the ad. "If you want to run this in color, we'll give you a twenty percent discount for two editions."

He nodded. "Looks great. Let's do it." He inclined his head toward the register. "The boots are behind the counter."

Tony walked around the end of the counter and reached for her bag. An explosion rocked the building, shattering the windows and throwing Meg and Tony to the ground.

Rod stood in the library of the Drake mansion, scanning titles of leather-bound books that graced the elegant cherry shelves. He couldn't help contrasting this collection with the diverse piles at Megan's place.

Though this library was more attractive, more organized, Meg's stacks were gathered from appreciation and interest rather than height or color. The Drakes probably didn't have a clue what books occupied their vast collection. None of the bindings appeared creased from use.

The door opened. "I should have realized you would be the detective in charge of Sherri's case." Kyle Drake closed the door behind him and held out his hand. "Good to see you again, Rod. Too bad it's under such lousy circumstances."

"I'm sorry about Sherri. How is Ty holding up?"

Kyle motioned to the leather armchairs arranged in front of the fire crackling in the obsidian marble fireplace. "About like you'd expect. He's devastated. We all are." He sank into the soft leather. "Do you have any idea who did this?"

"We're following leads." Rod pulled a notebook from his pocket. "I'll need to talk to all of you."

Kyle settled against the back of the armchair, appearing relaxed yet attentive. "Of course. We want to help catch whoever did this to Sherri. Ask anything you want."

"When was the last time you saw Sherri?"

"Must have been Sunday afternoon, maybe four o'clock."

"Did she seem upset?"

"Upset?" Kyle frowned, rubbing his jaw. "No, I'd say she was excited about Ty returning home yesterday."

"Ty was out of town?"

"He was in Pensacola last week at some computer geek convention. He drove most of the night to surprise Sherri. Got here about three o'clock in the morning." His face twisted. "Ty was the one surprised when he discovered she was gone."

Computer geek convention? He didn't remember Kyle showing such disdain for his brother. Ty was a world-class computer software programmer, sought after by the top companies. From what he heard, Ty could demand a king's ransom in salary and get it.

"So, what did you do after you left Sherri?"

Kyle's lips curved. "Checking on my movements, Rod?"

"As I'll be doing with everyone else in the house."

"I had a business dinner at Willow Bay until ten o'clock. Then I came home and went to bed." Amusement crossed his face. "Alone."

"What time did you leave for the dinner?"

"Around six o'clock."

"What about the two hours prior to you leaving the house?"

"On the phone with potential contributors."

Potential contributors? The Senator didn't run for re-election for another couple of years. "Isn't this too early to crank up a re-election campaign?"

Kyle laughed. "Oh, we aren't gearing up for Dad's senate run. Don't worry. You'll learn the big secret in a few days. We're not ready for a press conference yet."

"You're still working for your father?"

He inclined his head. "Campaign manager. For now."

"I need the name of your dinner companions."

Kyle rose and circled the desk. "Let me write their names and numbers for you. They already returned to their homes in Massachusetts and California. I'm sure Otter Creek's budget can't handle flying you to opposite ends of the country to confirm my alibi."

Rod scanned the names, fighting to keep his expression neutral. He wondered how much trouble he'd have getting the two most powerful senators on the phone to confirm Kyle's story. If Kyle wasn't fundraising for his father, why dine with men whose names regularly appeared in headlines?

"Anything else I can help with?"

"Were Sherri and Ty having any problems?"

Kyle remained silent a moment. "I'm not sure. Dad and I are gone ten months out of the year. Maybe on a trip home or two in the last year, I noticed some tension between them." He shrugged. "Ask Ty. Should I have him come downstairs? I think he'll be able to talk to you now."

Before Rod answered, his cell phone rang. "Kelter."

"Get over to Tony's." Ethan's voice almost crackled with tension. "Somebody just blew up Meg's car."

CHAPTER FOUR

Rod slammed on the brakes and shut off his engine. Staring at the mangled, smoldering remains of Meg's prized Corvette, he threw open the SUV's door and removed his sunglasses.

He waved over the fire chief. "What can you tell me, Bo?"

"Your boys won't have to give the blue bullet any more speeding tickets."

"Should spare a few trees. Any chance this was a mechanical or electrical problem?"

"An accident, you mean?" The chief shook his head. "This was definitely a bomb. We'll stick around a while longer to make sure it doesn't re-ignite."

"Thanks." Rod surveyed the charred mass again, his jaw clenched. The way Ethan told what happened on the phone, Megan was lucky to be alive. If she hadn't stopped at Tony's store, she would have been in the car when it exploded.

Ethan evaded emergency equipment and stopped at Rod's side.

"Where's Meg?"

The police chief nodded toward the store. "Inside, trying to convince Tony to let her replace his windows."

"She all right?"

"Says she is." Ethan turned to face him. "Right now she's fine. She won't be when reality sets in."

Shock trumped all other emotions at this point. Give Meg some time to adjust and raw fury would fuel her temper. Nobody touched her car without drawing back a bloody stump.

Rod frowned, concerned about her emotional well-being. Two attempts on her life in two days. According to Bo, no chance this fire was an accident. Who wanted Meg dead? The trail shooter? Made more sense than two people wanting to kill the unflappable editor within 48 hours. "I'll talk to her. Watch the fire crews. Don't let them trample whatever clues are left."

Glass crunched under his shoes as he stepped inside the store. He found Meg pacing, cell phone pressed to her ear.

"No, Zoe, you don't need to come down here. Just send J.J. to take pictures. I'll write this up." Meg ran her fingers through her hair and jerked her hand away with a gasp. She stared for a minute at the blood oozing from her index finger.

Rod yanked a clean handkerchief from his pocket. Meg must have glass fragments in her hair. He lifted her hand, removed the glass shard and gently pressed the cloth over the cut.

Meg stared at him, an odd look on her face. "What?" she said to Zoe. "No, I'm fine. Just a piece of glass. Look, stay on the assignment I gave you. I need that cookie article and the Parks party coverage before 4:00." She ended the call.

"Are you all right?" Rod asked.

"How do you think I am?" She scowled at him. "Some lowlife just blew up my Corvette! No, I'm not all right. I'd stomp the car murderer into the ground if I knew who to stomp."

"I'll find out who did this. Trust me." He checked her finger again. Good, no oozing. He needed his first-aid kit. "Come with me." Keeping her hand in his, Rod led her to his SUV and opened the back door.

When she was seated, he said, "Are you too sore to bend over a little?"

Meg blinked. "Why?"

"I'll help you get the glass out of your hair."

"Shouldn't you be bagging evidence or something?"

His eyebrows rose. "Not until what's left of your car cools off. Will you let me help or not, Cahill?"

She rolled her eyes, but bent over at the waist, her long blond hair flipped over her head. "You're starting to sound like Josh."

Rod chuckled, sliding his fingers along her scalp. After a couple of minutes, he realized how soft her hair felt in his hands. Like silk. He jerked his hands away.

Meg stiffened. "What's wrong? Did you cut yourself too?"

"Nothing." He drew in a deep breath to steady himself and almost groaned at his mistake. The fragrance of apples drifted from her hair into his lungs.

"You can sit up," Rod said, his voice thick. He retrieved his first-aid kit and pulled out band-aids and antibiotic cream.

"What are you doing now?"

He glanced into her blue eyes. "Uh, I need to bandage that finger."

"Oh. Right."

"Did the EMTs check you?"

The look she gave him surpassed scornful. "And let those vampires siphon another gallon of blood from my veins? Forget it. Besides, the blast blew me onto my fanny. No way am I letting those guys check for bruises."

He could think of many things for them to check besides her well-formed backside, but refrained from commenting. "Was your car having any problems?"

Another look from the reporter, this one filled with fury. "My 'Vette was in perfect condition except for the boots."

"Did you see anyone near it before the explosion?" Rod smeared antibiotic cream on Meg's cut.

She shook her head. "I was at the back of the store with Tony, showing him the new ad layout."

"Anyone else in the store at the time?"

"Nope."

Rod tore open the band-aid wrapper. "Have you ticked anyone off recently?"

"Not enough to blow up my car."

"Except maybe Sherri's killer."

She blanched. "Except him."

"You're sure Sherri's attacker was a man?" He wrapped Meg's finger, then let go and crumpled the wrapper.

Meg sat silent a moment. "If it wasn't, this woman was strong and had long, muscular legs like a man."

Pleased at the new sliver of information she volunteered, Rod helped her down and escorted her into the store. He waved Tony over. "Notice anybody hanging around the Corvette before it exploded?"

"Didn't pay much attention to the parking lot except to notice it was full. When all the customers cleared out, Meg showed me a new ad she wanted to run for me in the *Gazette*."

He glanced around the store. "Where were you?"

Tony pointed to the round table outside his office.

Rod walked to the area in question and stood beside Meg's laptop. "Is this where you were standing?" The shop owner's height was close to his.

Tony nodded and Rod scanned the line of sight from his position. He could see the charred remains of Meg's car from here. "Any cars driving by that were out of place?"

"Not that I remember."

Following more questions and unrevealing answers, Rod handed him a card. "If you think of anything, call me."

"Do you need me for anything else?" Meg asked.

"Would it do any good to ask you to stay at the *Gazette* office until I pick you up tonight?

She smiled at him.

"That's what I thought." Rod massaged the tight muscles in his neck. "Look, at least promise you'll be extra careful. My gut tells me this is related to Sherri's murder."

"Which means the murderer wants to finish what he started."

"He wants to kill the only witness."

"Some witness. I can't remember anything once I hit the stone wall."

Rod's eyes narrowed at her bitter tone. "He doesn't know that."

"Maybe I should take out a full-page ad in the paper and enlighten him."

"I appreciate the wheels, Nick." Meg snatched in mid-air the keys her brother-in-law tossed her.

"Try not to destroy my Jeep." He leaned against the fender of his car, blocking her view of the Otter Creek police station.

"You're a riot, Santana." She cranked the engine and flipped the fan to the high setting.

"You didn't ask for Madison's Jeep." A quiet statement from Nick, not a question.

Cold chills swept over Meg's body despite the heat blowing from the vents. "I don't want somebody mistaking either of my sisters for me. In this case, being one of identical triplets is a definite drawback."

Nick dropped a hand on her shoulder and squeezed. "Be careful, Meg."

She wrinkled her nose at him. "I already heard that today from Rod."

"Better listen to him. Keep your cell phone on you at all times and call one of us if you feel uneasy about anything. Trust your instincts. No hot-dogging."

"Yeah, I hear you. Thanks again." She waved and put the car in gear. Turning right from the police station parking lot onto Main Street, Meg drove toward the outskirts of town.

A few minutes later, she parked in front of a dirty white mobile home. Rust dotted the front of the structure along with streaks of dirt. Mud and sparse brown grass covered the expanse between her vehicle and the trailer.

Climbing from the Jeep, Meg evaded mud puddles and trudged to the door. A woman answered her knock dressed in faded pink sweats, ratty tennis shoes, limp gray hair brushing her shoulders.

"Megan."

"I'm so sorry for your loss, Mrs. King."

Tears welled in her eyes. "I can't believe she's gone. I talked to her Sunday afternoon." Wanda King slipped fingers beneath her glasses and wiped away the moisture. "Come in." She stepped aside, motioning Meg into her dwelling.

"Is there anything I can do for you?" Meg sat on the faded couch next to Sherri's mother. She glanced around, noticing that, as with every other time she'd visited the King home, nothing was out of place. "Anything you need?"

"You're so sweet to think of me, but I'm all right. Ty stopped by earlier this afternoon to check on me. He said the killer hurt you, too." She stared at the bandage on Meg's forehead.

"Just a few stitches." Meg cradled one of Mrs. King's hands between her own. "You said you talked to Sherri on Sunday. What time was this?"

The older woman furrowed her brow as she thought. "She called about dinner time. Maybe five o'clock."

"Did she seem all right?"

"What do you mean?"

Meg didn't want to upset Sherri's mother or interfere in Rod's investigation, but the question had been bugging her since she got out of the hospital yesterday. "Was anything bothering her?"

"She was in a rush. Some garden club meeting."

Meg nodded. The Otter Creek Garden Club met on the third Sunday afternoon of each month. Sherri had been pleased to be part of the prestigious group. The landscape and gardens at the Drake mansion reflected her passion for flowers.

"Did she mention anyone in particular when she called?"

Mrs. King shook her head. "Only Ty. He'd been out of town and she was looking forward to him coming home." Tears pooled in her eyes again. "It doesn't seem fair, does it? Ty and Sherri endured so much in the last two years. She was hoping I would be a grandmother by my next birthday."

"What did you think about Sherri's plan to build The Haven?" Sherri had dreamed of opening a shelter for abused women and children, talked for hours about the programs needed and purchased the land a month prior to her murder.

"I was so proud of her for that." A soft smile touched her lips. "She took a tragedy and tried to bring something good from it. You know, a lot of people would have crawled into a hole, withdrawn from the world after being the victim of violence. Not Sherri, though. She poured her energy into helping other rape victims recover their lives, though the police never found her attacker."

"Do you know what Ty's going to do about The Haven now?"

"I don't know, Meg. I hope he doesn't let it suffer the same fate as my daughter."

Rod searched the perimeter of the parking lot and the street the officers had blocked off, looking for evidence. The sharp wind cut through his coat straight to his bones. He shivered and tugged the coat zipper higher.

Hunching his shoulders in a vain attempt to keep warm, Rod studied the debris in each quadrant of his grid, bagging pieces, labeling each charred remnant. About two feet from the vehicle, he knelt and examined one piece closer. Though heavily damaged, he recognized the unmistakable shape. An LED, probably from a cell phone. He swiveled on one foot. "Ethan."

The police chief walked to his side. "What do you have?"

"Take a look."

Ethan studied the indicated piece in silence. A grim expression settled on his face. "Detonator for the bomb?"

"That's what it looks like to me."

"Did you talk to Meg?"

"Yeah. She says no one else has it in for her."

"So Sherri's killer is after her now."

Rod bagged what was left of the detonator and labeled it. "I think he's going to keep after her until he succeeds, unless we get him first."

"Has she remembered anything more?"

"She's sure it's a man."

Ethan stood. "That's not much. When will you talk to her again?"

"Tonight, after the *Gazette* press run is finished." Rod rose and faced his boss. "I want to take her back to the trail, walk her through Monday morning's events. Do you think she can handle it this soon?"

"From what Serena tells me, Meg hasn't really processed all that's happened. She's compartmentalized everything, rolling from one priority to the next, not allowing herself any downtime." Ethan jammed his hands in his pockets. "She might have a meltdown on the trail."

"Will you let me do this with her?"

"Not my call, Rod. You're the investigating officer. If you feel it's necessary, do it. I don't think we can wait for her memory to return on its own."

"I can't believe she's gone, Meg." Tyler Drake's face mirrored the anguish in his voice. "I walk through the house, still expecting her around the next corner or waiting for me in our suite."

He rose and stood in front of the library fireplace, his back to her. "What happened? Why did you ask her to go to the trail?"

Meg chose her words before answering. "She asked me to meet her there."

Ty swung around. "At four o'clock in the morning? Why? What did she want?"

"I don't know. Sherri didn't have the chance to tell me." Sherri said so little Meg didn't know if her friend had heard something about the Senator that scared her or heard him discussing someone or something else.

"I don't understand it." He ran his hands through his hair, leaving the brown strands rumpled. "What was so important that she'd go to a deserted area in the middle of the night? She didn't like to leave the house after dark."

Not since the rape two years ago. "I'm sorry, Ty. I don't have answers for you."

The muscles in his cheek twitched. "Don't have them or won't give them?"

Meg stiffened. "I told Ethan and Rod as much as I can. They will uncover the killer."

"I think you're holding out information. Are you trying to boost the *Gazette's* circulation by dribbling out facts? I'll bet Sherri's murder will sell a lot of papers for you."

Meg's face flamed at the acid overtone in Ty's words. "I'm not trying to profit from her death. I have a responsibility to Otter Creek to report the news, both good and bad. I won't apologize for doing my job, Ty."

"So you sensationalize her murder and get away with calling it news."

Blood drained from Meg's face. She knew Ty harbored some resentment against her because of an article about his affair with a student, but not to the extent revealed by his body language and voice. Hard to miss the hatred hanging over the room. "The people of Otter Creek need to know the truth."

"The truth?" Ty's fists clenched. "The truth is the murderer should have done us all a favor and killed you instead of my wife."

CHAPTER FIVE

"What's going on?" Rod stepped through the doorway into the mansion's library, his gaze shifting from Meg to Tyler Drake. Tension electrified the silent room.

"Meg was just leaving."

She stood and picked up her bag. "What are your plans regarding The Haven?"

"I haven't thought that far ahead." Ty stalked to the window and gazed at the late afternoon sun. "Goodbye, Meg."

The words, body language, attitude, all of it sounded final. Rod's eyes narrowed. What had caused the bad blood between Megan Cahill and Tyler Drake?

After excusing himself for a moment, Rod followed Meg into the hallway. He caught up to her near the front door and grasped her arm to keep her from leaving. "Are you out of your mind?" he snapped.

The muscles in her arm tensed. "Not lately. The way my luck is running, though, it's a distinct possibility."

"What are you trying to do? Hang a target on your back?"

She jerked her arm free, glaring at him. "My job, Detective."

"Stirring up trouble?" His voice dropped to a whisper. "Maybe incite a killer? He's already tried to take you out today."

"I need information about The Haven for my editorial. Who better to get the information from than Ty?"

"Ever heard of a phone, Cahill?"

Meg moved in close and pointed her bandaged finger at him. "You know as well as I do how much more you pick up in face-to-face interviews, Kelter." She scowled. "Besides, he hung up on me." She turned away from him and opened the door.

"So you bulldozed your way in here?"

"I asked the maid nicely to take me to Ty."

"What's the deal between you two?"

"Later. Ty's waiting for you and I have a paper to put to bed in a few hours." She walked out, slamming the door behind her.

Rod rubbed his face with his hands, teeth clenched. Megan Cahill had to be one of the most infuriating women on the planet. And one of the most beautiful. Man, he needed to get out in the dating scene more.

He returned to the library, gave a perfunctory knock on the door and stepped inside. Ty hadn't moved from his place at the window.

"I'm sorry about Sherri, Ty."

Turning from the window, Ty waved Rod to one of the leather armchairs in front of the fireplace and sat in the other. "Does it ever get any easier?"

Rod almost groaned. He was the last person to ask for advice about healing from the loss of a loved one. Some mornings he still thought he smelled Erin cooking breakfast and heard Kayla running through the house on her bare feet. "Eventually." He pulled out a notepad and pen.

"So, I guess you aren't here as a friend."

"I'm here as a friend and a cop. I understand you were out of town last week."

Ty nodded. "Computer programming seminars down in Pensacola."

"How long were you there?"

"Drove down last Monday and came back Sunday, late."

"Long drive. Why didn't you fly?"

Ty shrugged. "Needed some time to think."

"About?"

"Life. Politics. Whatever."

Rod resisted the urge to roll his eyes. Too bad it wasn't possible to subpoena thoughts. "What time did you discover Sherri was gone?"

Ty stared into the dancing flames, his expression sober. "About four o'clock."

Rod nodded and made the notation on his pad. The time fit with the timeline Meg had given him. "When did you talk to her last?"

"Saturday night after a business meeting, around 11 o'clock."

"Did she act as if anything was bothering her?" Rod held his pen suspended over his notepad.

Ty dragged his gaze from the flames and shook his head. "She was fine. Talked about going to her church Sunday, then meeting with the garden group she belonged to in the afternoon."

"Did Sherri mention anyone by name last week when you called?"

"Just Dad and Kyle. We didn't know they were coming back to town." His eyes narrowed. "She also mentioned Meg."

"How did she like living here in the mansion with the Senator and your brother?"

"She didn't mind. They were gone most of the time anyway."

"Did she want a home of her own?" Most women would. Erin had hated living in the same house with his parents the first few months of their marriage. The alternative, though, had been living alone all week in a strange city while he trained at the police academy and came home on weekends. Not the best option for newlyweds.

"Look, Rod, Sherri loved my father, and he needed a hostess for fundraisers. You know he hasn't been serious about any woman since Mom died."

"She could have been a hostess for him and still had her own home."

"I would have bought us a separate house if she'd asked for it, but she didn't. Sherri loved this place, especially the gardens. She said the grounds were perfect for the type of gardens she'd always wanted to design."

"Did she get along with your father and your brother?"

Ty froze. "Are you insinuating one of them killed her? That's crazy."

"I'm not insinuating anything. I'm asking questions I need answered. Did Sherri get along with your family?"

The agitated husband jumped to his feet and paced in front of the fire. "Of course she did. She had nothing but good things to say about Dad."

"What about Kyle?"

He sighed. "Same. Look, you're wasting time, Rod. You're supposed to find Sherri's killer, not interrogate me about my family."

"How long were you married?"

Ty pulled up short and swung around. "Seventeen years. Why?"

Rod paused. "Have any recent tensions in your marriage?"

"What kind of question is that? It's none of your business. You might have been close friends with Kyle in school, but that doesn't give you the right to ask personal questions."

Rod rose, wary of the volatile emotion surging through his friend. "As the lead investigator in your wife's murder, I'll ask any question necessary to capture her killer. There aren't any secrets in a murder investigation. So tell me what I want to know or I'll find out from other sources." He waited a moment. "I'd rather get the information from you."

Ty dropped into the leather armchair again. "Sherri was the most loving, incredible woman I've ever known; she almost sparkled." When his voice grew thick, Ty paused, wiping moisture from his eyes. "Until two years ago."

"The rape."

He nodded. "She was never the same after that. Afraid of the dark, not wanting to leave the house after sunset unless I was with her. I loved her, more than I've ever loved anyone in my life, but it wasn't enough."

"What do you mean, it wasn't enough?"

"She became obsessed with The Haven."

"Obsessed?"

"What would you call it when someone spends more time working on plans for a charity to help abused women and kids than with her own husband?"

Rod studied his friend for a moment. "Focused?"

Ty snorted. "She was obsessed, Rod. Night and day. No time for me. No time for anything except The Haven. Does that sound normal to you?"

"Sounds like she poured her frustration and fear from the rape into helping other victims of violence. Do you know of anyone who wanted to hurt Sherri?"

Ty shook his head.

"Sherri didn't work a regular job?"

"No. She worked occasionally with a landscaper to design gardens for her clients. Nita's Landscape Design."

Rod wrote down the name and slipped the notepad into his pocket. "That's all for now. Is the Senator home?"

A wry smile curved Ty's lips. "He's in a meeting at the Otter Creek Town Hall."

Pausing at the door, Rod said, "By the way, does your family still use monogrammed buttons?"

"Sure. Sherri didn't, though. She said they were too heavy." Speculation lit Ty's gaze. "Why?"

Meg bit another corner off the chicken salad sandwich Serena had brought her. She chewed and read Zoe's article on the mayor's Christmas party, editing as she read.

Finished, she opened the article file on her computer and entered the changes. Zoe's writing had improved in the last three months as she became more adept at using active verbs and vivid descriptions. If the *Gazette's* circulation increased, Meg could promote her to full-time journalist and hire a part-time receptionist.

She grabbed Zoe's article and laid it on her desk. "Good job on this, Zoe."

The girl glanced at the changes and grinned. "Not as much blood this time, Boss."

"Kill those unnecessary adverbs and adjectives and we might save money on red ink pens."

Zoe looked hopeful. "Enough for me to write full time and ditch the phones?"

"Maybe in the spring."

"Yes!"

"If circulation goes up and stays up. We can't count the surge we'll see from the murder."

"No worries, Boss." Zoe waved her hand as if brushing aside Meg's conservatism. "Once people see the quality we provide to the community, they'll want to keep receiving that service."

"I hope you're right."

"Ms. Rollins called a few minutes ago. She's coming in with the Drake murder article."

Relief washed over Meg. She figured she could count on Ruth to meet the deadline, but a good editor always had a backup plan just in case. And the backup plan was her under a pen name. She was glad she didn't have to use it this time. "Send her back when she arrives."

Returning to her desk, Meg opened the two letters to the editor which arrived in the morning mail. Mrs. Anderson complained again about the library hours not being long enough. Meg whole-heartedly agreed with her. Then again, few people in town kept her weird hours, except maybe law enforcement.

Rod's schedule was as erratic as the policemen in her family, though he seemed to be at every major crime or accident scene the paper covered. She knew he couldn't be at all of them because she'd heard Nick talking to Ethan about taking some of the investigative load off Rod's shoulders.

So maybe he didn't work every crime or accident scene. Maybe she had noticed the handsome red-haired cop more in the last few months. She scowled. The last thing she needed in her life was another cop. And if that wasn't enough of a deterrent to her interest, he still mourned the death of his wife and daughter. Hard to compete with ghosts.

"What caused that look?" Ruth Rollins settled in the chair across from Meg's desk.

"Do you know if Rod's dating anyone?" Meg closed her eyes and hung her head as Ruth laughed at her. Why didn't she ever think about how words sounded before they flew out of her mouth? She ought to take out an ad in the paper and ask him for a date, get the humiliation over with now.

"Is there a reason for the interest?"

"Just curious, that's all." Heat rose in her cheeks as she opened her eyes. "I've seen him around a lot recently and never noticed one woman in particular."

Ruth grinned. "He was seeing one of the female officers for a while, but she moved on to another police force to be near her family. There's been no one for several months." Her blue eyes twinkled. "Should I put a bug in Ethan's ear?"

"No." Meg shifted in her seat. "So, how did the article turn out?"

"Duck and run, huh?"

"Ruth."

"Oh, all right, I'll stop torturing you." She pulled the article and flash drive from her tote and handed them to Meg. "The article is a few words shy of the word limit. I hope that's okay."

"Okay?" Meg grinned. "I may cut my own salary to hire you permanently."

"Don't start planning bread and water rations just yet. You haven't read the article. I'll stay while you edit. Is there something else for me to work on in the meantime?"

"I still need copy for the proposed new water system. Want to play phone tag with the town council?"

"Sure."

"Great. There's a phone and computer on the desk across from Zoe's. Work there as long as you want."

With Ruth settled at the desk, Meg closed her office door and read the article, wisps of memory floating into her mind as she read. Sherri's grip on her arm. Her scream. The fear on her face. The sound of their feet as they fled. The running footsteps of their pursuer.

Meg drew in a shaky breath and dashed away the tears gathering in her eyes. Not now. She didn't have time to deal with the memories until after the press run tonight. She needed a clear mind, focused. Deadlines didn't wait for mental glitches and nightmare memories to disappear.

She plucked her red pen off the desktop and forced herself to see the article as an editor, not a participant or victim. She trimmed a few words here and there, moved a couple of paragraphs to the end of the article, then downloaded Ruth's file from her flash drive and entered the changes.

She read through it once more, printed a copy and took the original and edited versions to Ruth.

"Well, what did you think?" Ruth asked.

Meg grinned at the older woman's flushed face. The Christie award-winning author looked nervous. "How large of a name plate should I order for your desk?"

The tense look on her face vanished. "It was all right?"

"I should have hired you sooner." Meg turned both copies of the article around and laid them on the desk so Ruth could see the difference. "I cut a few words, most of it descriptions. We'll save that for the filler articles. The biggest change I made was simply to move the background information paragraphs to the end. When you write for newspapers, put the important information on the front page above the fold. Background information to complete the article is on the inside."

Ruth scanned the edited version. "There's not much difference."

Meg chuckled. "No, ma'am. You did a great job, Ruth. If I didn't know better, I'd think you had some experience in journalism." She tilted her head. "Would you be interested in doing some freelance writing for me on a permanent basis?"

"Let me think about it. This article wasn't hard to write because you gave me all the information I needed. I'm not sure about doing them continually if I have to do the research for those along with writing my novels."

"Don't sell yourself short. I didn't give you all the information included in the article." Meg's lips curved. "You cornered Ethan or Rod, didn't you?"

"Ethan owes me a few favors."

Meg laughed. "I'll bet. How many council members talked to you?"

"Only two." Ruth grimaced. "The others are in meetings or dodging calls."

"So, what's the consensus on the water system?"

"Jackson and Hoyt say it's a done deal, that the vote next week is just a formality."

"Wait a minute." Meg dropped into a chair at the side of Ruth's desk. "You're telling me the same council that debated for six months on whether to continue opening the library on Sundays is approving this multi-million dollar contract in a span of three weeks?"

"And that's not all. Neither of the two council members I talked to knew much about the company with the winning bid."

"Something is up with that. See if you can talk to more council members before 4:00. If not, use what you have." She stood. "You interested in doing a series of articles on this?"

Ruth grabbed the phone handset. "Absolutely. Will I get a raise?"

Meg laughed and returned to her office. Something was definitely going on with that water contract. But what?

CHAPTER SIX

Rod parked his SUV in the empty slot in front of the *Gazette*. He climbed out of his vehicle and scanned the deserted street. The back of his neck tingled. He couldn't shake the feeling that someone watched him from the shadows.

His gaze scoured the area, anticipating movement in the darkness. Dead leaves and a few pieces of paper blew in swirls down the street and sidewalk. Nothing else stirred except his breath. The feeling in his feet disappeared from exposure to the sharp wind. Rod eased his hand away from his weapon and entered the well-lit newspaper office.

He checked Megan's office first. Empty. He pivoted and followed the noise of the press into the back room. Opening the door, he watched the press machinery at work for a few seconds before his gaze sought Meg. After a moment, she glanced up and waved. Meg leaned close to the printer, said something to him and walked to Rod's side.

"Fascinating, isn't it?" She grinned, eyes sparkling. "The smell of ink and paper and the roar of machinery get me every time."

Rod grunted. "Gives me a headache."

"We'll be finished in about 20 minutes. Want to wait in my office?"

"You have Internet?"

"Of course. Help yourself." She waved him off and returned to the press.

Rod closed the printing room door and, in Meg's office, sat in the leather chair. His eyes widened as the comfort of her seat registered. Department-issued chairs didn't hold up to the luxury of this one. He'd spring for the money from his own pocket except he wasn't at his desk for long periods of time.

He surfed the Internet for references to the Drakes. Most references linked to the Senator. A few mentioned Kyle in his role as the Senator's campaign manager and public relations man. Ty was mentioned only once in relation to the Senator, the rest referenced his computer programs.

Meg stepped into the doorway and Rod glanced up. "Ready?" When she nodded, he exited from the Internet search engine and logged off.

He stopped Meg at the outside door with a raised hand. "Wait here." Rod took his time unlocking the SUV, scanning the street, probing the shadows for lurkers. A shadow of movement near the library door caught his attention. He tensed, his hand moving automatically to his weapon.

The Watcher's lip curled. His hand clenched the grip of his pistol. Too close to the police station, but oh, he was tempted. So many shadows in which to hide. His index finger slid into the trigger guard and settled on the slender piece of metal that would end his problem with the witness.

Megan Cahill. Fury flared at her name, at the sight of her with the cop. Always nosing into other people's business, stirring up trouble. He hadn't wanted to kill

Sherri. Megan forced his hand. It was her fault Sherri was dead.

He would make sure Meg paid.

A cat strolled from the doorway and ambled down the stairs to the street. Rod relaxed. Oscar, the library's mouser. And any other business who fed him. Guess that made him sort of the town cat. He motioned to Meg and opened the door for her.

"Is there a problem?"

"I don't think so."

Meg paused, the buckle of her seatbelt in hand. "That doesn't sound convincing."

He circled the SUV and climbed into the driver's seat. "Just being cautious, Megan." He cranked the car and backed into the square. "When did you eat last?"

Meg sat silent a moment. "Lunchtime, I think."

That's what he thought. Ethan had warned him that she forgot to eat most of the time when she was on deadline. So, instead of heading to the trail, he turned in the opposite direction.

"Where are we going?"

"You need to eat. Ethan's orders."

She twisted in the seat, frowning in his direction. "And you always do whatever he tells you?"

"Only when he's right. Is Burger Heaven okay?"

She moaned. "Perfect, if you include a milkshake."

A few minutes later, Rod swung into Burger Heaven's parking lot. "Want to eat here or on the way to the trail."

"Here."

A wave of sympathy rolled through Rod at her prompt response. He didn't blame her for not wanting to relive Monday morning's nightmare any sooner than necessary. Inside the restaurant, he said, "Tell me what you want. I'll wait for the order while you choose a table. You look beat."

"At least you didn't say I looked beat up."

His eyebrows rose. "Do I look stupid?"

She laughed, told him to order a mushroom and Swiss hamburger and chose a table at the back corner of the restaurant.

He noted the choice of a table where both doors and the cash register were in view and his back hugged the wall. Rod smiled. She'd noticed the seating choices of the cops in her family.

He unloaded their tray. "Chocolate shake okay?"

She grinned. "How did you know I'd like that?"

"Nick and Ethan talk about your sisters. Many discussions include chocolate. I guess the Cahill women are chocoholics?"

Meg sipped her shake before replying. "Serena loves dark chocolate and Madison craves Goo-Goo Clusters."

"What's your vice?"

"Snickers."

"What about your mother?"

She laughed. "Death by Chocolate ice cream."

He kept her talking throughout the meal, hoping to distract her from the unpleasantness ahead. As she chewed the last bite of her burger, he found to his amazement that his own burger and fries were gone and he was full. He'd ordered food for himself so she wouldn't be uncomfortable, but he never expected to eat much of it. He usually didn't. "Ready to go, Meg?"

Emotion flickered over her face. "Not really, but I guess it has to be done."

The Churchill Trail parking lot was empty. Rod scanned the surrounding area, then helped Megan down. "Let's walk around the trail and come up on the scene from behind."

"Do we have to do this?" Her voice cracked on the last word. She stiffened. "Sorry. That slipped out without permission. Ignore the outburst."

Rod shot her a glance, amusement surging to the forefront. He had to give the spunky editor credit for courage. Most civilians would have cracked long before this point. "Have you remembered anything more?"

She drew her coat closer around her body. "Flashes, but no time to think them through." She shuddered. "Didn't want to, either."

"I wouldn't push you to do this if I didn't think it might help." He took her hand in his and gave a gentle squeeze. "After this morning's attempt on your life, we can't wait for your memory to return over time."

Meg frowned. "Did you have to bring up the 'Vette? When you find out who blew up my car, I want two minutes with him. Alone. I want him to know how much I loved that car."

Rod's lips twitched, silently agreeing, wishing he could grant her request. Might be an interesting two minutes, time the bomber would never forget. "How long did you own the car?"

"I bought it in 2000. The owner wanted to upgrade. That was such a sweet ride."

"Fast one, too."

She turned her head. "You wouldn't be making reference to my speeding tickets would you, Detective? That's pretty low considering what's left of my car is languishing in evidence bags at the station."

Rod chuckled. "Your driving habits are legendary around the department. Every time Ethan discovers you were issued another citation, he goes ballistic."

"That's one of the reasons I drive fast. To escape Ethan's lectures." She tilted her head, mischief animating her features. "Plus, it's fun and I'm a good driver."

Grudging admiration for her driving skills surfaced. Not that he would ever tell her she drove better than most of the officers in the department. Wouldn't pay to encourage Megan to burn more rubber on Otter Creek streets. "You might want to slow down for a few months. Ethan's riding Henderson hard."

"I heard. You don't have to worry. Without the 'Vette, speed isn't as appealing."

"Have you thought about a new car yet?"

She shook her head.

"Ferarri's are nice. Wouldn't mind test driving one myself."

Her laughter sounded strained. They walked in silence for another quarter of a mile. Rod slowed as they approached the half-mile bench. "Time to go to work, Megan."

Megan's heart pounded, a cold knot forming in the pit of her stomach. She loosened her grip on his hand, but instead of letting go, he threaded his fingers through hers. He appeared determined not to let her walk through this alone.

"Talk to me as we walk through it. Don't hold anything back, no matter how weird." He pulled her closer to his side. "This will be hard, Meg, but I'll help as much as I can. Remember, you're safe now. I won't let him hurt you."

She shuddered. She knew he felt it because his hand tightened on hers. "Let's get this over with."

She paused at the bench. "Sherri was waiting for me there." She pointed at the right side. "I sat beside her for a few minutes. She started to tell me about the Senator, but she stopped. She heard something."

Meg turned to look down the trail, again seeing what she saw early Monday morning. Heavy, impenetrable darkness.

"What are you thinking? Talk to me."

She swallowed hard. "It was so dark. We couldn't see anything. I remember thinking the darkness seemed oppressive, thick."

"What did you hear?"

"What I told you before, twigs breaking, like an animal walking around out there. I'd seen a cat on the way to meet Sherri, but this sounded bigger, heavier."

"What did you do next?"

"Sherri grabbed my hand and we started down the trail toward the parking lot."

The coldness of the night seeped into Meg's bones. One spot of warmth remained on her body—the hand Rod held in his. She trudged down the trail, retracing her steps with Sherri. Each stride brought resurgent echoes of the fear she'd experienced.

"We heard footsteps behind us. Running. We panicked and started running right about here."

Rod urged her forward. "The footsteps. Describe them. How did they sound?"

Meg replayed the memory, hearing the footsteps again in her mind. "Heavy, like a man." They moved a few feet further and she pointed at the scarred tree. "He shot at us here. There's the mark on the tree trunk."

A gust of wind blew Meg's hair across her face. She shoved the locks aside, noting that her hand trembled. She fisted her hand and buried it deep in her coat pocket. "Sherri stumbled. I dropped back here because she wasn't as fast a runner."

When they rounded the final curve, she stopped. Moonlight illuminated the stone wall, guardian to the trail entrance. Her body trembled, waves starting from deep inside and working their way out. She gritted her teeth and willed the shaking to still. Her body didn't listen.

"Easy, Meg. We're almost finished." Rod slipped his arm around her shoulder. "You're doing great. What did you see when you reached this point?"

She looked toward the parking lot, empty of vehicles except for his. "Sherri made it to the car and was unlocking her door. I thought we were going to make it, Rod." She turned to him. "When I reached the stone wall, he pushed me from behind. I hit the wall. The impact stunned me so much I couldn't move."

Meg gripped Rod's hand tighter. "It was like a nightmare where you're so scared and you want to run, but you're frozen in place. I wanted to help Sherri, tried to rise, but I couldn't move." Tears trickled down her cheeks. "He ran past me to the parking lot."

"Did you see his face, get a look at his clothes, anything?"

She shook her head. "I saw dirt and stones, my hands against the ground. Then Sherri screamed and I heard another shot."

"What did you do?"

"I pushed myself to get to my knees." Her voice broke. "I didn't hear anything else from Sherri. Then I heard the footsteps again, this time coming in my direction." A violent shudder shook her frame.

Rod brought her into the circle of his arms and held her. "What happened next, Meg?"

"I turned to face him, but I was unstable, still on my hands and knees." She fell silent as the memory rushed to the surface. "I saw his shoes."

"Close your eyes. Describe them."

"Jogging shoes, black."

"In your mind, lift your gaze a few inches. What color were his pants?"

Surprise surfaced, admiration for the detective rising. She'd never thought about the man's clothes. "Black."

"Light-weight material or heavier like jeans or corduroy?"

She considered that a moment before answering. "Jeans."

"Good, Meg. What happened next?"

"He drew back his foot and kicked me."

"What? Where?" Rod's arms tightened around her. He hadn't known about the kick.

"He was aiming for my head, but I turned away at the last second." She grimaced. "He connected with my back. Left me with bruised ribs. The kick sent me headlong into the wall."

"What did he do then?"

"He pressed his gun to the back of my head and cocked it."

"How did it sound?"

"Like Josh popping all his knuckles at once."

Rod burst into laughter. His voice rumbled in his chest under Megan's ear. Nice, very nice.

"Did he say anything?"

"No. I started to lose consciousness then. I thought I was going to die, right there." She sighed. "I remember smelling pine and wondering if my sisters would put pine wreaths on my grave. Isn't that strange?"

Rod scanned the trees on either side of the trail. Cedars, maples, oaks. No pine. Had she smelled the shooter's aftershave, cologne, shampoo? Or was it a wisp of memory from some other time?

He stood there a few more minutes, holding Megan. She'd stopped talking after mentioning the pine smell and he should have let her go. He didn't. She felt so good in his arms. Arms that had been empty for too long.

When she shivered, he unlocked his hands and let his arms drop. Rod dragged his attention back to business. "Thanks, Megan. I'll drive you to the newspaper office so you can get the Jeep and go home."

Inside the SUV, Meg said, "You won't tell anybody about the tears, will you?"

"Why not? Afraid the news will ruin your tough girl image?"

"Tough newspaper editors aren't supposed to cry."

"Who says? I'd worry if you didn't shed a few tears."

"Well, at least go light on the details when you talk to Ethan. I don't want my sisters to worry about me. They're already hovering. I couldn't handle it if they camped out at my place."

Rod's eyebrows shot up. "They'd do that, even newly married?"

She grinned. "Maybe not for as long as when they were single, but they'd do it."

"You girls are close, aren't you?"

"Close enough that I'm concerned about their safety." She sounded grim. "Except for Madison's limp, we're all dead ringers for each other." Meg sighed. "Sorry. Bad choice of words. The point I'm trying to make is there's a possibility the shooter might mistake one of them for me."

Rod considered that for a moment. "That's why you chose to use Nick's Jeep, isn't it? You didn't want the shooter to think Madison was you."

"I'll do whatever it takes to protect them."

"Would you consider leaving town for a couple of weeks? Put the paper together somewhere else and e-mail it to J.J."

She scowled. "Anything but that. I'm not running."

Somehow, he suspected that would be her answer. He parked in front of the *Gazette* office. "Stay here while I check the Jeep."

"You're kidding, right? Do you know anything about cars?"

"Not as much as you. But even I would recognize an unusual puddle underneath the car and I know what a car bomb looks like. Can you say the same?"

She wrinkled her nose at him, but tossed him the keys.

Satisfied nothing had been tampered with, he helped Meg from the SUV and opened her car door. "I'll follow you home."

"You don't have to do that."

"You're wasting time, Meg, and I need my beauty rest."

She burst into laughter, as he had intended. Meg shook her head at him, but dropped the argument.

Rod replayed the cycle of events at the trail in his mind while following her home. Meg's description of the gun's noise led him to believe the shooter's weapon was a .38 revolver. Hopefully the coroner would recover the bullet intact that killed Sherri. If they were lucky, ballistics might match the slug.

Rod parked behind the Jeep in Meg's driveway. He accompanied her to the front door, scanning the neighborhood. Was someone watching them? He'd been careful to check for a tail on the way to Meg's, but it wouldn't take much to figure out she was headed home for the night.

Rod held out his hand for her key. "I want to check the house." He unlocked the door, drew his weapon from the holster and stepped inside the living room. When he was certain it was clear of threats, he motioned her inside. "Wait here."

Minutes later, he returned. "All clear. Is Josh staying with you again tonight?"

She shook her head. "He goes on duty at 11:00 o'clock. Nick and Madison are coming over in a few minutes."

"I'll stick around until they arrive, then."

Meg led him to the kitchen. "Would you like some hot cocoa?"

He studied her face, noting the lines of strain showing around her mouth. "Need a little comfort food?" he asked, his voice quiet.

She retrieved two mugs from the oak kitchen cabinets. "According to Serena, chocolate fixes whatever ails you."

Rod sat on the same stool at her counter he'd occupied the night before. "What made you go into journalism?"

Meg filled a kettle with water and set it on the stove burner. "Love of the written word. I love to read, have ever since I was four. Mom taught me to read as a defense mechanism. I drove her crazy asking her to read Dr. Seuss books to me. She got tired of reading *Go, Dogs! Go!* and *The Cat in the Hat*. She'd read them to me so much she could quote them in her sleep."

"How did that lead you into journalism?"

"I read so much as a kid that I began analyzing how books worked. I started writing my own stories. But my stories weren't fiction. They were tales about the adventures my sisters and I had in school or things that happened on our vacations. They were all true stories told with my own spin."

"What kind of stuff do you read?"

"Everything. Good, bad, classic, atrocious. I like mysteries, police procedurals and romantic suspense books the most. I also read a lot of non-fiction. It's amazing what you learn in books if you know where to look."

"Should I worry about you breaking and entering any time soon?"

She stared at him a moment, then laughed. "You saw the books on picking locks, huh? I was thinking about doing an editorial on the most burglar-proof locks."

"And you wanted to test the manufacturer's claims."

"Exactly." She poured the now boiling water into the mugs and dumped a packet of cocoa mix into each cup. She stirred the chocolate mix and slid one mug in front of him.

"Thanks. You didn't answer my question, you know."

"I don't plan on breaking and entering, but it might be a good skill to have."

Rod grunted. "I don't think I want to hear any more. I'd hate to have to turn you in to one of the cops in your family."

The doorbell rang. Meg glanced at the clock. "Right on time."

"Check the peephole, Meg."

She glared his direction, but complied with the request. She unlocked the door and admitted Nick and Madison.

Madison pulled up short when she noticed Rod sitting at the counter. "Did we interrupt something?" Her eyes glittered with curiosity.

"Waiting for you." Rod smiled at her. She was a mirror-image of Meg, but so different in personality. Madison seemed more delicate, gentle in nature. Meg, on the other hand, sported a take-no-prisoners attitude mixed with grit and stubbornness.

He finished the cocoa while the girls talked and carried the mug to the sink. Rod caught Nick's gaze and motioned him outside. To Meg, he said, "I'll talk to you tomorrow. Call me if you think of anything else."

On the porch, he turned to Nick. "Keep an eye on her tonight. She walked through the crime scene with me."

"How did she do?"

"Gave me a couple more pieces of information, but it cost her. She may not sleep well."

Nick leaned against the door frame. "Want me to talk to her or just let it go and see how she copes?"

"Let's wait it out for now. If she starts showing signs of having problems, I'll talk to her about seeing a counselor."

Nick grinned. "I'm glad you volunteered for that duty. Meg on a rampage is something to see."

Rod climbed into his SUV, and with a wave, headed home. He flipped open his cell phone and punched in his speed dial number for Ethan.

"Blackhawk."

"It's Rod. Anything new on the Drake case?"

"Coroner's office called about fifteen minutes ago. They recovered the bullet intact. It's a .38 caliber."

"Maybe a Beretta?"

"Possibly."

"Fits with what Meg told me tonight. She remembered hearing the shooter cock the pistol."

"So taking her back through the crime scene worked?" He sounded pleased.

"It brought a couple of memories to the surface."

"What else did she remember?"

"The smell of pine."

"Pine? As in trees?"

"Yeah, but there aren't any pine trees on that part of the trail. I suppose it's possible the wind might have carried the scent to her, but the smell must have been strong for her to remember it. I didn't smell that scent tonight and the breeze blew in the same direction as Sunday night.

"Another thing. Meg only mentioned the smell after she remembered hearing the gun cocked. She said she wondered at the time if her sisters would put pine wreaths on her grave."

Ethan remained silent a moment. "She's one tough lady."

CHAPTER SEVEN

Meg stumbled into the kitchen, tracking the scent of brewing coffee. She hoped Maddie made the full 12 cups. Two hours of sleep interspersed with nightmares left her with brain fog and sluggish movements. Meg yawned, jaws cracking.

"How did you sleep?"

She scowled in the direction of her brother-in-law's deep voice.

"That good, huh? It might help to talk about it, Meg."

Without replying, she grabbed a large mug from the cabinet and poured a cup of Serena's Home Runs blend. After she'd sipped half the cup, Meg sat at the counter opposite Nick. "How do you stand this? How can you sleep at night?"

"Some nights I don't." He grinned. "Those sleepless nights don't aggravate me nearly as much now that my bed's not empty, though."

Meg groaned. "Way too much information for this early in the morning, Nick." Her brother-in-law topped off her mug. "These nightmares are normal, right?"

"The dreams are your mind's way of coping. In dreams, you try every logical avenue to change the outcome of what happened. Time will make the dreams less frequent, but they won't ever fade entirely. Another tragedy may bring them back for a time."

"Great. Another nightmare to add to the memory banks. As if what happened to Mandy wasn't horrible enough to keep me awake some nights."

"It will pass, sweetheart."

Not soon enough for her sanity. "Is Madison awake?"

"Not yet."

"You will keep an eye on her?"

Nick smiled, love for Madison shining from his attractive eyes. If you liked chocolate eyes, that is. She was partial to lighter-colored eyes. Like Rod's. Her cheeks heated as she remembered the strength of his arms round her the night before. Meg yanked her attention back to the present.

"Always. Stop worrying about her. You should be more concerned about your own safety. When are you leaving for the office?"

Meg glanced at the clock and estimated the time it would take her to shower and dress for the day. "Thirty minutes."

"Okay." He stood. "While you're getting ready, I'll check out the vehicles to make sure no one left us another nasty surprise."

"Worried about your Jeep?"

Nick paused, his hand on the door knob. "Cars can be replaced, Meg. You can't."

Rod scanned Ruth's article on Sherri's murder. He had to admit, for a woman who didn't habitually write for the paper, she had done a great job. She had gathered facts the public would be interested in plus an interview with Ethan, all without compromising their investigation.

He scanned the paper until his gaze fell on Meg's editorial about Sherri's dream for The Haven. True to her word, she stayed away from the case, focusing instead on the necessity for keeping Sherri's vision alive.

Meg had a knack for writing. Her impassioned plea had him mentally reaching for his wallet to donate to the cause. Every week during the course of his work, he saw evidence of the need for The Haven's ministry in their community.

He knocked on Ethan's office door, paper in hand. Rod waggled the paper at his boss. "Did you see this?"

"Not yet."

He laid the latest edition on the desk. "Ruth did a great job." He grinned. "So did you."

Ethan chuckled. "Not an easy thing to dance around Ruth. She knows when I'm holding something back. What about Meg?"

"She wrote about The Haven in her editorial, never mentioned the events at the fitness trail."

The police chief nodded. "What's on your schedule today?"

"Interviews, starting with Senator Drake."

The Watcher balled the *Gazette* and threw it across the room, rage boiling in his gut. Why wouldn't she leave this alone? She was going to ruin everything. His destiny awaited. He had to stop Megan Cahill. Permanently.

Rod waited in the Drake mansion library in front of another crackling fire. The door opened and Warren Drake, wearing a dark suit and tie, entered the room. He looked ready to walk onto the senate floor and deliver a speech.

Drake's gray hair glistened in the sunlight shining through the windows as he extended his hand. "Good to see you again, Rod, though it's under horrendous circumstances."

"Thanks for seeing me this morning, Senator."

"Anything I can do to help find Sherri's killer." He waved Rod toward the chairs by the fire.

"Did Sherri mention a problem recently?"

"What kind of problem?"

"Anything that caused her enough concern to mention it to you."

"You know, I haven't been home much this year. Spent most of my time in D.C. and abroad. I really didn't talk to Sherri much except to check in once in a while and let her know when I would be in town."

"What about this trip?"

Drake frowned. "What do you mean?"

"Did you inform Sherri you were coming home Sunday?"

Face coloring, he shook his head. "Last minute change of plans."

"When did you arrive?"

"Around seven o'clock. I didn't pay attention to the time."

That statement struck Rod as strange. As a kid, he remembered the Drakes were always punctual for events. When he spent time in their home, he'd noticed the clocks in every room. "Did you see Sherri or talk to her?"

"No. I came in here to work as soon as we arrived."

"Anyone with you?"

"Kyle and Don Brandenburg."

Brandenburg? Rod sat back in his chair. "Don works for you?"

The Senator smiled. "In a way. He works for Kyle managing campaign funds."

A bean counter. Well, that fit with Don's nerdy personality in high school. "How long has he worked for Kyle?"

"Oh, a few years now. You'll have to ask Kyle for the exact date."

"Did you make any phone calls Sunday night?"

"Phone calls?" Drake's smile dimmed. "I'm sure I did. Why do you want to know that?"

"Who did you call, sir?"

"That's none of your business."

"I need an answer to the question, Senator."

"I don't like your tone, Rod. You used to be friends with my sons. I expected more respect from you than this."

Rod had wondered how much cooperation to expect from the Senator. Looked like he had his answer. "My friendship with your sons has nothing to do with this matter. I'm investigating a murder. That takes precedence over loyalty and ties to old friends." He let the silence build a moment, then said, "I'd rather learn the information from you, but I can get it from the telephone company if necessary."

"I suppose that's what you'll have to do. That's an invasion of privacy and I've done nothing wrong."

"How did you get along with Sherri, Senator Drake?"

The senator sat frozen for a moment. "You're accusing me of killing her?"

"No, sir." Of that he was positive. Warren Drake was about 75 pounds overweight. In his physical condition, Drake couldn't have run a half mile after Sherri and Meg. That didn't, however, let him off the hook for hiring someone to kill Sherri and any potential witnesses. "I'm asking if you and Sherri had any disagreements."

"I'm hardly here enough to say more than two sentences to anybody. Sherri was a sweet, attractive woman whom my son loved dearly."

"Do you know of someone who might have wanted to harm her?"

He shook his head. "Not unless you count the scumbag who raped her. But you still don't know who that is, do you, Detective? Maybe he's the one who killed her."

Rod's face flushed. Although he worked for the Knoxville police department at the time of the rape, the unspoken accusation of ineptness still stung. He stood. "I need to search Sherri's suite and other areas she frequented." He handed over the search warrant.

The senator rose. "I suppose that will be all right. Ty drove to the funeral home to make the arrangements for Sherri's service. I'll have the maid escort you upstairs."

"That won't be necessary. Just give me directions. I'll find it."

Moments later, Rod opened the door to Sherri and Ty's suite. The living room was neat, with only a copy of the *Gazette* on the coffee table. Nothing else was out of place. He scanned the cherry bookshelves. One, obviously Ty's, had books on computer programming and graphics, and stacked issues of computer magazines. The other bookcase held a hodgepodge of paperbacks and gardening books and magazines.

In the kitchenette, Sherri's collection of herbal teas and various blends of coffee filled the cabinets along with a few snack foods. Nothing out of the ordinary.

Rod searched the bedroom and noted Ty's aftershave. Old Spice. Definitely not pine-scented. Their framed wedding picture sat in the middle of the dresser. He remembered the day they got married. They all had big dreams then. No one would have guessed Sherri's life would end in a senseless tragedy.

He opened the closet door and found fewer clothes than he expected for a walk-in closet the size of his main bathroom. Sherri chose basic colors, aside from the dresses he recognized from society page pictures and news clips, dresses worn in hosting the senator's dinners and lunches.

He paused as he reached a section of larger clothes. Sherri had never been large. Why would she have a section of clothes too big for her to wear? He removed one top, examined the label. *Marti Maternity*. His gut clenched and his mind flashed back to the shopping sprees he and Erin enjoyed when she was expecting Kayla.

Rod returned the shirt to its place and continued the search. He turned to leave and noticed a shoe box at the back of a shelf in a dark corner. There were no other shoes boxes in the closet. Sherri had used shoe cubbies to organize her footwear.

He pulled the box from the shelf, lifted the lid and peered inside. Journals, the kind found at Wal-Mart. Rod thumbed through the five books. The earliest date was January 1, 2000. At a glance, it looked like Sherri consistently wrote for five years. Did she stop journaling in 2005 or were the next years kept somewhere else? Maybe someone took the journals because something incriminating was in them.

Rod carried the box with him into the living room and opened another door into the second bedroom, used as a study. Two desks occupied the room, one large, one small. The large desk looked like a work area for Ty.

On the smaller desk sat a laptop and an assortment of gardening books and magazines. He touched a key on the keyboard and the computer shifted from sleep mode. Maybe Sherri switched to a computer journal. The crammed desktop calendar and multi-colored slips of paper posted various places indicated she spent a lot of time in here.

He called up the word processing program and scanned the files. Rod tried to open the 2005 Journal file, but discovered it was password protected. He didn't have time to fiddle with possible passwords. Maybe one of the computer geeks at the lab could open the files. He shut down the computer, unplugged it, and carried it to his car along with the shoe box.

"How are you this morning?" Ruth's concerned gaze missed nothing. "I didn't think it possible, but you look more tired than yesterday. Did you stay late last night?"

Meg glanced up from the article she was editing and wrinkled her nose at the older woman. "I think I look pretty good for two hours of sleep."

Ruth sat across from her. "Were you hurting?"

"Some." She shrugged. "Nightmares kept waking me."

"Understandable considering the trauma you've been through in the last few days. Have you written any of this down yet?"

Meg dropped her red pen and sat back in her chair. "Why should I do that?"

"You're a writer. We think better with a pen in our hand or a keyboard under our fingertips. You might remember more details to provide Ethan and Rod, but the most important reason to write your experience down is the chance to deal with your emotions on paper. Exorcise your demon, so to speak."

"I didn't think about doing that." She should have considered it. She was a writer, after all, even though in non-fiction. The stream of consciousness writing some of her novelist friends talked about might clear the clutter that plagued her brain at night. "That's a good idea, Ruth. I might take my laptop to bed with me and do a brain dump before turning out the light."

Ruth smiled. "So, what's our assignment for today, Boss?"

"Cornerstone Church's Christmas cantata promo and the water system project, along with updates on Sherri's case and any other emergencies that pop up."

"Is that all?"

"That's just for this morning." Meg grinned. "I have another list for this afternoon."

"I may go back to writing novels. It's less work."

Meg chuckled. "Want to tackle Cornerstone's write-up since you're part of the choir?"

"Sure. How many words?"

"Aim for 200. Is there any legwork you want me to do?"

"Ask Rod if he's made any progress on the murder investigation. I would also like to include statements from Sherri's mother and father in my follow-up article for the next issue."

"I'll see what I can do." Meg could easily get a statement from Sherri's mother, but she didn't know if her father was still in the area. She hadn't seen or heard about Gerald King in years.

She would start with Rod, since he was the closest target interview and his car remained parked in the police station lot. Meg grabbed her notepad and pen and stuffed them in her bag. "Zoe, I'll be at the police station for a few minutes. Call my cell if you need me."

"Will do, Boss."

Meg stepped onto the sidewalk and breathed in the crisp December air. Not quite cold enough for snow, but soon. She loved the crunch of snow and ice under her feet and the challenge of keeping her 'Vette under control on the weather-stricken roads.

She scowled. Except this year she wouldn't have the 'Vette.

In between deadlines, she needed to find a new car. Her mind whirled with the possibilities. She just wished her budget kept pace with her taste in vehicles.

"Hey, Meg!" Rod waved at her from the sidewalk in front of the station. "Got a minute?" He jogged toward her.

She checked for traffic, stepped off the curb and into the square to meet him at the grassy median. An engine revved, followed by squealing tires. As if in slow motion, Meg looked to her left. A black SUV bore down on her.

CHAPTER EIGHT

A bystander screamed. Rod dove for Megan, knocking her out of the SUV's path. The vehicle roared past, trailed by a cloud of misty exhaust. He scrambled to his feet, leaped over Meg, weapon in hand.

"Police! Stop!"

The driver of the vehicle ignored Rod's shout. Other pedestrians in the square scattered. As the vehicle sped from the square, Rod caught a partial license plate number and holstered his weapon.

Zoe dashed out the newspaper office door and plowed through the gathering crowd. "Boss! Are you okay?" She dropped to her knees and tried to help the struggling Megan to an upright position.

"Take it easy, Meg." Rod laid a restraining hand on her shoulder. "Wait until the EMTs check you."

She glared at him. "I'm not messing with those EMTs again. They'll want to cart me off to the hospital and I've had enough of that place this week."

"But, Boss, the detective hit you pretty hard."

Meg turned her scowl to Zoe. "Josh hit harder when we played football in the backyard. I'm fine. Now let me up. Everybody is staring at me."

Rod slipped his arm around her back and one under her knees and lifted her in his arms. After Zoe thrust Meg's bag into her hand, he carried Meg toward the police station.

"You're making a scene, Kelter. Put me down."

He glared down at her red face. "Shut up, Cahill." When she opened her mouth, no doubt to smart off, he simply raised an eyebrow and she subsided. Smart lady. Too much guff from her and he would call in reinforcements.

The desk sergeant saw him climbing the stairs and rushed to open the station door. "You'll have to let the squad in on your pick-up line, Detective. The beautiful women are falling at your feet now."

"Falling?" Rod rolled his eyes. "I had to tackle this one. Where's the chief?"

"Office."

Megan kicked her feet. "Put me down."

Rod tightened his grip around her. "Keep pushing me, Cahill, and I'll transport you to the hospital in cuffs."

She growled, but finally fell into a seething silence. The calm before the storm, he knew. The first opportunity without an audience, he was toast. He carried her into the squad room, and the workers and cops fell silent.

Meg buried her face in his neck. "You are going to pay for this," she whispered.

"I figured that." He carried her into Ethan's office.

Ethan jumped to his feet and came around the desk. "What happened?"

"SUV tried to run her down in the square." Rod slowly set Meg on her feet. "Tell me if something hurts, Meg. No holding back or being the tough editor."

She scowled at him. "You didn't have to carry me. I could have walked in here under my own steam. I am beyond mad at you, Kelter."

"Yeah? Get in line, honey. You aren't the first person I ticked off today." Despite Meg's bravado, she swayed where she stood. He slipped his arm around her waist to steady her. Stubborn woman.

Ethan grasped her arm and helped her sit in a chair. "You need to see a doctor, babe."

"Quit hovering. I'm not an idiot. If I needed to go to the hospital, I'd tell you. The car didn't hit me. Rod did."

"May I quote you on that?" Ruth Rollins walked into the office and stepped between Rod and Ethan to sit beside Megan in the second chair.

"Be my guest." Meg lifted a trembling hand and tucked strands of her hair behind her ear. "You would have made a great defensive tackle for the Cowboys, Detective."

More concern swept through him. He knelt beside her. "Are you sure you're all right? I did hit you pretty hard." He'd been so afraid he was too late, that he wouldn't reach her in time. "You'll probably have a bruise on your ribs to match the one on your back."

"Did you get the plate number?" Ethan asked.

"A partial. Tennessee tag NJR 3. Black Lincoln Navigator, late model."

"Good work. Remind me to give you a raise." Ethan motioned to one of the officers in the squad room and gave him the information. "Start with Navigators in Dunlap County and Otter Creek."

After the officer left to begin the computer search, Ruth said, "Meg needs something sweet to counteract the shock."

Rod stood. "I'll take care of it." He ignored Ethan's surprised expression and strode to the employee break room. Grateful to find it empty for once, Rod took a minute to pace, bleeding off the adrenaline. If he'd been a second or two slower, both of them would be at the hospital right now. Maybe in the morgue.

His fist clenched. Had the shooter tried to take Meg out again, the third time in three days? If so, the move was either incredibly bold or desperate to run her down in broad daylight. For that matter, how did the shooter know when Meg would leave the *Gazette* office? Was it a chance encounter? Would he have tried to run her off the road if she'd driven the Jeep instead of walking across the square?

When he'd settled enough, he crossed to the vending machine, slipped quarters into the slot and selected a Snickers bar. At the drink machine, he chose a Coke. He knew from being with Serena so much that the Cahill women preferred Diet Coke, but Meg needed the sugar right now.

Ethan met him half-way across the squad room. "You all right?" His dark eyes studied Rod's face.

"Adrenaline rush."

He nodded. "Did the car clip you?"

Rod shook his head. "Think you could talk Meg into protective custody?"

"Already tried that. She handed me my head on a platter."

"Mine, too." He started toward the office. "I wish she wasn't so stubborn. It may end up getting her killed."

A Snickers bar dropped into her lap. Meg smiled. "You're back in my good graces, Kelter."

"We need to talk." Rod's voice sounded grim. A signal from Ethan and Ruth patted her on the hand and left the office.

She tore open the wrapper. "About?"

"Protective custody."

"We already had that discussion. The answer's still no." She took a bite of the candy.

"Meg, this attempt on your life was too close. If I hadn't been there or if I'd been a step or two slower, you could be in the hospital or the morgue."

"That's not how it turned out. And we still don't know that this incident was deliberate. It might have been an accident."

"You're right," Ethan said. "We don't know that. But if it was Serena or Madison, would you want us to take that chance?"

"I can't do my job from seclusion. Deadlines won't wait for me to come out of hiding."

"You promised you wouldn't dig into Sherri's murder," Rod said. "Did you find a way around it? Are you investigating?"

"Investigating is your job. I interview."

Color climbed into Rod's cheeks. "You didn't answer my question. It's getting to be a habit, Cahill."

"There were two questions and the answer to both is no." She frowned. "I've managed to get the information Ruth needs without interrogating your suspects, though it hasn't been easy."

Ethan tilted his head. "Is there some other story you're working on that might trigger an incident like this?"

"The only other major story I'm working on is the water system project, and right now no one knows it's a story. We're still nosing around to see if there is a story worth pursuing."

"So you haven't seen the Drakes again?"

"Not yet."

"Meg." Rod's voice carried a hint of steel.

She smiled and sipped her Coke. "I can't promise I won't have to interview them for Ruth's articles, but I will let you know beforehand. Fair enough?"

"I want your word you'll call me or Ethan soon enough that we'll have time to send in the cavalry."

"I promise. Should I report my agenda each day as well?"

"That'll do for a start," Ethan said. "Where do you need to go this afternoon?"

"I'm covering a Christmas party and interviewing Sherri's mother and, maybe, her father." Her eyes narrowed at the look that passed between Ethan and Rod. "What?"

"I'm going with you," Rod said, holding out his hand to her. "What's first?"

She grasped his hand, already stiffening from the tackle. Meg knew she'd have trouble standing without help. Not that she planned to tell these overbearing cops how much she hurt. "Don't you have a job to do? I don't need babysitting services."

"I need to talk to the Kings anyway and I had a couple of questions I wanted to ask you before I dove for the touchdown." He opened the office door. "Maybe this way I'll be able to keep you out of trouble instead of diving to the rescue."

"Dream on, buddy." Meg eyed him. "You any good at taking pictures?"

"Fair, why?"

"You're hired. And by the way, I'm driving."

Ethan's laughter followed them into the squad room.

Rod squeezed his eyes shut and clamped one hand more tightly around his phone and the other around the Jeep's door handle. "You sure you can't work it in?"

He half listened to the computer nerd explain priorities in the lab. Apparently, his request fell near the middle of the list. "Okay. I'd appreciate whatever you can do to move me up the list, man."

Rod opened his eyes again and cringed. "Who taught you to drive, Meg? Dale Earnhardt, Jr.?"

Meg laughed. "Lighten up, Rod."

"Next time I see Henderson, I'm going to tear a strip from his hide for letting you dodge all those tickets." He longed to press on the brake pedal and slow her down. Did she always drive like this? "Slow down, Meg, or I'll write you a ticket myself."

She grinned, but eased up on the gas pedal.

Rod breathed easier as the needle neared the posted speed limit. One good thing, he'd noticed that Meg always wore her seatbelt. "Where are you taking me for lunch?"

Her lips twitched. "Who said anything about lunch?"

"You're driving, you're paying."

"I guess that's fair, especially since you paid the tab last night." She flipped on the blinker. "Joe's Tacos okay? We're running late."

"Fine."

Rod waited until Meg had finished her tacos and Coke before broaching the topic uppermost in his mind. "Did you know Sherri kept a diary?"

Meg shot him a glance. "She did?"

Guess that answered his question. "I found five diaries in her closet, from 2000 to 2004. When I checked her laptop computer, she had files in her word processing documents. They're labeled by the year date, from 2005 forward."

"Did you read the computer files?"

"They're password protected and the lab's backed up on other cases right now. Do you have any idea what Sherri might have used as a password?"

"You already checked the obvious ones, birthdays and anniversary date?"

"Yeah. No dice."

Meg's brow wrinkled. "Nothing comes to mind right off hand, but let me think about it."

Disappointment weighed heavy. He'd hoped Meg could help. The computer geeks at the lab could probably break the password, but he didn't want to wait a few months. The files might contain nothing that helped, but he'd like to read them for himself sooner rather than later to make that determination.

Meg turned into the long driveway of the Holt Plantation. Puzzled, Rod said, "Why are we here?"

"Gardening Society Christmas luncheon."

Oh, joy. A luncheon with the flower matrons of Otter Creek. "Let me guess. This is where I earn my lunch by taking pictures."

"You got it."

Rod eyed her, suspicion growing. "What am I photographing?"

"Otter Creek's flower gurus."

"And?"

Meg grinned. "And the house, garden and grounds."

In December? What sane person wanted pictures of a dead garden in the middle of winter? Great. Cold feet, cold hands, cold everything. The brisk wind from earlier had turned raw and biting. "Where's your regular photographer?"

"This is his day off."

Meg almost felt sorry for Rod. Almost. He stepped into the rear of the room, camera in hand, shivering, cheeks and eyes red. A little payback for embarrassing her earlier, but she needed pictures for the paper's weekend edition. Her lips curved. Probably not the outdoor shots, though.

She snagged a copy of the luncheon program and jotted a few notes for the write-up when Francis Malone's words caught her attention.

"Money for dues and other fees may be given to Maeve Drummond. She is our new treasurer. Have a wonderful Christmas, ladies. See you in January."

Meg remained seated in a chair in the corner as the twenty or so women milled around the ornate dining room. The Gardening Society had already elected a treasurer to replace Sherri within two days of her death?

Rod crossed the room to her side. "What's wrong?"

She needed to practice her poker face. The handsome detective was starting to read her expressions too well. "Sherri met with the Gardening Society's executive committee Sunday afternoon." She inclined her head toward the women clustered around the fireplace. "That makes them some of the last people to see her alive. Maybe they can tell us what was on her mind."

"Meg." His voice carried a warning. "You promised to stay out of the murder investigation."

She rose. "They've already replaced her as treasurer, Rod. She hasn't even been buried yet."

She singled out Francis and drew her to the side. "Maeve's the new treasurer? Fast work, isn't it?"

A sympathetic look crossed the older woman's face. "Not really, dear. Sherri asked us to meet Sunday and handed in her resignation. She's the one who recommended Maeve to the committee as a replacement."

Resigned? Meg bit her lip. Sherri never mentioned she was thinking about stepping down. She loved her Gardening Society work. "Why did she resign?"

Francis spread her hands. "Like I already told Detective Kelter, she hoped her schedule would be too full to continue in that position by next fall. She didn't explain any further."

Meg blinked away sudden tears. So, Francis didn't know the reason. Meg knew, after talking with Wanda King and learning the background to Sherri's resignation. "Is there anything particular you want us to mention in the article? Maybe the date and time of your next meeting?"

Francis gave her the information and returned to the waiting committee.

Meg and Rod climbed back into the Jeep. She cranked the engine and set the vehicle in motion. "Do you have Sherri's laptop?"

"At the station. Why?"

"I think I know the password."

CHAPTER NINE

Leaning on his desk, Rod watched over Meg's shoulder as she typed in the keystrokes. The dialog screen winked out and the text for Sherri's journal popped up. "What did you type?"

"Jordan Tyler Drake."

He thought about that for a minute, but came up blank. "Who is that?"

Meg turned her face away and sat still for a moment. "The name of the son she wanted to have."

Memories of the birth of his daughter flooded his mind, memories that Ty wouldn't have with Sherri because someone ended her life too soon. Rod squeezed Meg's shoulder. No wonder she sounded so choked up.

She wiped tears from her face and turned to him. "Come with me to Mrs. King's place and bring the laptop. The battery is fully charged. I'll drive while you read Sherri's journal." She gave him a watery smile. "I'll even keep to the speed limit."

He held out his hand and helped Meg to her feet. "Deal."

In the car, Megan turned off the radio and drove in silence. She burned with curiosity, but held her tongue in check. If she pushed too hard, Rod would clam up and she would learn nothing.

Megan had to admit she kind of liked Ethan's sidekick. A little. Okay, more than a little. Enough to do something about it? An intriguing idea. She appreciated his sharp sense of humor and the fact he didn't back down from a fight with her. He hung in there, just like her father, Josh, Nick and Ethan. Of course, it didn't really matter what she thought of him. She doubted he thought about her as being anything other than Ethan's sister-in-law and a nosy editor.

Finally, she couldn't stand the silence any longer. "Have you learned anything yet?"

Rod glanced up from the screen. "Did Sherri mention any problems at home in March?"

Meg blinked. "That was two kidnappings and two weddings ago in our family. Can you be more specific?"

"Did she say anything about having a problem with Kyle?"

"Kyle?" Her hands tightened on the wheel. "No. Did he hurt her?"

"Not physically. She found out something about him, something that disturbed her enough she was afraid to go to Ty or the Senator with it."

"Did she say what it was or are you holding that back because of your investigation?"

"Didn't say from what I've read so far."

Sherri was concerned about Ty's reaction? Meg frowned. She knew from discussions with Sherri the last few months that Ty felt increasingly distant, separated from his brother and father. Sherri thought that same distance was creeping into her marriage as well. That was why she'd begun pushing Ty so hard to have a baby. She hoped a child would bring them closer, weave tighter bonds in their marriage. Did Ty's adoption have anything to do with Sherri's murder?

"What?"

She glanced at his face, fighting a smile. He'd keyed into her facial expressions again. How interesting. "I wonder if Ty's adoption has anything to do with this."

"How?"

"I'm not sure. I just know Sherri mentioned Ty was thinking about trying to find his birth mother. The Senator doesn't want him to and that's causing friction between them."

"How does that tie into Kyle?"

She shrugged. "He's the Senator's right-hand man. Maybe he pressured Sherri to convince Ty to back off on the search."

"Where are your facts, Cahill? That's strictly supposition."

"That's your job, Kelter."

A few minutes later, they turned into Mrs. King's rock-covered driveway. Her old Ford Tempo was parked beside the trailer.

Meg climbed from the Jeep and again picked her way around the mud puddles. More rain had fallen overnight. She lifted her hand to knock on the door, but froze before it connected with the wood. "Rod."

He walked up behind her and pulled her aside to examine the smear on the door. "Blood." He drew his weapon.

Rod eased the door open with his foot. He stepped into the trailer and the stench of death hit him, twisting his stomach into knots. "Stay outside, Meg."

"No. I can help you with first aid."

He grasped Meg's shoulder and pushed her back onto the top stair. "You can't help her, Meg. I need you to stay out here. Will you do that for me?"

She pressed her lips and nodded.

Satisfied she wouldn't follow, Rod checked each room for intruders, but the home felt empty. Following the odor, Rod ended his search in the back bedroom. Mrs. King lay in bed, a bullet hole in her forehead.

He holstered his weapon and walked outside, breathing in the fresh, crisp air.

"Well?" Meg's white face drew his gaze.

"I'm sorry."

"How? Heart attack, a fall?"

He wished he could tell her the cause of death was accidental, but it wasn't. Someone had murdered Sherri's mother. "Someone shot her."

She dropped onto the bench beside the path.

He berated himself silently. Meg already had a shock today with the SUV trying to run her down. He should have been more sensitive and at least made her sit before divulging such bad news to her.

Rod sat beside her and pulled her into the circle of his arms. "I'm sorry."

"Why?"

"I should have tried to break the news in a more sensitive manner."

"There is no easy way to deliver that kind of gut-wrenching news. Why would someone kill her? Was it a robbery?"

He pulled out his cell phone and punched in a number he didn't use often. When a male voice answered, Rod said, "Wes, this is Rod Kelter. I stumbled on a murder scene on your turf. 427 Barnett Lane. Tell your boys I'm in a red Jeep parked in the drive. I don't want them to shoot me by accident." He ended the call and slipped the cell phone back in its holder.

"Why didn't you call Ethan?"

"Not our jurisdiction. On county roads, Sheriff's department gets the call."

"Will they keep you informed?"

"Of course. Professional courtesy." He stood and pulled her to her feet. "Come on. Let's wait in the car. We're going to be here a while."

Within minutes, the first responders barreled down the road and scattered mud and rocks as they skidded to a stop. Before they opened their doors and approached the Jeep, Rod had his window rolled down and his badge visible.

"You the one who called this in?"

"Yeah."

"What have we got?"

"Found the homeowner in the back bedroom with a bullet in the forehead." Megan gasped and Rod covered her hand with his. "This may be tied in to a murder case I'm working. Your vic is the mother of my vic."

The cop motioned to the other patrolman. "You can give your statements to Officer Neese and be on your way." He looked at Megan, speculation in his gaze, before returning his attention to Rod. "You the only one to enter the crime scene?"

He gazed at the cop through narrowed eyes. Why was the guy looking at Meg like that? "Yeah," he said, his voice edged with steel. Rod handed him his card. "Call me when you finish processing the scene."

The man examined the card, nodded and slipped it into his pocket. "Will do, Detective." He strode toward the trailer.

Two hours later, Megan eased past the emergency vehicles parked in the roadway and headed for Otter Creek. "You think they believed us?"

Rod turned in his seat to face her. "Why wouldn't they? We had no reason to kill Mrs. King and there's no evidence to say otherwise."

"I had the feeling that first cop didn't take everything you said at face value."

"We're trained to be suspicious of everybody. Sometimes the perpetrator of the crime is the one who calls it in."

"You told the officer Mrs. King's death might be connected to Sherri's murder. Do you think that's true?"

"It's a distinct possibility. Cops don't like coincidences."

She nodded. "Neither do journalists. You're sure Mrs. King didn't walk in on a robber?"

Rod didn't say anything for a minute.

"Come on, Rod. I have to report this in the paper. You're not the investigating officer, but you did see the scene. Give me something."

"She was in bed. It looks like someone shot her while she slept."

"In bed? Not on the bed?"

"In bed."

"She was killed during the night. Could you tell how long she'd been dead?"

"That's the ME's job."

Megan grimaced. Interviewing a cop was akin to interviewing an aardvark. "You don't think it was a robbery?"

"It's not my crime scene, Meg. I shouldn't be talking to you about this."

"Off the record, then."

He scowled at her.

She sighed. "All right. Can you tell me if she was as neat a housekeeper as I remember?"

"Nothing was out of place."

Definitely not a robbery, then. Mrs. King kept everything neat in her trailer. She figured a thief wouldn't care if he left a mess after killing the woman.

Then another horrible thought stuck deep in her soul. Had she brought death to Mrs. King by going to see her so soon after Sherri's death? Did the killer think Megan was using Sherri's mother as a source of information to track him down and expose him?

She glanced at Rod. "Do you think her death could be my fault?"

He blinked. "What?"

"Do you think I caused her death?"

"How? You didn't pull the trigger or print her address in the paper. You didn't quote any inflammatory statements she might have made."

Her hands gripped the steering wheel. "But I visited her the day after Sherri died."

"What?"

Meg clenched her teeth. Rod's voice sounded colder than the freezing temperature outside. "Maybe the killer found out and thought I was pumping her for information."

"Did she know anything about Sherri's killer?"

"I don't think so. She didn't seem to be holding back."

"Maybe she knew more than she thought. If the shooter is the same one that killed Sherri, he wanted to plug any potential leaks that might lead back to him."

If it was the same killer and he'd learned she talked to Mrs. King, he would come to another inevitable conclusion. If Meg had talked to both Mrs. King and Sherri, then she was a definite liability.

Great. She was a repository of information that might be important, except that she couldn't make all the pieces of the puzzle fit yet. As far as she knew, she still had pieces missing. And maybe a screw loose from hitting the stone wall with her head.

"You're too quiet. What are you thinking?"

"I need to stay away from my sisters." She licked her dry lips. "I think he's going to try again and I don't want them caught in his trap by accident."

Much as he hated to admit it, Rod feared Megan was correct. If Sherri's killer had murdered Mrs. King, Meg was his next target and his earlier failures would make him that much more determined to finish the job.

Darkness had fallen by the time Megan parked the Jeep next to his SUV. The lot had a few cars left in it, but most of the civilian employees had knocked off for the day. Ethan's truck still remained in place. Rod figured the police chief was waiting for an update, but he didn't want Meg driving home without an escort.

A gust of wind rocked the Jeep. Looked like a storm might be brewing. "You headed home?"

She shook her head. "Office. I need to write this article while the details are fresh."

He glanced at the newspaper office windows. Lights still burned and he noted Zoe working at her desk. "Call me before you leave the office."

She frowned, but didn't argue for which he was grateful.

Rod slammed the passenger door and watched until Meg entered her office. He ran up the station stairs two at a time.

"No beautiful woman in your arms this time, Detective?" The desk sergeant grinned at him.

"Must be losing my touch." Rod crossed the squad room and knocked on Ethan's door. "Meg's back at the office."

Ethan pushed aside some of the paperwork on his desk. "Is she all right?"

"So far. The woman's got a lot of sheer grit."

Lightning lit the sky. Thunder rumbled loud enough to rattle the window in Ethan's office.

"Fill me in."

Rod recounted what he'd found, adding, "It looked like the same caliber weapon that killed Sherri, Ethan."

"Sheriff's department call?"

"Not yet."

"I'll call the Sheriff later tonight if you don't hear from them." He glanced at his watch. "I've got a few more things to wrap up before I leave and I don't want Meg to go home alone."

Rod grinned, way ahead of his boss. "I already planned on making sure she arrived home safe."

"Good. Why don't you knock off for the day. Start fresh tomorrow. Maybe the Sheriff's people will find something to help on our case."

Lights flickered in the station as Rod stood. "Call me if you learn anything."

He waved at the desk sergeant and dashed down the stairs to the parking lot. Wind whipped his hair, moisture thick in the air. The first drops of cold rain stung his face.

If he hurried, he might make it into the Gazette office before the rain started in earnest. He ran to the SUV, cranked the engine and drove around the square to the newspaper office.

He threw open the car door. A bolt of lightning struck the transformer down the street and the lights winked out around the square. Rod grabbed his flashlight and dashed to the Gazette office.

Meg froze in the complete darkness. Her heart slammed against her chest wall. In an instant, she found herself gasping for air. She couldn't get enough air. She had to get out of there. She couldn't breathe. Why wasn't there enough air?

A deafening clap of thunder spurred her into movement. She hurried forward. A sharp jab of pain shot down her leg. What was it? The corner of the desk? She felt her way out of the office. Once she left the doorway, nothing but open space and pitch black greeted her.

Where was the door? Why weren't there any lights on the square? She heard something to her left. A step, a breath. Someone was in the office with her.

Panic set in. Reasoning fled. She plunged forward, ran into a man's chest and screamed.

CHAPTER TEN

Rod grunted at the impact, but reflexively lifted his hands to steady Megan. Even without the lights, he knew it was her.

"Megan, it's me." He shook her a little to get her attention. "It's Rod."

As soon as he said his name, she stopped screaming. The silence almost shocked him. Meg's body shook, then he heard her gasping for air. "Megan?" He jerked the flashlight from his pocket and aimed the beam at her face.

Her panic-stricken expression galvanized him into action. Rod laid the flashlight down on Zoe's desk, beam shining toward them. He cupped her face with his hands. "Slow down your breathing. Breathe with me. In. Out. In. Out." He kept his voice low, tone steady. "Come on, Cahill. Don't make me call those EMTs. In. Out."

She gripped his wrists, her gaze locked on his face.

Within minutes, her breathing settled into a more normal rhythm. He drew her into his arms. "It's okay, Meg. I'm so sorry." He eased back enough to examine her dimly lit face. "I didn't mean to scare you."

"Not your fault." She concentrated on steadying her breathing for another minute or two. "The darkness," she whispered.

Rod rubbed her back gently. "You're afraid of the dark? Never expected that from a lady who would give Dale, Jr. some stiff competition."

A wry smile crossed her face. "Didn't used to be afraid of the dark."

"A panic attack?" He frowned. "Is this a leftover effect from Monday morning?"

She remained silent a moment. "Maybe." Meg shivered. "It was so dark on the path I felt like I couldn't breathe."

"Is that how you felt a few minutes ago?"

She nodded and Rod tightened his arms around her. "The transformer blew down the street. Electricity is out around the square."

He should let Meg go, but she was still trembling. And, in truth, she was a perfect fit in his arms and that fascinated him.

Rod's hand moved of its own volition into Meg's hair. Blond silk. Now he understood why Ethan had a thing for Serena's hair. He wondered if her skin was as soft as it looked. Just one touch to satisfy his curiosity and he'd let her go.

His hand untangled from her hair and curled around the back of her neck. Satisfaction bloomed in his gut. He'd guessed right. Baby soft skin.

"Rod?" Her voice came out as a whisper.

His gaze dropped to her beautiful, lush mouth. "What?"

"Are you going to kiss me or not?"

His lips twitched. "Do you want me to?"

"Would you hurry up already? You're killing me here."

Before he could second guess himself, he settled his lips on hers. Impressions flew at him. Soft, sweet, incredible. This was a stupid move. He knew it as sure as he knew his own name. He wasn't ready for any kind of relationship. Was he? And, besides, this was his boss's sister-in-law. But he couldn't break Meg's spell and move away from her, not yet.

Rod deepened the kiss for a moment, reveling in the unique taste of her. Seconds, maybe minutes passed before he made himself lift his mouth from hers. He ran a shaking finger down her cheek. "Meg, I don't know what to say."

"Don't." She stepped out of his embrace. "Don't spoil an amazing kiss by apologizing."

He grinned. "Amazing, huh?"

"Strike that. More like stupendous. But you can't quote me on that. I'll deny it."

He laughed. "Let's check outside, see if the guys need help directing traffic. You can stand under the awning. It should keep you dry."

"Can I carry the flashlight?"

"Sure. Want to keep it handy?"

"I can't write down the action on a notepad without light. I need enough information to put together an article."

He snatched the light from Zoe's desk and gave it to her. At the door, he paused and looked back at her. "Meg, I know the storm knocked out the power, but don't wander off, okay? I don't want to give the killer an opportunity to take a run at you during all the chaos."

She straightened and saluted him. "Yes, sir. Orders received, sir."

Rod chuckled and opened the door. She was definitely feeling better. Her smart-mouth editor side had surfaced again.

Minutes later, he dashed to the protected area where Meg stood taking notes. He wiped the rain from his face. "They have it under control now. I'll follow you home."

She nodded and stuffed the notepad into her bag and handed him the flashlight. "Let's go."

Meg sighed, relieved at the sight of her porch light burning and Josh's SUV in the driveway. She'd rather not have a repeat panic episode and, after the day she'd experienced, would prefer not to be alone overnight. She figured tonight's nightmares would include black SUVs, old trailers, and impenetrable blackness.

She ran to her porch with her bag, Rod a step behind her. Josh opened the door for them.

"About time you got here." He leaned against the frame. "I was ready to send out a posse."

"A transformer blew in the square. There's a blackout in the center of town."

Josh straightened. "Looks like you're soaked, Rod. Need some coffee or a towel?"

"No, thanks."

"Here." Meg handed her bag to Josh. "Take this inside and make me some hot cocoa. I need a chocolate fix."

His eyebrows rose. He studied her face, then Rod's, but nodded and left them on the porch without saying anything. She knew that wouldn't last long. Just as long as it took for her to shut the front door.

She faced Rod and found his gaze locked on her. "Thank you for not ratting on me to Josh. Are you going home or back to the station?"

"Home. Ethan wants me to start fresh in the morning."

"What's the plan for tomorrow?"

His lips twitched. "Aside from keeping you out of trouble, tracking down the black Navigator, more interviews, the usual."

"That's a hard job, you know." She inched closer to him.

"Which part?"

"Keeping me out of trouble. The Cahill triplets are trouble with a capital T."

Rod lifted his hand and cupped the back of her neck. He bent his head to hers. "Believe me, I know."

His brief, whisper-soft kiss left her with an ache in her heart as she watched him drive away. She waited until the lights of his car disappeared, then went inside and shut the door on the darkness.

Meg found Josh in the kitchen, stirring the packet of hot cocoa mix into hot water in a mug. He glanced at her face and froze.

"Oh, no." Josh laid down the spoon and glared at her.

"What?"

"First Serena, then Madison, and now you. I'm doomed."

She plopped down on a bar stool. "What are you talking about?"

"You're in love with Rod Kelter, aren't you?"

"Are you crazy?" Her stomach turned a flip. He couldn't be right. "We're not even dating."

Josh placed the mug of steaming chocolate in front of her. "You're in the early stages, snoopy."

Meg frowned at his childhood nickname for her. "What makes you say that?"

"It's all over your face. Serena has the same expression when she looks at Ethan. Madison has it when she looks at Nick. You've been bitten by the love bug."

She sipped the hot liquid. "I think you're imagining things, but say you were right. Why does that spell your doom?"

Josh sighed. "The Cahill offspring are falling like dominoes. I'm the next in line and the only one left. Mom's already hinting about Madison's business partner, Del. I think she's picking out names for grandchildren."

Meg laughed at his horrified expression. Some good woman deserved her awesome brother. And now that she thought about it, Del did blush a lot when Josh was around. Maybe she'd call Madison later. Compare notes.

She finished her mug of cocoa, hugged her brother and traipsed to her room. Meg readied herself for bed, thought more about her brother's statements and chuckled. No way. Rod Kelter was a great guy when he wasn't getting in her way as an editor, but she couldn't be in love with him. It was too soon. They hadn't had a real date yet. And the man had baggage, the kind Meg doubted he had unloaded.

Rod replaced the picture of his wife and daughter on his bedside table and grabbed the phone handset. "Kelter."

"It's Ethan. Sheriff Benson just called."

"Hang on." He yanked open the table drawer and pulled out a pen and pad. "Okay. Go."

"Mrs. King died sometime Tuesday night, probably around midnight. No sign of forced entry. No footprints under the windows."

"After Sherri's murder, I doubt she left her doors unlocked."

"Not likely," Ethan agreed.

"So the perp had a key." And that narrowed the list of suspects if Sherri's mother didn't leave a key under her mat or under a fake rock. He didn't remember seeing either. The area around the trailer was bare.

"That's what the lead detective thinks."

"What about the husband?"

"Can't find him. The neighbors said he hasn't been around in years."

"Anything missing?"

"Doesn't seem like it."

That ruled out robbery as a motive for the killing. "What about the bullet? Any luck with that?"

"It's a .38 caliber."

"That's fast."

"Crime scene techs found it in the mattress. They've sent it off to the lab for comparison."

"The same gun?"

"That's my guess. Benson thinks the cases are connected."

"Is he going to cooperate?"

"He says they'll investigate things from their end and report any findings if we'll do the same."

Rod laid down his pen. "Okay. I'll be in the office early tomorrow, but probably out the rest of the day."

"I'll call if something comes up."

The moment Meg entered the *Gazette's* office the next morning, she spotted the Starbucks cup at the edge of Zoe's desk. "Please say that's mine."

Zoe laughed. "Thought you could use a strong pick-me-up after the SUV incident yesterday. How do you feel?"

"Like a truck hit me." She smiled. "Actually, I'm sore, but mobile. I guess I owe the detective for that." And for dreams of hot kisses interspersed with the nightmares. Meg sipped the coffee and sighed. "Peppermint mocha. You're an angel, Zoe."

"That's what my boyfriend says too."

"Did you call Ruth?"

"She wants an interview with the mayor about the water system but his office is giving her the runaround."

Perfect. She felt just bad enough and mean enough to corner Henry Parks today. "Tell her I'll take care of it myself. Are you covering the Junior League's Christmas sale?"

"I planned on it." She wrinkled her brow. "That's okay, isn't it?"

"Of course. You'll do a great job with the story. You're the best shopper I know. Take J.J. with you. He'll take some sharp pictures."

Zoe beamed. "Thanks, Boss."

Meg checked messages, slipped on her coat and headed for Town Hall. The wind wasn't nearly as raw today, so she left the Jeep parked in front of the office and walked. By the time she arrived, she'd finished her coffee and the brisk air had cleared the muzzy sluggishness from her brain.

She took the stairs to the second floor and opened the door to the mayor's outer office. Velda West eyed her over half-glasses.

"Can I help you, Ms. Cahill?"

"I need five minutes of the mayor's time."

"He's buried in paperwork. He won't be available until late this afternoon." She gave a cold smile. "I'll be sure to let him know you stopped by to see him."

"This is important, Velda."

"Everybody says that, Ms. Cahill. Would you like to make an appointment for tomorrow?"

"Isn't the mayor up for re-election next fall?"

Wariness grew in the older woman's eyes. "Yes. Why?"

"I'm sure the mayor wants to keep his name in front of his constituents. Might be better for his reputation if his name is associated with the good things he's doing for Otter Creek. Dad admires his ideals and commitment to the town. Surely Mayor Parks can spare a few minutes to talk about the new water system."

Velda glanced at the mayor's closed door, then Meg. "I'll check, but I can't guarantee anything. He's a very busy man."

But apparently never too busy to solicit votes. Velda stepped out of the mayor's office and motioned her inside.

Buried in paperwork? Meg wanted to laugh. Parks had three pieces of paper on his desk. She had three piles of papers on hers. "Thanks for taking a minute for me, Mayor Parks."

"Always glad to talk to you, my dear. How's your father enjoying his vacation?"

Meg grinned. She knew her father's name would get her in the door. Parks always jockeyed to keep in her father's good graces. After all, Dad was the president of the only bank in town and, as such, had a lot of pull in town business. "He says Mom loves Hawaii. He's not too keen on the sand, though."

Henry Parks laughed, his portly belly jiggling. "I'll have to take the wife and kids there. I bet they'd love it."

And Meg figured that by the end of the day, the mayor would have a vacation planned to Hawaii for himself and his family. Something inside drove him to match or best the leaders in their town.

"Now, what story are you here researching, my dear?"

She pulled her notepad and pen from her bag. "The new water system. What can you tell me about it?"

"Well, as you know, Otter Creek's water pipes were laid back in the 1920s when we had 300 residents. Over the years, we've grown so much that the small pipes popular back then can't keep up with the demand for water. The system is strained and we're having more and more pipes burst because of the pipes degrading with age and the constant pressure of adding new customers to the system decreases the water pressure."

Meg paused in her writing. "What are you recommending to help with the problem?"

"I'm asking the town council to approve a proposal for a new water system. The contracted company would replace the old pipes with larger, stronger ones. The work would be completed in phases, so not everyone would be inconvenienced at the same time." He smiled. "We're hoping the good citizens of Otter Creek will open their homes to neighbors and friends across town for a day or two as the need arises."

"How many companies are bidding for the project?"

"Right now, one."

"One? Is the council going to solicit other bids?"

Color climbed into the mayor's cheeks. "We've asked a few other companies to submit a bid. So far, none of them have responded."

Meg sat back in her chair. "When are you voting on whether or not to approve the bid?"

"The next council meeting."

That was Tuesday. "How much was the bid?"

When he named the multi-million dollar figure, her jaw dropped. "Isn't that kind of high? How can they charge that much for so little work? It isn't a complicated project. They dig up old pipes and replace them with new ones."

Parks frowned. "The man-hours alone should put the price tag well over their quoted price. They have an excellent reputation in the business world."

"Which company is it?"

"De Marco Water Works."

"When's the projected starting and ending date?"

The mayor relaxed again, no longer uneasy. "If the contract is approved Tuesday, they will begin work immediately. They want to be finished by the end of the summer."

A tap on the door interrupted them. Velda said, "Mayor, you have a meeting in ten minutes."

"Thanks."

Meg stood. "I appreciate your time, Mayor Parks. I won't keep you, but I do have one more question. Who recommended De Marco Water Works to the council?"

"Senator Drake. Good to see you again, Megan."

She waved and exited the office. What connection did Senator Drake have with De Marco Water Works? Coming down the stairs, Meg noticed a commotion near the lobby doors. After a moment, the sea of people parted and allowed Senator Warren Drake to enter the building.

Meg smiled as she watched him work the crowd like a pro, shaking hands, slapping backs, something to say with a smile to each person he greeted. She hurried down the last stairs as he reached the elevator doors. "Senator Drake. Can I speak with you a moment, please?"

He swiveled and extended his hand, a broad smile on his face. "Megan, what a pleasure. I haven't seen you in ages, my dear. You've grown into a beautiful woman."

Man, Drake was in full politician mode. "Thank you, sir."

"I only have a minute. How can I help you?"

"I'm working on an editorial about the proposed new water system in Otter Creek. I understand from Mayor Parks that you recommended De Marco Water Works. How did you hear about the company?"

His smile morphed into a straight line. "You'll have to talk to Don Brandenburg, my dear. He's the one who recommended them to me. I've got to run, now. Great to see you again." Drake brushed past her to board the elevator.

With her next breath, she froze. The scent of pine. In an instant, she was back at the trail, hearing a gun being cocked behind her ear. Her knees weakened so that she had to lean against the wall to stay on her feet. She couldn't pass out here. Talk about causing a scene.

Meg waited for the lobby to clear before stumbling outside. She looked over at the police parking lot. Rod's SUV was gone. Frustrated, she found an unoccupied bench out of the pedestrian traffic flow and dug out her cell phone. She punched in his number.

"Kelter."

"It's Meg."

"What's wrong?"

She smiled a little. The guy was good. First, he'd learned to read her face, now her voice. "I ran into Senator Drake a few minutes ago."

"What? You weren't supposed to go near the Drakes without letting me know."

"Stuff the macho cop routine, Rod. It wasn't intentional. He was entering Town Hall as I was leaving. You remember me mentioning the pine smell that night on the trail?"

"Yeah."

"Drake's cologne is that same scent."

CHAPTER ELEVEN

"Where are you now?" Rod slid from his SUV and glanced around the driveway of the Drake mansion.

"Outside Town Hall."

"Are you returning to your office?"

"No, Flint's."

The department store? "Why Flint's?"

"The scent will drive me crazy until I identify it. I'm going to the men's counter and find that cologne."

"Stay in populated places, Meg. Call me when you're finished."

Rod pocketed his cell and rang the doorbell. He didn't like Meg driving around in the open, but short of tossing her in jail he couldn't do anything about it.

The maid led him to the dining room where Kyle waited for him.

"Rod, come sit with me." Kyle shook his hand. "I asked Charlene to bring us coffee and pastries. I hope you don't mind, but I had an early meeting and I'm starved."

"Coffee sounds good."

"Great." He motioned to Charlene to pour two cups and invited Rod to sit. After the cook left, Kyle said, "I heard about Sherri's mother on the news this morning. Is that why you're here?"

"Partly."

"What happened to her? Was it a botched robbery?"

"It's county jurisdiction. Sheriff Benson is in charge of the investigation."

"But didn't you discover Mrs. King's body?"

Rod sipped his coffee. He had no intention of discussing an on-going case with Kyle Drake. "Was Sherri close to her mother?"

A flash of irritation showed in Kyle's eyes for a second and disappeared. "I haven't been around much recently, but they were in the habit of calling each other three or four times a day. Sherri felt responsible for taking care of her since her father left."

"How long ago was that?"

"About the time we graduated from college. Maybe that fall. I went to work for Dad after I toured Europe during the summer and I remember Ty calling to tell us when I was settling in D.C."

Thirteen years and Gerald King hadn't tried to get in touch with his family? "He never contacted them again?"

"Not that I ever heard. One of his friends claimed to have seen him on the streets in Knoxville a couple of years after he left, but Ty couldn't find him."

"Any idea why he left?"

His mouth full of lemon pastry, Kyle shook his head.

Rod made a note to ask Ty about his father-in-law. It was possible King came back, but would he still have a house key after all these years? Wouldn't Mrs. King have changed the locks since then?

"Do you know who had a key to Mrs. King's house?"

"Sherri did. She was always running over there, taking food or craft supplies to her mother." He dropped his gaze to his coffee cup and studied the steaming liquid. "Look, I don't like talking behind Ty's back, but you'll find out any way."

"Find out what?"

"Ty also has a key to the King place."

"How do you know that?"

"I heard him talking to Sherri once about going over to her mother's to fix something. When Sherri offered her key, Ty told her he had one of his own." Kyle paused. "You know, Mrs. King lived out on a rural road. Not much traffic through there. Maybe a vagrant wandered into her home."

"Maybe." But Rod didn't think so. Most of the vagrants he'd run across didn't have a gun. And if it had been a homeless person, why not take things like food or money? Mrs. King's purse had $120 in the wallet.

"Listen, Rod, I was sorry to hear about the loss of your wife and daughter. I found out months after it happened and I didn't see you when Dad and I were in town for a few days after that."

Rod closed his notebook. Though the sadness resurfaced, it didn't seem as severe or maybe he'd grown used to the pain. Maybe a certain blonde-haired editor had something to do with it. "Thanks."

"You're young." Kyle grinned at Rod. "And decent to look at. Anybody new in your life?"

The question caught him by surprise. Meg's face appeared in his mind. Rod stood and tucked the notebook and pen into his pocket. "Don't have much time for that right now."

"Is there anyone on your radar?"

"Why the twenty questions about my social life?"

Kyle chuckled. "Didn't want to poach on your territory. That's all."

"You don't stick around long. Why should I worry?" Rod leaned his hip against the dining table. "Got anybody in mind?"

"Megan Cahill."

Rod straightened, fighting to keep his expression neutral. "That wouldn't be a good idea right now."

"Why not?"

"She's a material witness in a case in which you are a suspect."

"What?" Kyle jumped to his feet. "Are you crazy? We're friends, man. From grade school. You know I wouldn't kill anybody. You can trust me."

"I trust no one in an investigation. Everybody is a suspect, including you." Rod strode to the door, Kyle trailing behind, still protesting his innocence. On the porch, he turned to Kyle. "Leave Megan alone, Kyle. She's not your typical flavor of the week."

A speculative look rose in Kyle's eyes. "You are interested in her."

Rod frowned. "Just stay away from her."

Meg crinkled her nose and shook her head. Yuck! "No. That has too much citrus."

The counter girl frowned and handed Meg a cup filled with ground coffee beans. "Sniff this and we'll try a few more."

Meg's eyebrows rose. "I like the smell of coffee, but why do you want me to sniff it?"

"It sort of cleanses the smelling senses. After sniffing several perfumes or colognes, haven't you noticed the scents all smell alike?"

"Yeah."

"The ground coffee will keep that from happening."

"Can I quote you on that?"

"What do you mean?"

Meg grinned. "After this experience, I might write an editorial on the finer points of selecting cologne and perfume for a loved one."

"Are you trying to find a scent for your boyfriend?"

She shook her head as a picture of Rod formed in her mind. No way would she get him pine-scented cologne, not after the trail incident. Now maybe if she found something a little musky, Meg might indulge herself. After all, he'd gone out of his way to be kind to her. When he wasn't acting the macho cop and annoying her.

The counter girl brought another four colognes for Meg to sniff. "These are the last of the woodsy scents."

Meg breathed in a whiff of the first three, shaking her head after each. When she tried the last one, she froze. "That's it." She looked at the label. *Sherwood.* Like the forest. How appropriate.

"That's our most expensive cologne."

She named a price that made Meg wince.

"Would you like me to wrap this for your husband or boyfriend?"

"I don't want to buy that." The girl looked so disappointed that Meg didn't have the heart to leave without buying something from her. She'd been a great help. "What have you got in musky scents?"

The smile reappeared on the counter girl's face. She thrust the coffee cup back in Meg's hand. "Sniff more of this and I'll bring some for you to try."

A few minutes later, as Meg stood by the cash register, the counter girl glanced up from Meg's debit card with a startled look on her face. "You're the woman who was attacked on the trail the other night with Sherri Drake."

A knot formed in Meg's stomach. "Yes."

"I was so sorry to hear about Sherri. She was a nice lady."

Meg glanced at her name tag. "You knew her, Lucy?"

Lucy handed back her card. "She came in every couple of months to purchase cologne for her husband."

"Do you remember what kind? Was it Sherwood?" Did Ty wear that kind of cologne? She thought back to her interview with him, but he hadn't stood close enough or she would have smelled that pine scent.

Lucy shook her head. "Oh, no. Sherri hated that kind of cologne. She always bought him British Wave. It's a spicy scent."

"Did Sherri come in recently?"

"No. Ty did, though." She busied herself tidying the counter, color staining her cheeks.

"What happened, Lucy? Did he say something to you?"

The girl's face twisted into a scowl. "He didn't, but that woman on his arm sure did." She bagged Meg's purchase and scooted it in front of her.

Again? Meg felt sick. How could Ty do that to Sherri after all the promises he'd made the last time? "What woman?"

"Candy Wilson. Candy. What kind of name is that for a grown woman?"

Meg handed her business card to Lucy. "If you think of anything else about Sherri, Ty or Candy, call me."

The girl studied Meg's card. "You're investigating?"

"Sort of. I'm helping a friend."

Minutes later, locked inside the Jeep, Meg pulled out her cell phone and punched in a number now very familiar. "Can you meet me for lunch?"

"So, what's up?" Rod bit into the chicken salad crescent Serena had put in front of him. Oh, man. He closed his eyes and savored the taste. It was a miracle Ethan didn't put on tons of weight with cooking like this on hand all the time.

The bell over The Bare Ewe's door tinged. Rod's gaze automatically shifted to the front of Madison's yarn store and surveyed the two women walking in the door. Doubtful the two blue-haired women were serious threats to security, he returned his attention to Meg.

"Thanks for meeting me here. I was afraid we might be overheard in a restaurant." She took several swallows of her Coke before continuing. "I found the pine scent at the cologne counter at Flint's."

He wasn't surprised. When Meg wanted information, not much seemed to stop her. "What was it?"

"Something called Sherwood. It's the most expensive brand in the store."

And not a cologne for a run-of-the-mill thief. He'd have to follow up with Flint's and see if they could give him a list of customers who bought that brand. "Okay. What else did you learn?"

She paused in her chewing to stare. After she swallowed, she said, "How did you know there was more?"

"When a beautiful woman invites me to lunch, there's got to be more than a product name she could pass on over the phone."

"Beautiful?" she whispered. Her cheeks turned pink.

"I take that back." He smiled at the disappointment in her eyes. "A better description would be breath-taking."

Meg smiled. "With compliments like that, I'll have to come up with other excuses for dates with you."

"Dates?" Serena placed a steaming mug of coffee in front of Rod, her gaze shifting from him to her sister. A smile formed on her mouth. "Did I hear that right?"

"You aren't supposed to eavesdrop, Serena."

"Don't change the subject." Serena tilted her head. "Are you and my sister dating, Rod?"

He felt Meg's gaze on him. How was he supposed to answer that? He didn't want to hurt Meg. So he hedged. "It's complicated."

Serena grinned. "That wasn't a no."

Rod chuckled. "Okay, it wasn't a no."

"Serena, don't you have somewhere to be? Like somebody's kitchen?" Meg's face looked flushed.

Her sister laughed. "All right, you win for now. I'll leave the other sandwiches in the refrigerator if you want more, Rod."

"These are great, Serena. Thanks."

After Serena left, Rod turned his attention back to Meg. "What else did you learn at Flint's, Meg?"

"I talked to the counter girl in the men's cologne section. Sherri used to come in every few weeks to buy cologne for Ty."

Rod pushed aside his empty plate and lifted the mug of coffee to his lips. "What kind?"

"British Wave, definitely not Sherwood. Lucy said Sherri didn't buy that scent for Ty."

"And?"

"And Ty came in to buy cologne for himself not too long ago, but he wasn't alone and the woman he was with wasn't Sherri."

Rod set down his mug with a thud. "Ty was having an affair?"

"You're not surprised, are you? This isn't the first one."

"It isn't?"

Meg looked puzzled. "He had a relationship with one of his students."

Try as he might, he couldn't remember hearing about that. "You sure it wasn't Kyle?"

"Kyle has so many women a new one wouldn't make the news."

The tension in his gut lessened at Meg's disgusted tone. She knew about Kyle's constant stream of women. "Ty's affair made the news? When?"

"Almost two years ago."

About the time Erin and Kayla died. No wonder he didn't remember the story.

Meg's gaze sought and held his. "I'm the one who wrote the story."

"That's why he threw you out yesterday?"

"Ty lost his job at Camden University because of my story. I guess he still harbors some hard feelings."

Rod grunted. That was putting a mild spin on how Ty felt about Meg. "Who was the woman with Ty at Flint's?"

"Candy Wilson."

He wrote the name on his pad. "I'll check her out." His cell phone buzzed. "Kelter."

"It's Ethan. We got a hit on the Black Navigator."

"Who?"

"Judge Wyatt."

Rod's hand tightened around his pen. "Any others?"

"No other matches, Rod." Ethan paused. "Want me to meet you at the courthouse?"

"I'll take care of it." He ended the call and stood. "I've got to go."

"What's wrong?"

"We traced the license plate of the SUV that almost hit you yesterday."

Meg jumped to her feet. "I'm going with you."

"Meg."

"Don't feed me the police business line, Rod." She grabbed her bag and shoved her chair in place. "I promise not to get in your way, but my showing up might rattle whoever was driving the SUV."

"No."

"Look, either you take me along or I'll just follow you. That might not be too safe since I seem to inspire accidents near cars these days."

Rod grimaced, but didn't say anything more. He'd rather keep her close until he had the killer behind bars. After that, he'd figure out what to do about the haunting journalist who had started appearing in his dreams.

Meg stared out the SUV's front windshield. "What are we doing here?" The courthouse loomed in front of them, white columns rising three stories. She twisted in her seat.

"The SUV is registered to Judge Wyatt." Rod opened the door and waited for her on the sidewalk.

Meg scrambled for her bag, hopped out and joined him. "What's the plan?"

"You keep quiet. I'll ask questions."

"That's it?"

"You have a better one?"

"Yeah, I get to ask questions as well. We tag team him."

"Want to wait in the car, Cahill?"

She narrowed her eyes. "Fine. No questions." Unless, of course, she couldn't help herself.

They climbed the courthouse steps in silence. Near the top, a crowd of people surged down the stairs. One man knocked into her in his haste to get down the stairs. Rod slipped his arm around her back to steady her, but didn't move it until they reached the hallway outside Judge Wyatt's chambers.

In the outer office, Rod explained to the judge's assistant that he needed to see Wyatt on police business. After a couple of minutes, the assistant motioned them into Wyatt's inner sanctum.

The judge's black robe hung on a coat tree in a corner of the office. Floor to ceiling bookcases lined the walls. Meg envied the book space, but not the volumes in his collection. All law books.

"Detective Kelter, what can I do for you?" Wyatt nodded in greeting to Meg and motioned them to the seats in front of his desk.

"You own a Black Navigator, plate number NJR 378?"

Alarmed, Wyatt got to his feet. "What's wrong? Did someone hit my car in the parking lot?"

"Your SUV was involved in an incident yesterday."

"What kind of incident?"

"It came within inches of hitting Miss Cahill."

The judge sat abruptly. "Where? When?"

"In the square around 4:00 yesterday afternoon."

"I was in court at that time, Detective. My bailiff can verify that." He turned his gaze to Megan. "Are you all right, Ms. Cahill?"

"A few bruises, sir."

Rod pulled out his notepad. "Who has access to your keys, sir?"

"My wife and my son." He rubbed his jaw. "My wife is out of town visiting her mother in California. She's been gone since Sunday morning."

"Then I need to speak to your son, sir."

"Of course, but I insist on being with Tommy when you question him. He's still a minor."

"It was an accident. You've got to believe me." Tommy Wyatt's dark eyes radiated fear.

Rod sat beside the sixteen-year-old boy on the couch. "Tell me what happened, Tommy."

"Mom left her keys here when she flew to see Grandma. I saw them on the counter and took them." He hung his head. "One of my friends gave me a ride to the courthouse."

"You took my car for a joyride?" Judge Wyatt's voice rose.

Tommy flinched.

Rod shot the judge a glance and held up his hand like a traffic cop. "What did you do when you arrived at the courthouse?"

"I took the Navigator for a spin around the block a few times."

"Bet it drives like a dream."

Tommy glanced at Rod, a plea for understanding on his face. "It's so smooth."

"Gas pedal responds easily?"

Red suffused the boy's face. "Too easy. I meant to speed up a little, but I guess I pressed down too hard."

"Detective, I'll pay any medical expenses or damages caused by my son. I'd take this as a personal favor if you'd go easy on the boy." He glared at his son. "I guarantee he won't be driving anything faster than a bike for the next six months."

"You were lucky, Tommy." Rod's gaze held the boy's. "If you had hit Ms. Cahill, you might have critically injured her or even killed her, and leaving the scene of an accident is a crime. Do you understand that?"

"Yes, sir." Tommy hung his head. "I'm really sorry, Ms. Cahill."

Meg patted his knee. "I'm just glad it wasn't an irate reader."

"Have you taken a driver's education course?" Rod asked.

The teen shook his head.

Rod stood and turned to the judge. "Enroll him in a course by the first of the year. I want confirmation that he completed the program. If he drops out or fails, I get his license until he passes. Deal?"

Relief washed over the judge's face. "Thank you, Detective. Tommy will deliver the proof of passing or his license to you himself. I owe you and Chief Blackhawk."

Outside, Meg said, "That was nice of you. You could have caused that boy a lot of trouble."

"Nice?" Rod jerked the passenger door open. "That boy hurt you, could have killed you. I wanted to pound his face into the dirt."

She smiled wryly. "Judge Wyatt would have objected to that."

Rod lifted her into the passenger seat. "You were so lucky."

Meg's hand cupped his cheek. "It wasn't luck. It was you."

He pressed her hand with his for a moment, stepped back and slammed the door.

Ethan sank deeper into his chair. "The judge's son?"

"Yeah." Rod ran a hand through his hair. "Joyride around the block. He hit the gas too hard. I told Wyatt that his son had to enroll in driver's education and pass or his driver's license was mine."

Ethan nodded. "Good call. Wyatt's okay with that?"

"Said he owed us."

"At least this one wasn't a legit attempt on Meg."

"This time."

"Coroner called just before you arrived."

Rod sat up straighter in the chair. "What did he find?"

"The bullet that killed Sherri is the same type that killed her mother. He's sending it to the lab for comparison."

"What about Sherri's coat? Was it missing any buttons?"

Ethan shook his head. "And none of the buttons were personalized."

"Will he fax the complete report?"

"It should be here any time. Did you talk to Ty today?"

"Kyle. Ty was with the funeral director. Sherri's funeral is tomorrow morning."

"Anything come out of the interview?"

"Not much. Kyle says Ty has a key to Mrs. King's house and Mr. King dropped off the scene about 13 years ago." Rod stopped. Kyle's comments about Meg came back. He frowned.

"What else?"

"Maybe nothing. Kyle showed some interest in Megan, so I warned him off."

Ethan stared at him for a minute. "Did you warn him off as a cop protecting a witness or something more personal?"

Rod felt the heat rise in his face. "Serena talked to you, didn't she?"

"Which is it, Rod?"

"I don't know, okay?" His fists clenched. "I don't know how I feel right now."

CHAPTER TWELVE

"Kill the story about the SUV."

Ruth's mouth dropped. "Why? It's a great eye-catcher."

"It will also embarrass Judge Wyatt if we print it." Meg sat on the corner of Ruth's desk. "And torture a sixteen-year-old kid who needs driving lessons."

"It was the Judge's son?"

"Joy riding."

"All right." Ruth frowned. "So, what are we using to replace that story?"

"I think we're onto something with the water system story. Did you get in touch with the other council members?"

Ruth nodded. "None of them know anything about the company. Did you see the mayor?"

Meg grinned. "Mission accomplished."

"How did you get past his bodyguard?"

"Velda?" She laughed. What a perfect description of the mayor's assistant. "I reminded her about the upcoming mayoral election next fall."

"And she wants to keep her job." Ruth smiled. "A new mayor would bring in a new assistant. Very good, my dear. So what did you learn from Parks?"

"He recommended De Marco Water Works for the water project based on the word of Senator Drake."

Ruth made a few notes on her pad. "What about a project timeline and a cost estimate?" When Meg gave her the information, she dropped her pen. "Do we have another bid to compare De Marco's against?"

"The mayor talked like it was a done deal and the vote was just a formality."

"What connection does Senator Drake have to De Marco? Why would he recommend it?"

Meg folded her arms across her chest. "I asked him that when I ran into him at the Town Hall. He was going on the word of his campaign finance manager. Brandenburg is the one who recommended De Marco."

Ruth frowned. "Well, we'll see about this deal being in the bag for the council. We need to talk to Brandenburg."

Meg stood. "I'll try to schedule an interview with him."

"While you're tracking him down, I'll research De Marco on the Internet."

Minutes later, Meg grabbed her bag and walked into the outer office. "I'm off to the Brandenburg home."

Ruth dragged her gaze from the computer screen. "Want me to go with you? Brandenburg is connected to the Drakes. I doubt Ethan or Rod would want you to go alone."

"I'll be fine. His wife's at home with the kids. Tell Zoe where I am when she returns."

In the Gateway subdivision, Meg slowed to admire the large houses. She wondered how much campaign finance managers netted in salary each year. Must be a chunk to afford a home in this neighborhood. The smallest house she'd seen so far appeared to be about 4,000 square feet. And that one wasn't the Brandenburg house.

She drove two more blocks, confirmed the address and turned into the gated drive. At the wrought-iron gates, she pressed the button on the panel and noted the security camera moving in her direction. After a moment, the gates slowly swung open to admit her.

She cruised up the meandering drive and parked in front of a broad staircase leading to two large double doors. She was definitely in the wrong business if Brandenburg earned enough to afford a mansion that easily topped 10,000 square feet.

A shiver of uneasiness zinged over her skin. With a house that large, the family might never know she was there. Well, it couldn't be helped and she wasn't here about the Drakes, at least not directly.

The maid opened the door at her ring. Meg smiled. "I have an appointment with Mr. Brandenburg."

"This way, Miss." She led Meg down the marble hallway to a large office.

Don Brandenburg looked up from his computer, a smile curving his lips. "Meg, come in. It's been ages since I've seen you. You look great."

"So do you." And she wasn't lying. In high school, Don had been the nerd of Josh's graduating class. Number cruncher extraordinaire with geeky looks. Now, Don looked like an all-star athlete. Healthy, fit, tanned. Based on his surroundings, she figured his buff physique came from a health club. She couldn't see him doing his own yard work in this neighborhood. "Being a campaign finance manager seems to agree with you."

Don laughed, his white teeth flashing in the light. "How's Josh? I hear he's a cop now."

"After his stint in the Army, he joined the Otter Creek PD. He loves the job, though he gets restless now and then. Says the natives are too quiet some nights. That's when he goes to the firing range."

He motioned for her to sit. "So, what can I do for my favorite newspaper editor? Need information about the Drakes?"

"Actually, I'm interested in you." She smiled. "Or, more specifically, De Marco Water Works."

"Sure. What do you want to know?"

"Mayor Parks says the town council is voting Tuesday on hiring De Marco for a project. The recommendation to hire them comes from you by way of Senator Drake. What do you know about the company?"

Don chuckled. "Quite a bit, actually. I own it."

Meg's eyebrows rose. "How long have you owned De Marco?" She grabbed a notepad and pen from her bag.

"I bought it five years ago."

"No offense, Don, but you're a bean counter. What caught your attention with the company?"

"I ran across De Marco in California while on vacation with my family. A friend of mine owned the company and I recognized the name on their work vehicles. They were working on Santa Lucia's water system at the time. I was impressed with their work ethic and courtesy."

"Impressed enough to just make an offer?"

A flash of irritation showed in his eyes. "Of course not. While my wife and daughters went shopping one afternoon, I looked up Jay Curtis, the guy who owned De Marco. I found out he was dying of lung cancer. Two-pack a day habit caught up with him."

He leaned back in his chair. "When I expressed interest in the company, he asked me if I wanted to buy him out. He was going to put the money from the sale into a trust fund to take care of his family after he died."

"How do you keep up with De Marco and the Drake campaign finances?"

Don laughed. "It's a good thing the Drakes aren't always running for office. The work becomes hectic as elections draw closer."

She wondered if the Drakes did more than PR for Don's company. "Bet it doesn't hurt business to have Senator Drake promoting De Marco."

"That's how it is in the business world. As a writer, you've seen that in action."

"Are the Drakes involved in De Marco?"

He frowned. "Of course not. They don't have time."

"Have they invested in the company?"

"I don't think that's any of your business."

"What was the bid figure for Otter Creek's water system?"

When Don named the same figure the mayor had given her, she said, "Isn't that a little high?"

"Quality is pricey, Meg." He smiled, though it didn't seem as friendly this time. "You get what you pay for." He stood and came around the desk. "I hate to cut this short, but I have a meeting in a couple of minutes. Is there anything else?"

"I'd like a list of projects De Marco's completed since you've been at the helm. The *Gazette* reader's love home folks' success stories."

"Sure." He checked his watch. "I should have time to put one together by 5:00."

She smiled. "Great. Can I stop by and pick it up?"

"I'll leave it with the maid for you." He held out his hand. "Good to see you again, Meg." Don closed the door behind her.

She stared at the office door. Sounded like Don wouldn't give her a chance for a follow-up interview.

"This way, Miss."

Meg jumped. The maid had slipped up behind her without a sound. She followed the woman to the front door with a murmur of thanks. Meg hurried down the stairs to her car, unlocked the door and tossed her bag on the passenger seat.

"Megan, what a pleasant surprise."

She froze for a split second. Rod was going to be furious, but an opportunity just dropped in her lap. She'd be a fool to pass on it. Meg turned to face Kyle Drake.

"Kyle." Meg's keys jangled in her hand. "I didn't expect to see you here."

"How are you? I heard you were hurt the other night."

"I'm fine." She edged closer to the car. "I guess you're Don's next appointment."

"Have to keep the money man happy. He pays all the bills."

"You must be pleased with his work."

"Why do you say that?" He sounded cautious.

Meg waved toward the mansion. "He looks as though he's doing very well financially."

He chuckled. "Oh, we give all our paid staff bonuses with campaign victories. And Don's got another business on the side."

The business must be funneling in big money for Don to afford a house that size. "I'm so sorry about Sherri."

"Thank you. We're all devastated by her death, Ty especially."

Meg wasn't convinced of that after what she'd learned from Lucy. A man indulging in an affair might be relieved at the untimely death of his wife. "Is he?"

Kyle frowned. "What kind of question is that? Of course he is. He loved Sherri."

"He has a funny way of showing it. Does the name Candy Wilson mean anything to you?"

"Is this about the college co-ed again? That's in the past. You already ripped into him about that. Cost him his job, too."

"This is a different woman, Kyle."

"You can't leave anything alone, can you?" He stepped closer. "Look, Meg, isn't Ty hurting enough without you dragging his name through the mud again over an alleged affair?"

She drew in a deep breath and smelled a clean, spicy scent. "This isn't about smearing Ty."

"Well, it certainly sounds like you have a vendetta against him. Maybe he's right. Maybe you won't ever give him a fair shake in that newspaper of yours."

Her face heated. "Since you think I can't be unbiased about him, do you have anything to say to Otter Creek about Sherri?"

"She was a wonderful wife to Ty. She loved him as much as my parents loved each other. Sherri was devoted to Ty. We'll miss her." He stared at her for a moment, speculation in his gaze. "You know, Meg, you're a really gifted writer. I've seen your work. Have you thought about doing something in writing other than small-town journalism?"

Meg blinked at the sudden change in topic and tone of the conversation. "What's this? Trying another tactic so I'll leave Ty alone?"

"As Ty's brother, I'm protective. As a professional in politics, I recognize and appreciate a gift with words when I see it. I could use a woman of your talents on my team, Meg."

"Your team? Don't you mean your father's team?"

He shook his head, a smile curving his lips. "No, my team. Dad's planning to retire. He's backing me to take his place in Washington next fall."

"Is that for publication?"

Kyle grinned. "Not yet. I'll make sure you get first dibs on the press release. So what about it, Meg? Interested in being the White House press secretary?"

"White House? Isn't that a little presumptive? You haven't won the Senate seat yet."

He laughed. "After a term or two in the Senate, I plan to run for President. If you sign on with me now, I'll take you all the way to the White House."

Rod turned his back on the window facing the squad room. He had holed up in the empty office next to Ethan's to make the long-distance calls to the men meeting with Kyle Drake Sunday night.

"I appreciate you taking the time to talk to me, Senator Young."

"Always glad to help when I can, Detective. I was sorry to hear about Mrs. Drake. Real tragedy. Now, what kind of information did you need?"

"I understand you were in Otter Creek Sunday night."

"Yes." Surprise edged his voice. "Had a business meeting with Kyle Drake."

"What time did you arrive at the restaurant, sir?"

"Just before 7:00."

"Who else did you meet besides Kyle?"

"Don Brandenburg and Ben O'Leary."

"And when did your meeting end?"

"Uh, I guess about 10:00 or 11:00." A sheepish tone crept into Young's voice. "I had a couple of drinks so the time's a little fuzzy."

Rod's lip curled. He'd bet the senator had more than a few. His affinity for booze was well documented in the media. "Did anybody leave for an unusual length of time?"

"Not that I remember."

So far, all the information he'd gathered from O'Leary and Young matched what he had learned from Kyle. "Why did you meet with Kyle and Don?"

Wry laughter from the other end of the phone. "War plans."

Rod frowned. "I don't understand."

"You don't know about Kyle, then?"

"Why don't you enlighten me."

"Kyle's positioning himself to replace his old man in the Senate."

After Rod left his number in case the senator remembered anything else, he hung up and grabbed his coat. He knocked on Ethan's door and stuck his head in. "I'm going to Brandenburg's place. I may be gone a while."

"Something come up?"

"Confirming Kyle's alibi for early Sunday night."

Minutes later, he rounded the large curve and stared at the two people standing in the driveway. What was Meg doing here with Kyle Drake? He parked the SUV and crossed the concrete drive.

Kyle swiveled and nodded at him. "Rod. You here to see Don?"

"Yeah."

"I have a couple of checks to hand him, then I'll get out of your way." He eyed Megan. "Think about what I said." He turned and took the stairs two at a time.

Rod studied Meg's expression. She looked stunned. "What's going on?"

"Before you start in on me, I didn't know Kyle would be here. I came to ask Don about his company."

"Company?"

"De Marco Water Works. The mayor wants De Marco to replace the old water pipes in town."

Rod's eyebrows shot up. He didn't know Don was tied to De Marco. "So, what did Kyle want you to think about?"

"Working for him."

A cold chill spread over his body that had nothing to do with the temperature outside. "Doing what?"

"PR." She ran her fingers through her hair. "The man has great ambition. I'll give him that."

He could still feel the silky strands against his palm. Instead of giving in to a burning desire to run his hands through her hair, he jammed his fists into his pants pockets. "Running for his father's senate seat, you mean?"

"That's just a step to his ultimate goal."

"Which is?"

"The White House."

His eyes widened. "Kyle wants to be President?"

"And he asked me to be the White House press secretary."

Rod rubbed his jaw. "That's quite a goal. You interested in his offer?"

Meg grinned. "I'd rather be the newshound than dodge them." She leaned against her car. "So, why are you here, Detective?"

"Confirming alibis for early Sunday night. Where are you headed next?"

"Jean's Tea Room. We're doing a piece on the Victorian Christmas decorations and the Christmas tea she puts together. The *Gazette* doesn't have a food critic, so I get to share my opinions of all the offerings."

"Tough job, Cahill. Does that mean you won't be interested in dinner with me?" The words were out of his mouth before he realized what was coming and could stop them. Maybe it had something to do with the way Kyle looked at Megan earlier.

"Dinner? As in a date?" She tilted her head. "Does this mean we're beyond the 'not a no' stage?"

A cold sweat broke out on his back. "Let's say we're at the exploration stage, okay?"

"That works. What time?"

"Call me when you finish with the Tea Room."

Meg thought a minute. "Why don't I just meet you at the office? I'll have to write up the story before my taste buds forget the marvelous flavors."

Rod chuckled. "Works for me. Later, Cahill." After she climbed into the driver's seat, he shut her door and watched her drive away.

His smile faded and a tendril of worry wrapped around his heart. What had he been thinking to ask her on a date? He'd had a handful of casual dates in the last few months, but he had a feeling anything with Meg was more serious. She had such strength, deep wells of it that he wished he could tap.

Megan Cahill deserved a whole-hearted relationship and Rod wasn't sure he was capable of that any longer. Not since he lost his family. The phone call from the Highway Patrol had ripped apart his world and torn his heart and soul from him. He still felt like half a man most of the time. The other half was buried with his wife and daughter.

Rod set his jaw and climbed the stairs. In answer to his knock, a maid led him to Don's office where Kyle was just leaving.

Don waved him into the room and closed the door. "Rod, haven't seen you in a while. What can I do for you?"

"I'm looking into Sherri Drake's murder."

"Bad business."

"Yeah. I need to know where you were Sunday night."

"What?" Don sat heavily in his chair. "Why me? I haven't seen Sherri in months."

"Standard police procedure to check the whereabouts of all family and friends. So, where were you?"

"You're serious."

"Very."

"Okay, well, I was here until about 6:30. I left to attend a dinner meeting at the Pond Restaurant. Stayed there until 10:30 or so and came home."

Rod pulled out his notepad. "Who attended your meeting?"

"Kyle, Senator Gray Young and Senator Ben O'Leary."

"Can anyone verify when you arrived home?"

Don scratched his jaw. "You know, my wife was asleep. The twins wear her out. She didn't move when I climbed into bed."

"What about one of your staff?"

He brightened at that. "The maid might have noticed. And we have a security camera at the gate with a recorded time on the tape."

"I'll need a copy of that, please."

"No problem."

"Have much contact with Ty?"

"Phone calls now and then and sometimes he'd put in a surprise appearance in D.C. Ty didn't involve himself in the Senator's work." Don frowned. "We did arrange for him to write a computer program that helps us with polling public opinion. Kyle thought the campaign could respond to public sentiment faster if we had our own program instead of waiting for the national ones to come out. He said by the time the results were published the public's concerns had moved on to something else."

"Did Ty mind doing that?"

He shook his head. "Writing the program only took a few days and he seemed pleased with the result. So were the Senator and Kyle."

"How well did you know Sherri?"

"As well as you can know a casual acquaintance. I didn't see her much. She stayed with Ty or at their home most of the time."

Rod's pen hovered over his pad. "What about the Senator's fundraisers? Wasn't she the hostess for those shindigs?"

"Yeah, but I was on duty during those events. Those were working dinners. My job was to raise campaign contributions, so I didn't say much more than hello to her."

"Did Ty come with her?"

"Sometimes. Other times he'd stay in Otter Creek if he needed to work on a computer project."

"What kind of relationship did Sherri have with her in-laws?"

"She loved the Senator a lot to keep hosting those parties for him. I heard her telling Ty once that she would have preferred staying home."

"What about Kyle? Any problems there?"

"Not that I know about. Where's all this leading? Do you think one of the Drakes killed Sherri?"

"I don't think anything right now. I'm just gathering information. When was the last time you saw Sherri?"

Don's forehead furrowed. "Must have been about a month ago. We had a fundraiser in Knoxville."

"How did she act?"

He shrugged. "Didn't seem to have a problem." Don hesitated. "Well, now that I think about it, she did seem a little distracted. But Sherri did her part. You know, schmoozing with the ladies."

"Did you ask her what was wrong?"

"Didn't have time, man. We're hot on the money trail right now. We're starting to pick up momentum for the fall election."

"I heard about that. What did Kyle promise you?"

Don looked sheepish. "Something in the Treasury Department."

Smooth-talking Kyle probably promised Don the job as Secretary of the Treasury. The guy knew how to win people over to his side. No change from his college days. "What does your wife think about staying on in D.C.?"

"Oh, she's all for it. Delia loves the high society and internal workings of the capitol's political scene. That's why I always thought it strange that she and Sherri hit it off so well. Sherri hated the parties. She only hosted them for the Senator's sake."

"You wanted to see me, Rod?" Delia Brandenburg hadn't changed at all since high school, except maybe to grow more beautiful. She had Barbie doll looks, blonde hair, blue eyes, perfect bow-shaped upper lip. She'd been on the arm of the star quarterback throughout high school.

"Thanks for taking the time from your children to talk to me."

"No problem. The maid's keeping an eye on them for a few minutes." She sat on the loveseat in front of the picture window. The waning afternoon sunlight streaming through the window glinted off her hair.

Rod smiled. "The first thing I want to know is how did such a beautiful woman end up with a number cruncher like Don?"

Delighted laughter spilled from her lips. "Brains won out over brawn when the football jocks wanted me to do their papers and homework for them in college. I ran into Don one day at the student union and he helped me with a math problem I couldn't solve." She grinned. "I figured cultivating a friendship with the brain of our graduating class might pay off in better grades. I never thought it would grow into love, but it did."

"Congratulations on such a beautiful family. Don showed me pictures of the twins."

Pleasure lit her face. "We tried to have children for a long time before we adopted the boys. We're so grateful to Senator Drake for helping us with the red tape. I don't know what I would do without the boys. They are my life."

"Is the difficulty having children something you had in common with Sherri?"

She nodded, the light fading from her expression. "She and Ty had been trying to have a baby for years."

"When did you see Sherri last?"

"Two weeks ago. We met for lunch at the Tea Room."

"Did she seem bothered by anything?"

Delia dropped her gaze, her face flushing.

"Delia, don't hold information back. Everything I learn about Sherri and the happenings in her world will help me find out who killed her."

"I don't like this. I feel like I'm gossiping behind people's backs."

"What you tell me stays with me unless it's relevant to solving the case. I need you to be honest with me, for Sherri's sake."

Her hands clenched in her lap. "Sherri was worried about Ty. She said he'd been acting out of character."

"Out of character, how?"

"New cologne, new style of clothes, being out of touch for hours at a time, skipping a class or two. I told her it sounded like he was going through some kind of mid-life crisis."

"What did she think?"

"She thought he was involved with another woman, again."

Rod's gut clenched. He'd hoped Sherri hadn't known about Ty's renewed infidelity before she died. "Did she say what she intended to do?"

A tear slipped down her cheek. "I think I really messed up, Rod."

"You told her to confront him?"

She nodded. "Ty claimed to love her and they were trying so hard to have a baby. How could he do that to her? How could he betray her like that? And it wasn't even the first time."

"Do you know if she talked to him?"

"She called me Sunday afternoon. Ty called her Saturday night and she told him she knew about the other woman."

"Why didn't she wait until he returned home?"

"Ty's temper is volatile. She told me she felt safer confronting him on the phone, out of arm's reach."

So Ty had lied to him. A cold feeling roiled in the pit of his stomach. Ty had claimed not to notice anything amiss when he talked to Sherri Saturday night. Rod had to consider the possibility his friends had an argument and, in the heat of temper, Ty decided to come home early and take her out of the picture so he could have Candy.

CHAPTER THIRTEEN

"Try this, Meg." Jean Sanford slid a plate across the table. Bite-size pieces of various scones dotted the surface. "Lemon, blueberry, raspberry, cranberry-orange and vanilla."

She watched, eager for Meg's response to every taste. Each bite melted on Meg's tongue, leaving her taste buds wanting more. "Wonderful, Jean. Are any of these new flavors only for the Christmas season?"

"The cranberry-orange isn't normally on the menu. I love to include cranberries during the holidays. They look so festive."

"Why don't you set a table with a full Christmas tea? Everything looks so good the picture alone is sure to bring you holiday shopper business."

Jean jumped up. "Great idea. Why don't I prepare it for you? On the house, of course."

Meg waved her hands. "No, no. Thank you, but I couldn't possibly eat all that." Not and eat dinner with Rod in a short while.

Jean hustled back and forth to the large kitchen, carrying out finger sandwiches, clotted cream, tarts, scones and shortbread. After selecting an elegant china teapot with matching cup and saucer, she arranged the food on plates and placed the plates in a three-tier plate holder. "What do you think, Meg?"

"This will make a beautiful picture." Meg pulled out her camera and snapped pictures from different angles, shooting close-ups of the food and teapot. "Are all your customers women?"

Jean laughed. "Most of them, but there are a few men who dare to enter this Victorian domain."

Meg stopped photographing. "Really? Who?" She couldn't imagine any of the men in her family stepping foot in this female-dominated atmosphere. All the boas, ornate furniture and fans, the hats to wear while eating would make them turn on their booted heel and run with a curl of the lips.

"Well, a couple weeks ago, Ty Drake brought his secretary in for lunch. They ordered a full Christmas tea and shared it." She turned away, a frown on her face.

"What's wrong?"

"Well, I don't suppose it matters now, but I didn't think his secretary behaved like a secretary."

"What do you mean?"

Jean's face flushed. "Maybe I shouldn't be talking about this. Seems wrong, somehow."

"Every piece of information is important in a murder investigation. If you want me to, I'll pass on the information to Detective Kelter."

"He won't mention my name, will he?"

Meg patted her arm. "I'll ask him to keep your name under wraps. Now, how did this woman behave?"

Jean glanced around, checking that none of her waitresses were in sight. "Well, to tell the truth, I think she behaved more like a girlfriend than a secretary. She sat too close, fed him bites of food from her plate, spent a lot of time gazing into his eyes." She shook her head, disgust plain on her face. "I'm surprised Sherri let him treat this woman to lunch."

Unless Jean misjudged the situation, Meg doubted Sherri knew about the lunch. "What did this woman look like?"

"Oh, she was a looker. Red hair, witchy green eyes, tall, almost as tall as Ty."

"People need to call for reservations, don't they?"

"They sure do, honey. We have very limited seating."

"Do you keep the reservations in a book or something?"

"Actually, we log reservations into a spreadsheet program on the computer at the front desk."

Meg packed the camera and notepad in her bag. "How long do you keep guest logs in your system?"

"You know, I don't think we've deleted any of them. They're in files by month and the year."

"Would you mind printing out a copy of November and December's guest reservation lists?"

"I suppose that would be fine. Do you really think it might help Detective Kelter?"

"I believe it will." If Jean wasn't mistaken about the date, it most likely coincided with the Senator's last fundraiser in Knoxville, a fundraiser Ty couldn't attend because of a programming deadline.

Rod watched Meg from her office doorway for a minute. He grinned at the intense concentration on her face as she typed on the computer keyboard.

When it appeared she came to a stopping place, he spoke. "Hungry?"

Her head jerked up. "Rod." She looked puzzled and glanced at her watch. She smacked her forehead. "We were supposed to meet a half-hour ago. I'm sorry. I was just going to write another paragraph and I guess I lost track of time." She maneuvered the mouse through a series of clicks and backed away from her desk.

"It's okay, Meg. You didn't answer my question, though. Are you hungry?"

"Starving."

His eyebrows rose. "Didn't Jean treat you to a full tea?"

She eyed him as she grabbed her bag. "You've been to Jean's?"

"Sure. It's not a favorite haunt of mine, but Erin and Kayla loved it."

"Sherri liked it, too."

He helped her into the SUV and climbed behind the wheel. "Did you go to the Tea Room with her?"

"A few times, but it was more Serena's style than mine. Sherri didn't ask me to go with her often."

Rod backed into the square. "Where would you like to go for dinner?"

"The Rodeo."

"You're in the mood for Tex-Mex food? Should I be worried?'

Meg laughed. "No. It's across the street from Flint's. I thought we might stop there after dinner."

"Doing some detecting on my dime, Cahill?"

"You have to talk to Lucy anyway. And maybe she'll give you a list of people who buy that pine-cleaner cologne."

Rod grinned. "Pine-cleaner cologne?"

"That's what it smells like to me now." Her hand clenched. "I pitched all the pine-scented cleaners at home into the trash about three o'clock this morning."

His amusement faded. "Couldn't sleep?"

"Pine-scented nightmares." She shivered. "I doubt I'll ever have another live Christmas tree in my home."

He reached over and took her hand in his. "Good thing you can buy an artificial tree, then."

"That's the easy part to fix. I just wish I could wipe out the memory that goes along with the smell."

He squeezed her hand. "The sense of smell is the strongest memory trigger for people. It may take a long time."

"I hope my family understands when I refuse to go into the living room on Christmas day."

At The Rodeo, Rod chose a table in the corner, away from the bar and most of the diners in the restaurant. After they placed their orders, Meg pulled a sheaf of papers from her bag.

"What this?"

"Reservations list for November and December at the Tea Room." She flipped a couple of pages and pointed to a highlighted name.

Ty Drake had been to the Tea Room a couple of weeks ago? The date of the reservation struck him as odd, but he couldn't put a finger on why. "How did you get this?"

"Miss Jean provided them. Did you see the name?"

Rod's lips twitched. "Sure, but you must know something I don't. What is it?"

"Did you notice the date? Sherri was in Knoxville at a fundraiser for the Senator during that time."

"So who did he take to lunch?"

"I think it was Candy. Jean's description of Ty's 'secretary' fit Lucy's description of the woman who was in the store buying cologne with him."

He smiled. "Guess it's a good thing I'd planned to talk to Lucy and Candy, isn't it?"

"Guess it is." She grinned.

Partway through the meal, Rod said, "I see you writing at all hours of the day and night. How can you do that?"

Meg laid down her fork. "What do you mean?"

"Aren't writers supposed to be sensitive, half-soused, in pajamas all day, writing at odd hours when the muse strikes?"

She laughed, her laughter so infectious he found himself grinning at her.

"Well, is it true or not?"

"Not." She wrinkled her nose. "Well, at least in my case it's not true. Deadlines don't wait for the muse to visit. If my writing muse is absent, I go out and find her. If she won't come home willingly, I drag her to work by the hair and make her get busy."

Rod chuckled. "You sound serious."

"I am. People who wait for the muse to strike to start writing don't write much. Newspapers don't wait for the muse. I have deadlines to meet every day. If I don't meet them, the paper goes to press with a lot of white space and very little news."

"Does Ruth have your work habits?"

Meg nodded. "That's why she's a *New York Times* bestselling author. Think about it this way. You go to work every day whether you're inspired or not. You investigate burglaries and murders and sometimes rescue dogs and cats."

Rod nodded. He had the scars to prove he'd climbed trees to bring down a few AWOL felines.

"I go to work every day, too. I interview people and take pictures, then I sit and write. It's my job. I'm good with words and I've discovered there's no appreciable difference between words written when my muse is hot or when she's cold. When she's cold, I struggle harder and longer to type the words, but the production is still there. It has to be there. But I have to show up with a pad and pen or a computer. The writing won't happen unless I sit down and tell the story."

"And you like what you do?"

"I love my job. I love to keep Otter Creek informed about what's happening. It draws people closer together, creates a sense of community. I help provide safety and security for my town. If there's a burglary spree, I help people be on the lookout for unusual activity. If there's a murder, people need to know there's a killer among them."

Rod nodded. He noted the same passion in Meg that he felt for his job. He helped balance the scales, satisfied the need for justice when he closed a case. The victims depended on him to hear their voice, their story and bring balance to the system. They depended on him to make a last stand for them.

He nodded at her empty plate. "Would you like dessert?"

She shook her head. "Later, maybe. Let's get to Flint's before they close."

"Tell me about Sherwood." Rod jotted down a few notes as Lucy described the men's cologne. "Do you keep several bottles on hand or special order?"

"We order two bottles a month. We have four customers who regularly buy a bottle every other month." She shrugged. "It works out where we sell two a month."

"What are the names of the four customers?"

Lucy gave him the list, one of which was Sherri Drake. She probably bought the pricey cologne for the senator since Ty didn't wear that scent. The other three men Rod had never heard mentioned in connection to the murder. He'd check them out, but suspected they wouldn't offer any new information to his case.

The counter girl smiled at Meg. "How did your boyfriend like the cologne we selected?"

Boyfriend? Cologne? Rod searched Meg's fiery expression.

"I haven't given it to him yet. I'll let you know later."

"Please, do." Lucy glanced over Meg's shoulder, her eyes widening. "You know that woman I told you about? The one with Ty Drake?"

"Yes?"

Lucy nodded toward the front of the store. "She's standing at the jewelry counter."

Rod pressed his card into the girl's hand. "Thanks, Lucy. If you think of anything else that might help, call me."

After she nodded, he strode toward the jewelry counter. Rod spotted the tall red head immediately. Meg was right. The woman was hard to miss. Candy Wilson leaned over the counter, talking to the clerk.

"No, that's too small. I'd like to see the half-carat one."

Her drawl reminded Rod of southern belles. He peered at the contents of the glass case. This southern belle had marriage on her mind. He wondered grimly if Ty had talked to Candy about marriage or if she was hoping to be the new Mrs. Ty Drake?

"Candy Wilson?"

Witchy green eyes studied his face. "Do I know you from somewhere? You look familiar."

"No, ma'am." He showed her his badge. "I'm Detective Rod Kelter, Otter Creek Police. I'd like to ask you a few questions."

She paled, her hand drifting to her throat. "Now?"

"Yes, ma'am. We can go to the coffee shop next door or to the station. Your choice."

Candy retrieved her purse from the counter. "Coffee shop is fine."

Rod motioned for her to precede him and fell into step beside Meg. After asking their preference in the coffee shop, he ordered black coffee for himself, hot chocolate for Meg and a cappuccino for Candy and sat beside Meg.

"Who's your friend? Another cop?"

"This is Megan Cahill, my date." He smiled. "We were just in the right place at the right time to find you."

"What do you want, Detective?" The hand holding Candy's cappuccino cup trembled.

"Tell me about Ty Drake."

"I work with him at Otter Creek Community College."

"Are you his associate, assistant, secretary, boss, what?"

A flush surged over Candy's face. "His secretary."

"And what about off the job?"

"I don't understand."

"Sure you do, Candy. What kind of relationship do you have with Drake outside the office?"

"We're friends."

"Friends." Rod sipped his coffee. "And when I start asking your co-workers, family and friends about your relationship with Ty Drake, will they agree with you?"

"Okay, okay." She pushed aside her coffee cup. "So we're involved in a relationship. He's an adult."

"You're having an affair with a guy whose wife was just murdered a few days ago."

Candy sighed. "Look, I'm sorry about Sherri, but I didn't have anything to do with her death."

Rod pulled out his notepad. "How long have you and Ty been seeing each other?"

"Six months."

Beside him, Meg stiffened. He pressed his leg against hers in silent warning. "Was it serious or just a fling, Candy?"

"He loves me."

Meg set her hot chocolate on the table with a thud. "Ty was married. Didn't that bother you?"

Rod nudged her harder under the table. If she didn't settle down, he would send her on an errand.

"He was going to get a divorce."

"When did he tell you that?" Rod asked.

Candy glared at him, defiance glittering in her eyes. "He didn't, but it was coming. I could tell. He was spending more and more time with me."

"Is that why you were trying on engagement rings?"

She lifted her chin, but said nothing.

"Did you get tired of waiting for the divorce, Candy? Maybe decide to speed things up and get Sherri out of the way?"

"No!"

"When did you see him last?"

"Sunday night."

Rod raised his gaze from the notepad, pen hovering. "Sunday night. What time was this?"

Her hands wrapped around her coffee cup and brought it to her lips. "He left my apartment late, maybe 3:00 in the morning."

"How long had he been there?"

A dreamy look came over her face. "Since Thursday."

CHAPTER FOURTEEN

"How could he do that to Sherri?" Meg stared out the window at the passing houses and street signs. Rod's interview with Candy Wilson twisted her stomach into a knot.

"A lot of people don't take their marriage vows seriously, Meg. You should know that from all the stories you've written on broken and abusive homes."

"But she loved him."

"Love isn't enough to hold a marriage together, Megan. It takes commitment from both partners to work toward the same goal."

She twisted in her seat to face him. "What are you saying?"

He sighed. "I probably shouldn't be saying this, but during an interview Ty mentioned Sherri's charity, The Haven. He said she had gone beyond interest into obsession, that she spent more time on plans for The Haven than she did with him."

"So you're blaming her for their marriage problems?"

"Don't put words in my mouth. If Ty was having some sort of crisis or issue, the rape and her handling of the aftermath probably made him more insecure, especially if she shut him out."

Meg sat in silence for a moment, studying his face, lit by the dashboard lights. "You sound as though you're speaking from experience."

"I am." He glanced at her before returning his focus to the road. "Erin was a rape victim, too. About two years after we married. She was so different I wondered sometimes if our marriage would hold together. It was tough, Meg. I loved her and told her so repeatedly, but my love wasn't enough.

"She never felt safe unless I was with her and my schedule was just as erratic then as it is now. The nights I worked third shift, Erin didn't sleep. She stayed awake and worried that someone might break in while I was gone. I bought a state-of-the-art security system for the house. When I addressed that concern, her worry shifted to my safety. She started calling me five, ten times a night to check on me."

His hands tightened on the steering wheel. "I bought a separate cell phone for personal use, one I kept on vibrate, so she wouldn't tie up my work cell phone. I checked the messages she left frequently, but had to quit answering every one of her calls. I couldn't do my job. That kind of radical change is hard for a partner to accept."

"Life is change. What about me?"

Rod frowned. "What about you? You aren't a rape victim."

"I'm still the victim of a violent crime. We've already discovered I'm newly afraid of the dark. Who knows how many obsessions might take over my life now."

"I wasn't talking about you, Meg. I know you're strong."

"Not on the trail. Not right now. Everybody's weak at some point in their life, Kelter. Even someone as infallible as you. Oh, wait. I'm forgetting that problem you had a few months back. What was it? Oh, yeah. Booze." Sarcasm riddled her words.

He parked in front of the newspaper office, anger tightening his features. "Maybe we should slow down, rethink this dating thing, Meg."

Rethink this dating thing? Her eyes narrowed. No problem. "Thanks for dinner." Before he could unbuckle, she flung open the door and climbed into her vehicle. She gritted her teeth and backed into the square. She needed a hot shower and a cup of hot chocolate, in that order. She did not need any man in her weak life.

Rod's headlights shined in her rearview mirror. He would follow her home. He was a cop before anything else.

A stop sign loomed a few feet in front of her. She pressed on the brake, expecting the vehicle to slow down. It didn't.

Meg's heart jumped into overdrive. The brakes were out? She hadn't experienced problems this afternoon. She dragged her mind back to the task at hand. This road had a steep downhill slope.

When her cell phone rang, she dug it out of her purse. Without looking at the readout, she knew Rod was calling to read her the riot act for blowing through the stop sign. "My brakes are gone."

"I'm going to pull around in front of you. When I'm in position, take your transmission out of overdrive so it won't work against me. And put me on speakerphone so you can keep both hands on the wheel."

Meg dropped her cell phone into an empty cup holder and eyed the speedometer. The needle passed fifty miles per hour and kept rising. She gripped the wheel tighter. She glanced in the rearview mirror as Rod started to pull around her. An oncoming vehicle in the next lane sent his SUV diving in behind hers. By the time the vehicle passed them, the Jeep speedometer cruised at 60 miles per hour down a stretch of road with a speed limit of 35.

Rod swung around the Jeep, his blue lights flashing, and floored the gas pedal. His SUV lunged forward. "Meg, ease toward the right. When I get in front of you, maneuver the Jeep onto my bumper, okay?"

"Got it."

Her voice sounded tight, but she was still in control. She smiled grimly. No guarantees when the Jeep came to a stop in one piece. It had to come to a stop in one piece. She didn't want to face Nick if she messed up his car.

This was going to be tricky, but if she were hysterical it would have been almost impossible for him to help her. And he didn't want to lose her despite what he'd said to her earlier.

The engine of Rod's SUV whined as he passed the Jeep and eased in front of her. He maintained his speed. If he slowed down, the Jeep would hit the back of his vehicle too hard and cause either him or Meg to lose control. He figured if he held steady, she would nudge into his bumper. He hoped he could slow both vehicles down and get them to a safe stopping place.

"Okay, Meg. Both hands on the wheel. Try to steer so that the nose of the Jeep is against my bumper."

"Right. Between curves, I'm going to start easing down my emergency brake."

Rod switched to speakerphone, dropped his cell phone into the seat beside him and gripped the wheel with both hands himself. He alternated between watching the approaching Jeep in his rearview mirror and scanning the road ahead for obstacles.

The first contact with Rod's bumper jarred Meg to the teeth. She grimaced and held on to the steering wheel through a curve. On the straightaway, she depressed the emergency brake until she heard a click. The Jeep jerked as the braking system began slowing her descent in small increments. She prayed nothing strayed into Rod's path as they bumped their way down the grade.

Rod's brake lights lit up as he slowed a little. She held tight as the Jeep rolled into the back of the SUV with a thud. Again, she set the brake a little more. Another jerk from the Jeep.

All the way down the mountainside, Meg repeated the process, gradually slowing the Jeep until at the bottom of the grade, she and Rod steered onto a wide flat spot of hardened dirt beside the blacktop.

As soon as the Jeep rolled to a stop, Meg slipped the transmission into park and turned off the engine. No sooner had she removed the key, Rod opened the driver's side door and lifted her out. She threw her arms around his neck, grateful to feel the steel band of his arms across her back.

"Are you okay, baby?"

"Aside from being scared out of my wits, I'm good considering the alternative."

"You are an amazing woman, Megan Cahill."

"Yeah? Well, this amazing woman will sink to the dirt if you let go."

Rod tightened his grip, chuckling. "Guess those driving lessons with DEI actually paid off."

A siren sounded in the distance. She lifted her head to look at his face. "You called in the troops?"

"Made sure we had help on the way in case we had a problem."

"We already had a problem."

He grinned. "All right. Another problem, like a deer darting into our path or my brakes giving out." He sobered. "I'm sorry, Meg."

"For what?"

"I should have insisted on checking the Jeep before you pulled out."

She laid her forehead against his chest. "I didn't give you the chance. I was so angry at you, I didn't think about anything but getting some breathing room."

"Hey, I suggested we slow down, not stop." He ran his finger down her cheek. "I don't want to lose you, Cahill."

She smiled. "Nice to know, Kelter. Gives us a common goal when those odd weaknesses appear. And I'm sorry, too, Rod. That comment about the drinking was way out of line." Meg eased out of his arms, testing the strength of her legs. Finding they would hold her up, she took off her coat and laid it on the Jeep's hood.

"What are you doing? It's freezing out here."

"Got a flashlight?"

"In the SUV. Why?"

"Get it, please. I want to check Nick's brakes."

He frowned, but strode back to the SUV and pulled out a heavy-duty flashlight and handed it to her.

Meg scooted under the Jeep and turned on the flashlight. She growled, anger surging. She slid out and stood as two Otter Creek police cruisers rolled to a stop beside them.

"You guys okay?" The officer climbed from his car and surveyed the damage to the Jeep and the SUV.

"We're fine." Rod handed Meg her coat. "Chief on his way?"

"Yeah. Should be here in a couple of minutes."

Great. She'd end up with a 24-hour bodyguard this time.

Rod swung around and stared at her. "Well, did you find anything?"

She gave him the flashlight and slipped on her coat before answering. "I hoped my brother-in-law didn't pay much attention to maintenance on his vehicles. I should have known he wouldn't take risks, especially since Maddie might drive his car on occasion."

"So what did you find?"

"The brake lines were cut. Neat slice, like with a knife."

"No question about this being deliberate?"

"None."

Two more SUVs from the Otter Creek PD screeched to a halt behind their vehicles. Ethan and Josh spilled out of one, Nick scrambled from the other. Wonderful. The gang's all here.

"Everybody okay?" Ethan asked.

"We're good." Rod waved them over to the Jeep.

"What happened?" Nick slid one arm across Meg's shoulders and hugged her.

"Brake line was cut." Meg laid her head on his shoulder. "I'm sorry about your car, Nick. I seem to be trouble on wheels for our cars this week."

"No sweat, Meg." He ruffled her hair. "That's why we have insurance. Where's the flashlight? I want to look."

Josh frowned at Rod. "Didn't you check the car before she got in?"

"Back off, bro," Meg said, a warning in her voice.

"Don't tell me to back off. You might have been killed on this mountainside. I want to know if Kelter let down his guard."

"I didn't check the car," Rod admitted.

Josh's fists clenched.

Meg stepped in front of her brother, placed her hands flat on his chest and shoved. "I didn't give him the chance. It's my fault, Josh."

"You want to blame somebody?" Ethan scowled at all of them. "Blame the perp who's trying to kill Megan. Put that emotion and energy into finding Sherri's killer before he succeeds in taking out Meg."

Ethan pulled out his car keys and tossed them to Josh. "Take Meg home and stay with her."

An hour later, Meg slid under the covers, a mug of hot chocolate on her bedside table and her laptop open and ready on the bed. After adjusting the pillows, she leaned back and shifted the computer to her lap.

She ignored the file she started earlier in the day and opened a new one. Meg had tried to ride the balancing line between Rod and Ethan's request and her freedom of the press. Tonight's incident with the car had pushed her over the line. Enough was enough. What if Maddie had taken the Jeep and driven it? She might have been killed. It was one thing to try to kill her. Now Sherri's murderer had stepped into no-win territory. She wouldn't let her family be caught in the crossfire.

Her bedside phone rang. The voice on the other end of the line brought a smile to her face. "How are you?"

Rod chuckled. "I'm supposed to ask you that question."

"You're the one working out in the cold."

"Not anymore. I'm at the station. We towed both cars to our garage. Nick's processing his Jeep. Maybe we'll get lucky and find a print, but I doubt it. Our perp hasn't made that kind of mistake yet."

Not yet, but after her editorial came out, he might slip up. "No repercussions from Ethan?" Silence greeted her inquiry. "Okay, what happened?"

"Let's just say I sympathize with Henderson's hide stripping now."

Meg blew out a breath. "Ethan or Nick?"

"Both. I deserved that and a lot more for putting your life at risk. There was a puddle of brake fluid in the slot where you parked the Jeep. I would have seen it if I had checked the vehicle."

"I disagree with that assessment, Kelter. I'm not exactly easy to corral. You can't take the sole blame for this fiasco. So, what happens now?"

"You don't go anywhere alone from now on."

"Yeah, I figured that. Not much of a problem since I don't have wheels right now. What about you?"

"More of the same. I have leads to follow up, more interviews."

"You interested in taking me to Knoxville?"

"Sure. Any particular reason?"

"Car shopping." She grinned at the answering groan.

After Rod hung up, Meg resumed typing. All the men in her family were going to be furious with her after this. Especially one red-haired detective who was growing on her.

Rod unlocked the door of his house and stepped inside the dimly lit kitchen. Clean counters and sparkling sink plus the smell of something sweet told him Serena had been at work in his kitchen.

He walked down the hall to his bedroom and changed into a comfortable pair of jeans and a sweatshirt. Back in the kitchen, he peered inside the freezer. Food containers filled almost every square inch of space. He pulled out a couple. Beef stew, chicken and dumplings, white chili. Man, Serena had stockpiled his favorite foods for this month.

He closed the freezer door and opened the refrigerator. Home Runs' chef service was the best money he'd spent in years. A fresh pitcher of tea, salad, eggs, milk, cheese, bagels. Two twelve-packs of Coke and a case of bottled water now occupied the place where a case of beer used to sit.

Rod sighed as he shut the refrigerator door and scanned his counter. He'd been alcohol free for seven months. Even now, Meg's comment about the alcohol rankled, made him more determined than ever to beat the addiction.

The full cookie jar drew his attention. He lifted the lid and drew in a deep breath. Molasses cookies. He grabbed two and bit into one. The spicy flavor tingled on his tongue. Perfect.

Finishing the cookies, he wiped the sugar from his fingers and went to his woodshop and turned on the heat. Waiting for the warm air to knock off the chill, Rod selected several pieces of wood and stacked them beside his table saw. He marked the dimensions he needed for the wood and set to work.

He mulled over the case while he cut the wood to the correct proportions, twisting pieces of the puzzle, searching for a way to fit what he knew into the final picture. The evidence, little that they had, pointed to the Drake men. The most obvious place to look first was Ty, but that didn't sit well with Rod. He believed Ty guilty all right. Guilty of stupidity, not murder.

A few hours later, he cleaned up his equipment and turned off the heat and the light on the bookcase. If he had time this weekend, he'd stain it to match Meg's other bookcases. The way he figured it, Meg needed at least four more bookcases to hold her collection of reading and research material.

For now, he needed sleep. Tomorrow presented unique challenges. The most important of those was regaining Ethan's confidence.

Friday morning, Ruth laid down Meg's editorial, a grim expression on her face. "Are you sure about this?"

Meg swallowed hard and shoved trembling hands into her pockets. "It has to be done. The killer's coming too close to my family. Maybe I can draw him out in the open. Maybe he'll make a mistake."

"And maybe you'll end up as dead as Sherri. Then what will that do to your family? To Rod? Did you think of that?"

"Of course I did. I don't know what else to do, Ruth."

"Let Rod and Ethan do their jobs." She frowned and waggled her finger in Meg's face. "This is foolhardy, Megan. It's like flashing a red cape and daring an angry bull to come get you."

Her gaze dropped to the editorial. The title almost jumped off the page. Murder: A Coward's Tool.

"Will you at least give Ethan a copy early so he'll be prepared?"

"And have him pull it before press time?" She shook her head. "I'll give him and Rod the first copies off the press before it hits the streets."

"What's to say I won't tell them myself before tonight?"

Meg's lips twitched. "I would fire you on the spot and then you wouldn't be able to keep an eye on me during the daytime. You are my watchdog today aren't you?"

Ruth colored. "How did you know?"

"You aren't scheduled to work this morning, yet here you are at 8:00 a.m., diddling around with the Internet."

"All right. You caught me. It was either me or protective custody. Ethan figured on less complaints with me as your shadow."

"He's right. Who's on duty this afternoon?"

Ruth shrugged. "We'll find out around lunchtime I expect. In the meantime, we have a paper to put together. What's on tap first?"

Meg handed Ruth the notes she'd typed from her interview with Don Brandenburg. "This is the information about De Marco. I'm going to do some research on the Internet, see what else I unearth. So far I see nothing illegal, just good-old-boy networking and support."

Ruth nodded. "I'll write a rough draft on the water system. Let me know if you find something I can use."

Megan settled in her leather chair and logged onto her favorite Internet search engine. She read through De Marco's website, jotting notes as she progressed. She clicked on the endorsements link. Her gaze fell to one name she knew well.

She picked up her phone and dialed. "Hey, Greg. It's Megan Cahill."

"It's been a long time, long enough to know that you aren't calling to ask me to take you back. Biggest mistake I ever made, turning you loose. So, what can I do for you?"

"How long have you been in Congress?"

"Ten years."

"So you've been there long enough to know what's happening behind the scenes, right?"

"You still in journalism?" Greg's voice sounded cautious.

"Yes, but this isn't on the record. I need some background information on a company."

"Oh, well, in that case, yeah, I do know most of what's happening around here. Some I can talk about, some I can't. Which company caught your interest?"

"De Marco Water Works."

"What's your interest in them?"

"They're bidding on Otter Creek's water project. I wanted to know a little more about them."

"Go to their website."

Meg's eyebrows rose. "I did, Greg. That's where I found your name. You endorsed the company. So are they as good as you wrote?"

"Absolutely. Did a fine job on my hometown's water system. Fast work, good quality."

"How about their pricing? Are they competitive?"

"A little expensive, but they only use American parts and local labor for their projects."

"So you're comfortable recommending their services to other communities?"

"No question."

"Uh, huh. So, what do you know about the Drakes?"

"No comment."

CHAPTER FIFTEEN

Greg's sharp tone intrigued Meg. The nice thing about interviewing a former boyfriend was the clues from his voice. And right now, he was worried. "Tell me what you know about the Drakes, Greg. Remember this is off the record—for now. If you stonewall me, that might change."

"Warren Drake's a great senator, Meg. Very influential on Capitol Hill. He's old school, you know. He and his cronies swap favors."

No news there. Who didn't swap favors on the Hill? "How are they tied to De Marco?"

"Don Brandenburg owns De Marco. He's Drake's campaign finance manager."

She pressed the phone tighter to her ear. "That's common knowledge. What else do you know?" Silence. "If I have to dig further, I'll get more people involved and something will slip into the press. Won't be long before your name is plastered all over the headlines."

Greg sighed. "All right, but swear you won't give up my name."

"I promise. Now, what gives?"

"The Drakes gave Brandenburg the money to buy De Marco."

"That's it?" Disappointment swelled inside Meg. "They gave money to a friend. Nothing illegal in that."

"Remember I told you they trade favors with their cronies?"

"You keep saying 'they'. Are we talking about just the Senator?"

"No. Kyle and the Senator. In fact, Kyle's becoming more of a player these days."

"Okay. So what?"

"They trade information for De Marco business."

Meg sat up. "What?"

"Business comes to De Marco as a favor to the Drakes. The Drakes know things. Important things about influential people."

"Blackmail? Why hasn't anyone turned them in?"

Greg's laugh was harsh and short. "Who would dare? If law enforcement knew, the dirt the Drakes have on people would leak. Nobody wants that, so they keep quiet."

"The victims would rather pay than stop the blackmail?"

"Recommending De Marco is cheap."

"You recommended De Marco, Greg." His sigh carried across the line. "What do the Drakes have on you?"

"Nothing I'm willing to tell the press or you."

"You know Drake's retiring next fall?"

He snorted. "Kyle's worse than his old man. I guarantee De Marco won't suffer when Warren steps down. Kyle will see to that. He takes care of his own."

"He promised to take care of you as well, didn't he?"

"I'd rather be in the majority than blackballed. Look, I owed you this one, Meg, but don't call me again. No one's worth risking my family, not even you. Leave me and my family alone."

Meg replaced the handset and slumped deeper into her chair. So the Senator and Kyle pedaled favors. Maybe Sherri found proof and one of the Drakes killed her. Meg thought about Sherri's problem with Ty. She suspected her friend was trying to have a baby to mend her marriage. Ty went through fertility testing with her. Did that signify some commitment to their relationship?

Greg's sudden hostility bothered her. Whatever the Drakes held over his head made him afraid for his family's safety. Curious, Meg searched the Internet for references to Greg Mattson. The oldest references were dated after Greg finished his degree in political science and began his Congressional run, near the time Meg broke up with him. Being a politician's wife never appealed to her and she never loved Greg enough to try.

She scanned through dozens of articles following Greg's political career before she stumbled upon a society page write-up of his wedding to Jenna Fitzgerald four years earlier. Meg smiled. In the picture, a gorgeous red-head beamed at her equally besotted husband.

A reference to adoption caught her attention. She scanned the article. Buried in the last paragraph was a reference to Greg and Jenna adopting a baby girl two years earlier. Was Greg afraid the Drakes would interfere with the adoption? Meg scowled. What did the Drakes have on him?

Maybe she should write an article on the Drake family. The Senator might agree to an interview if the article preceded naming Kyle as his endorsed successor. If Meg talked to the Senator and Kyle in an interview setting, she might piece together more information and feed those facts to Rod.

Rod would hate the idea and tell her he didn't need help doing his job. Meg wished she could convince Rod to let her work with him more.

Ruth tapped on the door and poked her head in the doorway. She opened her mouth to say something and stopped, staring at Meg's face. "You're up to something."

She walked to the chair in front of Meg's desk and sat. "Spill it."

Meg grinned. "We need to write an article on the Drake family. A great build up to the Senator's big announcement."

"Planning to beard the lion in his den?"

"Something like that." She retrieved the phone and dialed. "Senator Drake, please. This is Megan Cahill." After a moment, she said, "Senator Drake, would it be possible for you to see me for an interview this morning? I want to write a feature article on the Drake men, their history and their future plans. Maybe you can use this as a lead-in to Kyle's announcement. Yes, sir, he did tell me about that. Yes, sir, I do know the funeral's at 2:00. I won't keep you long, maybe 20 minutes. Eleven o'clock? Thank you, sir." She hung up, grinning.

"You need backup, someone other than a 72-year-old woman." Ruth stood and reached for the phone. After a moment, she said, "Ethan, I just thought you should know Meg's headed to the Drake place. You might want to send someone with her who carries a gun." After a pause, she replied, "No, she won't be dissuaded. It's for an article on the family as a whole, not on Sherri. Yes, all right, I'll tell her."

Ruth hung up. "Aside from threatening to toss you in jail again, he agreed to find someone to go with you. I wouldn't get too close to him, though. He's not happy with you."

Meg chuckled. "When is he ever happy with me?"

"Rod! Get in here!"

Rod rolled back from his computer and leaped to his feet. He'd never heard Ethan sound so angry. Well, not since last night's dressing down. Another reaming for not checking Meg's car?

He stiffened, stepped into Ethan's office and shut the door. "Yes, sir?"

Ethan scowled. "Megan's going to the Drakes for an interview. I have a meeting in five minutes with the mayor and you're the only one I trust to keep our intrepid editor in line."

"No problem, but wouldn't Josh prefer guard duty or Nick?" Rod's cheeks burned. "Neither of them trust me right now."

"They were both awake all night. And didn't you mention interviewing Ty this morning?"

"That's right."

"At least you can keep an eye on her. Go to the *Gazette* office before she finagles my aunt into going with her."

Rod grabbed his jacket and hurried to his car. He parked in front of the newspaper office and walked inside.

"Hey, Detective." Zoe smiled at him, a twinkle in her eyes. "What brings you here?"

"I'm Megan's escort to the Drake place."

She tilted her head. "I think she's waiting for you."

He knocked on Meg's office door.

"What?"

His eyebrows shot up. Sounded like she was gearing up for a fight. Rod opened the door. "Your escort, my lady."

She stood. "Did you bring armor, Sir Rod?"

He pulled back his coat enough for her to see his weapon. "Will this work?"

"Good enough." Bag in hand, she moved past Rod to the outer office. She paused at Zoe's desk. "I don't know how long I'll be gone. My cell's on if you need me."

"Okay, Boss." She grinned and winked at Rod. "Be seeing you, Detective."

In the car, Rod waited for Meg to buckle and backed into the square. "Are you sure about this? You absolutely have to do this? There's no other way?"

Meg glared at him. "That's three questions. Yes, yes, and no. I'm a writer, Rod. I interview people who make the news around this area. Otter Creek's famous family is in town. People want to know why."

"You can't send anyone else?"

"I'm not sending Ruth to interview a potential murderer. Ethan would skin me alive, not to mention the fact I love her too much to put her in danger. Zoe's committed to other stories for tonight's press run. That leaves me."

Her tone told him she rode a thin edge of control. He'd tied her hands somewhat when he asked her not to interfere in his investigation and not to reveal too much information in the articles she printed. He couldn't fault her for the way she'd handled the whole situation. In fact, she avoided the potential bias and abundance of information by having Ruth write the articles.

"Thanks for calling before you interviewed the Drakes on your own."

"You and Ethan both told me I had to or I'd end up looking at the world from the inside of a jail cell."

"But you could have done it anyway, Meg. I appreciate how you've handled the difficult situation we put you in." He glanced at her. "So who are you interviewing? I assume it's not Ty."

"I'm not exactly on his best friend list right now. The Senator agreed to talk to me at 11:00."

"About?"

"A variety of things. De Marco Water Works, the Senator's retirement, Kyle and the history of the Drake men as a whole. People love to read about hometown boys making good." She gave him a wry smile. "You can't beat a city councilman elected to the U.S. Senate and his two successful sons."

Rod nodded. "Okay. Let's talk ground rules."

"Ground rules?"

"Uh huh. I want you to interview the Senator in the library."

"Why?"

"Because it's next door to the small sitting room in which I'll insist on talking to Ty. Leave the door open when you're with Drake. Under no circumstances are you to go anywhere else in that house without me."

Meg was silent a moment. "You really think one of them killed Sherri, don't you?"

"I think there's a good chance it was one of them, but I don't have the proof yet."

"Door stays open, then." She twisted in her seat. "Same goes for you, right? You're leaving the door open as well?"

"Worried about me?"

"Yes."

"Don't be." He grinned. "I carry a big gun."

"Senator Drake, thank you for agreeing to the interview this morning." Meg sat in a burgundy leather armchair in front of the fireplace. "I know this will be a difficult day for your family."

"I never thought I'd see this day, having to bury my daughter-in-law. It's not natural to have to bury your children or their spouses."

"No, sir. I know your time is short so I'd like to tape this interview." Meg smiled and showed him her hand-held tape recorder. "I won't have to ask you to repeat anything while I take notes this way. That's all right, isn't it?"

The Senator frowned, but nodded.

"Great." She flipped the switch and the machine began recording. "Senator Drake, tell me about your family."

The question startled him. "My family?"

"Yes, sir. Tell me about your wife, Caroline. I understand you were high school sweethearts."

A soft look came over Drake's face. "She was the most beautiful girl in our graduating class. Eyes like coal, hair the color of a midnight sky. She was the love of my life."

"When did you marry Caroline?"

"Right after high school graduation, the next day in fact. We went to the justice of the peace because neither one of our families supported our decision to marry."

"Why not?"

"Bad blood between our families. Not quite as bad as the Hatfields and McCoys, but along the same lines. I don't even remember now what started the original dispute."

"Did your families ever change their minds?"

He laughed, an ironic tone dominating. "Sure, after I was elected to the town council. All the way through college, they waited for us to flunk out of school and divorce."

"What did you and Caroline major in?"

"I graduated with a degree in political science. Caroline earned a degree in library science." He smiled. "That woman loved to read more than anybody I ever met."

Meg nodded. "I suppose that's why she was so involved in literacy programs."

"She believed that learning to read would open the doors for anybody to be successful in life. She said education was the only way out of the ghetto, not food stamps or welfare aid."

"Smart lady. Teach them to take care of themselves and their own families, not depend on the government for aid." Meg flipped to a new page in her notebook. "What about your sons? Tell me about your family."

"We had Kyle twelve years after Caroline and I married, about the time I was elected to the State Senate. Caroline had wanted a baby for so long. She quit working at the Otter Creek library and stayed home to raise him. Kyle was a dream come true for both of us. She was so proud of him and his accomplishments."

"How about you? Do you feel the same way about Kyle?"

"Absolutely. Kyle is everything I ever wanted in a son. I couldn't ask for a better successor or a better man to carry on the Drake name after I'm gone."

"Why are you retiring next fall, Senator Drake? You seem the picture of health."

"Looks can be deceiving, my dear."

Meg stared at the man's placid face. "You're not well, sir?"

"I have cancer, Meg."

"But surely with treatments so advanced these days, the medical community can do something to help."

"No. It's terminal."

"I'm sorry, Senator. Do your sons know?"

He nodded. "That's part of the reason I came home, to tell Ty. Kyle already knew."

"You've talked a lot about Kyle, how proud you are of him. Tell me about Ty. He was adopted, wasn't he?"

"Caroline couldn't carry another baby to term after Kyle was born. She had four miscarriages and the doctor warned it was too dangerous to try for another baby. She was devastated. Caroline loved Kyle so much and wanted to share her love with another child. She spent months in a deep depression. The doctor encouraged us to adopt and that's what we did."

"How old was Ty when he came to you and Caroline?"

"Oh, he must have been about six months old or so. He was already eating a little baby cereal and fruit."

Six months? From what she knew about the adoption system, babies weren't in the system long. People were so desperate for babies, many adopted them from outside the U.S. because of a short supply and a long waiting list. Maybe it was different back then. "How did Ty feel about being adopted? Did he ever feel second best to Kyle?"

"Never. We told Ty he was extra special because we chose him to be our son. He was fine with our explanation."

"He never asked about his birth parents, where they were or why they let him go?"

Drake shook his head. "We told him that parents sometimes get into difficult circumstances and feel like they can't take the best care of their children. Rather than hurt them or subject them to the horrors of a drug-addicted parent or an alcoholic one, it was best to let someone else have the children, someone with the means to raise them."

"Is that the type of circumstance Ty came from, an addicted parent?"

He stiffened. "I really don't know. It was a closed adoption handled by our lawyer. I have no idea who the birth parents are, never wanted to know either."

"It's obvious you love your sons, Senator."

He smiled. "I would do anything for my boys. They are everything to me."

"What about grandchildren, sir?"

Drake sighed. "I'd hoped for a grandchild from Ty and Sherri, but that never happened. Now with my health going down, I'm not sure I'll be around to enjoy that pleasure. I hope my sons will have children someday, children to carry on the Drake tradition of service to the community and the country."

And that sentiment, Meg thought, was the lead-in to his grand announcement about Kyle.

"Enough about me, Meg. How are you? I understand you were injured as well Sunday night."

"I'm fine, sir. A few bruises.'

"Very fortunate, my dear. Such a foolish chance you took. You could have been killed."

Did he really mean should have been killed? Meg shivered. The library didn't feel quite so friendly any more. She was very glad Rod had insisted the door remain open.

"You lied to me, Ty."

Ty Drake turned from the mantel. "About what?"

"I asked you about your marriage to Sherri."

"And I answered truthfully."

"Who's Candy Wilson?"

Ty paled. "My secretary."

"That's all she is to you? A secretary?"

"Of course. What are you insinuating?"

Rod studied his friend's flushed face, then said, "Come clean with me, Ty. Each time you lie, you're making yourself look even more guilty. What will Candy say when I ask her about your relationship?"

"How should I know?"

"I called your hotel in Florida, Ty."

He swallowed. "So?"

"The manager told me you left the hotel on Thursday, not Sunday." Rod moved closer to the mantel. "So, where were you from Thursday to Sunday, Ty?"

"You're trying to pin Sherri's murder on me, aren't you?"

"You can answer my questions here or we'll go to the station. Your choice."

Ty's mouth gaped. "Are you insane? My wife's funeral is in a few hours."

"Then it would be best for you to answer my questions here." Rod's voice dropped. "Where were you, Ty?"

He thrust his fingers through his hair, his eyes closed. "All right. Candy's place. Satisfied?"

"What time Thursday did you arrive?"

"After midnight. Maybe one o'clock."

"Anybody see you?"

"Get real. I timed my arrival so I wouldn't see anybody."

"Did you leave her apartment for any reason in those three days?"

He shook his head. "Candy went to the store for more beer and food. I stayed in the apartment."

"You called Sherri Saturday night with your cell phone?"

"Yeah. We have caller I.D. She would have seen Candy's name on the screen."

"Were you planning to divorce Sherri?"

"No." Ty started to pace. "I loved her. No way would I divorce Sherri. We'd been together a long time, man."

"Were you bored with her?"

"Where are you getting this stuff?"

"Candy seemed to be under the impression you were ending your marriage to Sherri and coming to her." Rod shoved a hand in his pocket. "When I caught up with her last night, Candy was trying on engagement rings."

Ty groaned. "No, Rod. It's not true. Candy doesn't mean anything to me."

"Then why risk your marriage on a fling? Seems more Kyle's style than yours."

Ty finally stopped pacing and dropped onto the couch. "I just needed a break from her, okay?"

"A break? You had an affair because you needed a break?"

"It wasn't like that." His tone was defensive.

"Quit the snow job and just tell me the truth."

Ty let his head lean against the back of the chair. "Sherri wanted to have a baby so much. We tried for years. I finally agreed to fertility testing." His face twisted. "We found out my sperm count was low. It was my fault we couldn't have kids. Do you know what that did to me? How much I felt like a failure? The one thing she wanted in all the world and I couldn't give it to her."

"Did Sherri blame you?"

A bitter chuckle came from Ty. "No. I might have felt better if she had. Instead, she turned to adoption."

Rod sat across from him in a nearby chair. "She wanted to adopt a baby?"

"She obsessed about it, man. We filled out mountains of paperwork, endured multiple home visits, financial audits, anything imaginable. Then we learned it could take years before a baby became available."

"How did she react to the news?"

"She was devastated at first. But she talked to Dad about helping us adopt."

"Why talk to your father?"

"Dad's helped a few people adopting children over the years. He travels extensively, knows diplomats and dignitaries in countries around the world. Sometimes he helps cut through the red tape that hinders adoptions."

"Sherri asked your father for help?"

"She must have. In the last few months, she seemed happy, more than I've ever seen her since the rape."

"And yet you hurt her by turning to another woman?"

"I didn't mean to do that. It just happened, okay? Besides, Sherri didn't know. I was careful."

"Not careful enough, Ty."

Ty stiffened. "What are you saying?"

"You're still lying to me."

"No."

"Can it, Ty. Sherri confronted you about the affair on the phone Saturday night, didn't she?"

He remained mute.

"I'd say that gives you a great motive. You were in town so that gives you the opportunity. And how hard can it be to buy a gun off the street?" Rod clenched his fist. "You're a resourceful guy and you have money. You could easily score a gun."

"You're crazy, Kelter."

Rod heard Meg in the hallway with Senator Drake. He stood. "Don't leave town, Ty. We'll be talking again soon."

CHAPTER SIXTEEN

"Are you going to the funeral?" Meg twisted in her seat to face Rod.

"Yeah, though I doubt I'll learn anything new." Still disgusted with Ty's insensitivity to his wife, Rod forced himself to loosen his choke hold on the steering wheel.

"I should sit in the back. Ty still won't talk to me. He blames me for Sherri's death."

"He's shifting blame for a lot of things to everyone but himself." Just like Rod had done with the loss of his family, except he turned to a bottle to soothe his loss instead of another woman.

"Will you change clothes?"

His head jerked around. "Do I need to?"

"No, but I do. How about lunch at my place so I can change?"

Rod merged into another lane and turned at the next light. "Did you learn anything new from the Senator?"

"He's dying, Rod."

"What?" He hadn't heard any rumors about Drake's health.

"Cancer. That's why he's stepping down and grooming Kyle to take his place. Sort of handing over the dynasty to his son."

"Did Sherri know?"

"I don't think so. The Senator told me he came home to tell Ty, that Kyle already knew. If Ty didn't know, I'd say Sherri probably didn't either." Meg turned a puzzled gaze to him. "Do you think that's what she overheard Sunday night? Were we just in the wrong place at the wrong time and some lunatic picked the trail as the place to hurt someone?"

Rod thought through all he knew so far, precious little that it was, and shook his head. "Too much tracks back to the Drakes, Meg. The attack wasn't random."

She remained silent a while, then, as he turned into her driveway, she sighed. "I didn't think so, but it's hard to believe people you know could do something so evil."

"Anything else stand out as unusual?"

"Drake seemed touchy about the subject of Ty's adoption. It struck me as odd since it's been over thirty years."

"Would you consider giving me a copy of your interview transcript?"

She smiled at him and unbuckled. "If you give me a few hours to transcribe the notes, you can have the tape and a copy of the transcript."

Marcus Lang, pastor of Cornerstone Church, gestured toward the closed white coffin in front of the pulpit. "If Sherri could stand before you right now, she'd tell you not to mourn her passing. She's standing before the throne of God as we speak, waiting for her family and her brothers and sisters in Christ to join her when God calls us home."

Rod shifted uncomfortably in the pew. The last time he'd been in Cornerstone Church for a service had been for Erin and Kayla's funeral. Though much of that time was a haze, he remembered similar words from Lang's message then.

"She'd tell you that life is fleeting, like a shadow that passes and is gone. Sherri lived her life in such a way that she regretted nothing, was thankful for every experience God allowed in her life."

Beside him, Meg sniffed. He reached over and clasped her hand. A tear splashed on the back of his hand. With her hand in his, Rod thought about the preacher's words. In his line of work, he came face to face with death on a daily basis, some from natural causes, others not.

Life could end in an instant. Erin and Kayla's lives had ended in a head-on collision. Flashes of memory from last night surfaced. His hand tightened around Meg's. He came so close to losing her. And if he didn't get his act together, he might lose her anyway.

When the congregation stood for closing prayer, he slid his arm around Meg's waist. After the prayer, he waited with the others for the pall bearers to escort Sherri's coffin down the aisle. Ty walked behind, flanked by his father and brother.

Rod wondered which one of the three men pulled the trigger that placed Sherri in that coffin.

Walking from the cemetery to the car, Meg stayed in the circle of Rod's arm, more determined than ever to go through with her plan.

She glanced at Rod's impassive face. He wouldn't like what she was about to print. All the more reason to keep it under wraps until it went to press. She would deal with his fury afterward.

"What's next for you?"

Rod's gaze dropped to her face. "The station, then I'll be tracking a few leads. Need a ride somewhere?"

Meg shook her head. "Press time is in a few hours. I'll be at the *Gazette* office late." She stopped beside his car. "Stop by tonight before you go home."

His eyes narrowed. "What's wrong?"

"Just stop in, okay?"

"You can count on it."

Rod knocked on Ethan's office door. "You wanted to see me?"

Ethan waved him inside. "Ballistics report came back. The bullets that killed Sherri and her mother match."

"Can't say I'm surprised."

"You probably won't be surprised by something else I picked up, either."

"What's that?"

Ethan slid a piece of paper across his desk to Rod. "Senator Drake owns a Smith and Wesson, .38 caliber."

"I'll get a warrant so we can test the gun for a possible match."

"Already in the works. What happened this morning with the Drakes?"

Rod recounted the information he and Meg learned from the Senator and Ty, ending with, "Meg promised to give us the tape and transcript later today."

"Let me know when it comes in. I want to hear the interview."

Rod stood. "Will do."

Back in the squad room, Rod settled behind his desk and booted Sherri's laptop. This was as good a time as any to finish reading her journal entries. He scrolled through Sherri's earlier journal entries and began reading where he'd left off. He reached an entry dated November 1 and his eyes widened.

"I think that would be the best Christmas present I could give Ty. Mom's willing to help me do some of the leg work. What a great gift. The names of his birth parents.

What he does with those names will be up to him. I just want to give him the information. Maybe the knowledge will give him a measure of peace."

So Sherri and her mother were looking for Ty's birth parents. He shut down the computer and stood. Listening to Megan's interview with the Senator just moved up on Rod's priority list.

Meg folded the latest edition of the *Gazette* and laid it on her desk. Things might be a lot more interesting over the next 24 hours. If her editorial didn't spark another attempt on her life, she didn't know what would. Her whole family would be livid. She shuddered to think how Rod might react.

She picked up the phone and dialed a number from memory. "Hey, Maeve. It's Megan Cahill. Do you have time for a trim? Great. I'll be right over."

Grabbing her bag, Meg stopped by Zoe's desk. "I'm going across the street to Maeve's. Call me if there's a problem with the press run. I should return in twenty minutes."

Zoe's fingers hovered over the computer keyboard. "Okay, Boss."

Meg dashed across the square, opened Maeve's door and glanced around the empty beauty shop with a sense of satisfaction. She'd judged the timing perfectly. No nosy patrons to eavesdrop on her conversation with the town's guru of gossip.

An auburn-haired, petite woman waved Meg to a chair. "I have your seat reserved, my dear. I've wanted to get my hands on your hair for months."

"You have?" Meg swallowed hard. "Look, I only need a trim. Don't whack off a lot."

Maeve waved her concerns aside. "Yeah, I know. Still, your hair will be healthier with those split ends removed."

"Split ends?" She sat in the chair and waited for the grandmother of six to finish examining her hair.

"Yes, ma'am." The hair stylist draped the cape around Meg's shoulders and fastened it. "Noticed it when I styled your hair for Madison's wedding to that handsome policeman. Those two look very happy."

"They're crazy about each other. Almost as bad as Serena and Ethan."

"So what kind of information do you need, dear?"

Meg's face grew hot. "How did you know?"

Maeve laughed and began snipping. "Usually your mother or one of your sisters schedules an appointment for you and then dares you to break it. I've never known you to come in voluntarily."

She grinned. "Got me. Do you remember the name of the Drake family lawyer?"

"Arnie Castlebaum. Died back in 1997."

Meg's heart sank. "Rats."

"His son, Willis, took over the practice."

"I don't think Willis can help. I need information about something that happened thirty years ago."

Maeve moved around in front of Meg, her scissors flashing in the shop's bright lights. "Talk to Mildred Barrett. She worked for Arnie from the first day he opened his law practice. Retired when he handed the practice over to Willis."

"Do you know where I can find her?"

"Last I heard her daughter moved her to an assisted living facility in Kingsport."

Rod entered the *Gazette's* front office and paused. No signs of life. Where was Meg? Zoe's raised voice sounded behind the closed press room door. Of course. The press run. Meg was probably watching the presses.

He strolled into Meg's office and noticed the folded paper on her desk. Sitting on the corner of the desk, Rod unfolded the Gazette's latest edition and began reading. After finishing Ruth's piece on De Marco Water Works, he turned to the second page to Meg's editorial. The more he read, the tighter he gripped the paper's edges. By the time he'd finished, the paper bunched in his fists and his face burned.

How could she do this? Meg had as much as challenged Sherri's killer to come and get her before she pointed an accusing finger. Had she remembered something more and not told him or was she trying to smoke out the killer?

He leaped to his feet, newspaper still crumpled in one hand. Either reason didn't justify hanging out a red flag to attract attention. Rod flung open the door to the press room. No Meg. He motioned Zoe over to him. "Where is she?" he yelled.

"Getting a haircut."

He flinched, hoping she didn't cut much. He loved her silky strands, even though he wanted to strangle her with them at the moment.

Zoe grinned and pushed him out the door. "Go on. Maybe you'll catch her before she loses her locks."

Rod darted across the square and down three doors to Maeve's place. Meg was rising from the chair as he stepped inside the shop, chemical smells assaulting his nose. Undeniable relief rolled through him at the sight of her long hair still intact.

He scowled at her. Now if he could just keep her beautiful head hidden from sight until he nabbed Sherri's killer, he might be able to sleep nights. Maybe.

Meg's gaze dropped to the crushed paper in his hand. "Read something interesting?"

"Are you crazy?" His voice rose to match the heat burning his face.

"I think we already covered that topic."

"Not today. I knew you were up to something, but I didn't think you had a death wish."

Maeve breezed by him on her way to the cash register. "I'm locking up now, kids. Take it outside. Maybe the cold air will cool you down."

Meg handed the woman a twenty and ambled outside without another word to him. He caught up with her on the sidewalk in front of the *Gazette*.

Rod gripped her arm and hustled her inside to her office and slammed the door before swinging her around to face him. "Why?"

"Desperate people make mistakes."

"Don't you trust me to do my job?"

She looked startled. "Of course I do. This isn't about your abilities as a detective. I'm tired of being a victim and hiding behind you and my brother. I want Sherri's killer to know I'm after him now. The hunter is now the hunted."

"He'll come after you with everything he has, Meg, and whoever is with you could get caught in the crossfire. Did you think of that before you threw down the gauntlet?"

"But I'm the target."

"Innocent people die all the time. What if I'm not with you the next time he tries?" His hands circled her arms in a vice grip. "What if he succeeds? Did you think about what that would do to me?"

She paled. Her hand pressed against his cheek. "I'm sorry. I never meant to hurt you."

Rod dragged her against his chest and folded his arms around her. "If something happens to you, it'll rip my heart out." He rested his chin on the top of her head and sighed. "I'm growing used to your wicked sense of humor and grouchy bedside manner before your first cup of coffee. I'd hate to lose you now, Cahill."

She pulled away a little and smiled at him, and his heart lurched in his chest. Somehow over the course of the last few days, Megan Cahill had wormed her way into his heart so deep, he'd never get her out. He swallowed hard, his stomach knotting with the unfamiliar sensations swamping his emotions. His arms tightened around her.

Rod forced himself to face the truth. He had fallen for the woman in his arms. Hard. So hard that if he lost her now, his heart would be shattered.

"Same here, Kelter." A puzzled look crossed her face. "What's going on with you, besides being ready to cart me off to a cave for safekeeping?"

Rod drew in a deep breath. "I did some thinking about you, me, us."

"Okay." She tilted her head. "What did you decide?"

"I don't know exactly what we have together, Megan, but I want to find out. If you're interested."

A huge smile curved her mouth. She threw her arms around his neck and squeezed. "I am very interested, Rod Kelter. Does this mean our relationship can move out of granny gear?"

Rod chuckled, his arms tightening around her waist. "I guess it does."

"Good," she said and kissed him.

Meg gritted her teeth and waited for the explosion.

"Are you crazy?" Ethan wadded the newspaper into a ball and threw it across the room, glaring at her.

She twisted her mouth. "Rod already asked me that a few minutes ago."

"If you weren't my wife's sister, I'd tan your hide." He slapped his palms on his desk and leaned toward her. "I still might after this is over with. Do you realize you've put Serena and Madison in danger as well as the men on protection detail?"

Meg eased back in her chair, as far as the seat would let her. She'd never seen him this angry. "I did what I thought was right, Ethan."

He dropped into his chair and dragged his hands down his face. "You are a piece of work, Megan Cahill. I can't believe you printed that editorial. Why didn't you just parade around the streets with a bulls-eye on your back? Would have been just as effective."

Rod straightened away from the wall and came to stand behind her chair. His hands rested on her shoulders. "What now, Ethan?"

"We've got about twelve hours before this hits the streets. Either we nail Sherri's killer by six o'clock tomorrow morning or Megan's going into protective custody out of town."

"No." Meg jumped to her feet. "I'm not going into hiding like a scared mouse." How was she supposed to follow up on Ty's adoption if Ethan had her stashed somewhere and locked down? "What about the *Gazette*?"

"You should have thought about that before printing your editorial." Ethan folded his arms across his massive chest. "Go home and pack your bags, sweetheart. You might be going on a trip by sunrise."

He couldn't be serious. But looking at her brother-in-law's expression of stone, she knew he meant every word. She whirled to face Rod. "You're going to let him do this to me?"

Rod raised an eyebrow. "Let him? Honey, I'll help him cuff you and cart you off if necessary."

After a silent ride to her house in his car, Rod escorted Meg to her front porch where Josh waited for them.

He looked uneasy, shifting his gaze from Rod to Meg. "What's up? Ethan sounded like he could chew nails when he sent me over here."

Megan remained mute.

Rod rolled his eyes. "Megan's dangling herself as bait in tomorrow's paper."

"Aw, Meg." Josh scowled at her. "You girls can't stay out of trouble."

"Yeah, I know. We're triple trouble."

"With a capital T." He shifted his gaze to Rod. "So, what's the plan?"

"Don't let Meg out of your sight. If anything out of the ordinary happens tonight, call me."

Josh stiffened. "Why not Ethan? The last time you were in charge of her safety, she careened down a mountainside without brakes."

Rod maintained steady eye contact with the former soldier. "I'm aware of that. I doubt I'll ever forget it. You can trust me, Josh. She means a lot to me, too. I'll keep her safe when we're together. In the meantime, while she's in your care, Meg is still a material witness in my case. I need to know if our perp makes another run at her."

Josh studied his face a moment, apparently weighing Rod's words. "He won't succeed."

"I know, Josh."

Rod's muscles relaxed a fraction. The last time he'd seen the rookie was on the mountainside, ready to tear him apart for putting Meg at risk. Rod considered himself lucky the man didn't flatten him on sight, even if he was Josh's superior in rank.

Meg nudged her brother. "I'll be inside in a minute."

Josh turned his head and eyed Rod a moment.

Rod nodded, understanding the silent message, and shifted his position. Anyone trying to get a shot at Meg now would have to go through him first.

After Josh closed the door, Meg's hand slipped into Rod's. "What are you going to do now?"

"Go back to work. Did you finish with the interview tape?"

She dug into her bag and handed him a cassette. "A copy of the transcript should be in your e-mail at work."

"Thanks." He slid his hand into her hair. "I'm glad you didn't take much length off your hair."

She laughed softly. "Funny. My brothers-in-law say the same thing about my sisters' hair." Meg sobered. "I need to go to Kingsport tomorrow, Rod."

He blinked. "Why?"

"The Senator's reaction when I asked about Ty's birth parents. You'll hear it when you listen to the tape. Maeve told me the name of Drake family lawyer and the lawyer's secretary at the time of the adoption. I think this might be important information."

"I'll get back to you on Kingsport." He wrapped her hair around his hand and tugged gently. "Promise me you won't ditch your brother and track down this lead on your own."

She bit her lip.

"Don't do this to me, Cahill." He dipped his head closer and kissed her. "You mean a lot to me, enough that I will go to extreme measures if you push me too hard."

Meg scowled. "Threatening me with handcuffs again?"

"If that's what it takes."

"You'll talk to Ethan about Kingsport?"

"Yes."

He felt the tension in her body melt before she said a word.

"I promise to stay with Josh."

He closed his eyes, relieved at her words, and gathered her close. "Thanks, baby." Rod's cell phone chirped. He grabbed the phone, refusing to let Meg slip away from him just yet. "Kelter."

"It's Ethan. We got the warrant. I'll meet you at the Drake house."

"Okay." He closed his cell phone and dropped a light kiss on Meg's upturned face. "I've got to go. I'll have my phone if you need me."

Rod waited until the door shut behind Megan before leaving. He pushed the pedal to the floor and arrived at the Drake mansion just as Ethan and a prowl car swung into the driveway.

Ethan motioned to the other officer to go around back and turned to Rod. "Let's go."

The maid who opened the door looked stunned to see the two policemen on the doorstep. "May I help you?"

"Is Senator Drake here?" Ethan said.

"He asked not to be disturbed tonight, sir."

Rod pushed the door open wider and shouldered his way inside, holding his crime scene kit in one hand. "Tell the Senator we have a search warrant."

She gasped, then turned and ran down the hallway to the library. In less than a minute, the Drake men assembled in the foyer, varied expressions of hostility on their faces. Ty cast puzzled glances between his family and the police.

Kyle stepped forward, fury evident in his stiff movements. "What's going on, Rod?"

Ethan handed him the warrant. "We have a warrant to search the house."

"For what?"

"A weapon, for starters."

"You'll find plenty," Ty said, his tone wry. "We all have guns."

"I'm only interested in one," Ethan said. "The gun that killed Sherri."

Silence greeted his statement. Finally, Ty's hoarse voice intruded into the quiet. "You think one of us killed Sherri?"

"A ballistics test will confirm what I already know."

Kyle turned. "I'm calling the lawyer, Dad."

"Use the phone in the living room." Rod motioned to the officer who appeared in the doorway. "Officer Gates will stay with the three of you while you wait for us to finish searching the house."

"That could take all night," Kyle snapped. "This is a 10,000-square foot house."

"That's enough, son." Warren Drake sounded tired. "Let Rod do his job."

After Gates left with the Drakes, Rod nodded toward the library. "Let's start there first." He pulled a pair of latex gloves from his pocket and handed them to Ethan, then tugged a pair on his own hands.

A fire crackled in the fireplace. Three glasses with varying levels of liquid in them sat on the desk, waiting for the Drakes' return. An open decanter sat in the middle of the desk. Unless their tastes had changed, Rod knew the crystal contained brandy. "Take the desk, Ethan. I'll start on the other end of the room and work my way toward you."

He left the crime scene case by the door and searched the couch and armchairs. A few coins, pens and a paperclip. Next, he turned to the bookcases. He discovered that the maid didn't spend much time dusting the tops of the books, but nothing else.

"Rod."

A gun lay in Ethan's hand. "A Smith and Wesson, .38 caliber, and it's been fired recently."

Rod's hand clenched into a fist. If this gun was the murder weapon, one of his friends had tried to kill Megan three times in the last week. He snatched a clear bag from the crime scene kit and opened it for Ethan to place the weapon inside. Once the gun was secured, they strode to the living room.

Kyle and Ty jumped to their feet, gazes glued to the bag in Rod's hand. Ty's jaws clenched, but he made no sound.

Rod held the bag in front of Warren Drake. "Is this your gun, Senator?"

Drake stared at the weapon a moment before raising his gaze to Rod's face. "It appears to be."

"Are you aware it's been fired recently?"

"Don't say anything else, Dad." Kyle grabbed his cell phone. "I'll see what's taking Phillips so long."

"I suggest you find your father a criminal attorney," Ethan said, his voice soft. "Senator, come with us."

"Where are you taking him?" Ty asked.

"To the station."

When Kyle moved like he was going to interfere, Rod stepped between Ethan and Kyle. "Back off, Kyle. We're taking the Senator in for questioning, not arresting him."

Drake rose. "Everything will be fine, Kyle. Trust me, son. I'll take care of it."

No one said anything more as Ethan and the Senator left the room. Kyle ran a shaking hand through his hair. "You can't do this to him, Rod. He's sick."

"I know."

"How did you find out?" Ty glared at him. "I just found out a few minutes ago."

"The Senator did an interview with Megan this morning. He told her."

"And, naturally, she told you everything." Kyle mouth twisted into a wry smile. "So much for you being only friends. What happens now?"

"We'll talk to your father, see if he can help us with some questions."

"He didn't kill Sherri," Ty said. "Dad loved her. You know that."

Rod had to admit, it didn't seem the Senator's character to murder someone. He'd be more inclined to murder someone's reputation. "We build cases based on evidence."

A stunned expression settled on Kyle's face. "You have evidence that Dad killed Sherri? That's not possible, Rod."

Rod crossed to the doorway. "Hire a good lawyer."

CHAPTER SEVENTEEN

"That's about the dumbest move I've ever seen you make." Josh leaned against the kitchen counter. "Why'd you do it, Meg?"

Dumb. Yeah, that described her actions all right. Meg sipped her hot cocoa. "I was so angry after that scare with the brakes last night. Mad at myself for not looking under the car because I would have noticed the brake fluid. Mad at Sherri's killer for putting my friends and family at risk."

She set her mug down on her counter and slid onto a bar stool. "Josh, what if Madison had driven Nick's Jeep? She wouldn't know what to do or had anyone around to help her. We could have lost her last night or Serena if she'd borrowed the Jeep."

"Or you."

"Maybe." She traced the rim of the mug with her finger, steam rising from the hot chocolate. "Slowing the car was easier with Rod as a buffer, but I could have done it without him."

"So what's the point of running a challenge in the paper?"

"Draw the killer's attention back to me. I want him to know I'm coming after him. I will find him before he catches me."

"So how will you make sure the perp targets you and not Madison or Serena?"

"I'm not going near either of them until you guys slam the cell door behind him." She glanced at her watch. "You up for a drive?"

"Meg's right." Rod stopped the tape player sitting on Ethan's desk. "Drake doesn't want Ty poking into his adoption." Why? None of this made sense to him. It was thirty years in the past. Who cared about the details now except Ty?

"Has Drake always been against Ty looking into his past?"

Rod shook his head. "Ty never showed any interest in his birth mother or father as he grew up. He seemed satisfied that his adoptive parents loved him enough to choose him from all the other available children. What triggered the need to find his birth parents?"

"Maybe trying to have a baby with Sherri. In any case, sounds like you should go to Kingsport tomorrow with Meg." Ethan handed him a piece of paper. "Check this out."

Rod scanned the report on the button he'd found at the trail. The lab had lifted a print from the surface belonging to Warren Drake. "The coat in his closet was missing a button. Guess we found it."

Ethan stood. "The Senator's been stewing on his own long enough. Let's see what he has to say."

Rod opened the interview room door. The Senator turned his head and watched them. "Do you need anything to drink, Senator?"

"So the police chief's playing the bad cop?"

Rod sat beside Ethan across the table from Drake and laid a file folder in front of him. "This is a murder investigation, not *Law and Order*. We'll be here a while. I don't want you dehydrated."

Drake stared at him a moment. "Very well. I'd like some water, please."

After Ethan returned with the water, Rod said, "Senator, when was the last time you were at the Churchill Trail?"

"Why?"

"That's not how it works, Drake." Ethan folded his arms across his chest. "You answer questions, not ask them."

"I don't remember."

Rod removed a picture from the folder, a close-up view of the button he'd found in the trail's parking lot, and slid it across the table. "Do you recognize this?"

Drake examined the photo. "It looks like a monogrammed button. We use similar buttons, but that doesn't mean it belongs to a Drake. Anyone could use a monogrammed button. We don't have proprietary rights to the design."

"True." Rod slid the picture back into the folder. "But this particular button has your fingerprint on it."

"I see." Drake lifted the cup of water, hand shaking, and drank.

"The weapon we found in the study at your home is registered to you."

"It's not illegal to have a gun."

"It's illegal to murder someone with that gun. Where were you Sunday night starting at midnight?"

"At the house. I made a few phone calls and went to bed. Look, is this really necessary? I already answered your questions about my activities."

Rod noted the Senator's heightened color. "Can anyone confirm that?"

"Maybe the maid, but I doubt it. The staff and the rest of the family were in bed by that time." He stopped. "At least, I thought they were."

"You thought they were?"

Drake frowned. "Sherri must have left sometime after midnight, but I didn't see her leave."

Ethan leaned forward, his gaze intent. "She saw you. She heard you."

The Senator froze. Rod could almost see thoughts racing through his mind.

"Heard what?"

The politician had to be wondering what secret Sherri had divulged. "She called Megan and asked her to meet at the trail. Did you follow Sherri, try to reason with her?"

"No, of course not. I was asleep. Ask Ty. He woke me around 4:00 a.m."

"Plenty of time for you to kill Sherri, then drive home and climb into bed," Ethan said.

"When we test your coat, will it have Sherri's blood on it?" Rod asked. "We found it hanging in the hall closet, Senator. Planning to take it to the cleaners?"

Drake, his complexion gray, deflated before Rod's eyes. He propped his elbows on the table and dropped the weight of his head into his hands. "Okay. All right. Enough, Rod."

"You have something to tell me, Senator?" Rod's hands clenched under the table. Was the father of his old friend guilty of murder and attempted murder?

"I did it. I killed Sherri." The words were muffled behind his hands.

Rod stiffened. A slight movement from Ethan shifted his attention to the police chief. Ethan shook his head slightly. Rod stayed silent. Something seemed off. Too easy, maybe.

"Do you want to make a statement?"

Drake nodded.

Ethan turned on the tape recorder sitting in the middle of the table. "I want to remind you again, Senator Drake, that you have the right to an attorney. Do you want one present before we go any further?"

Drake's hands dropped to the table. "No."

"What happened Sunday night, Senator?" Rod asked.

"Sherri heard me talking to another senator on the phone."

"What did she hear that upset her so much?"

"You have to understand, Rod. Sherri loved me, looked up to me as a father figure. Her father might have been there in body while she was growing up, but he checked out mentally before he came home from active combat."

Rod stared at him. "She loved you like a father, yet you shot her?"

Drake flinched. "I didn't have a choice."

"What did she overhear, sir?"

"Blackmail. She overheard me blackmailing another senator."

"You asked for money in return for not divulging a secret?" Ethan asked.

Drake shook his head. "I never asked for money, just votes to help pass bills or endorsements of De Marco Water Works."

"Let me get this straight." Rod crossed his arms. "You're telling me you killed Sherri so she wouldn't expose you, for discovering something a good private investigator or reporter could dig up at any time?"

"Kyle's running for my senate seat next fall. I didn't want the scandal to hurt his chances."

"What scandal?" Ethan said. "That's good old boy politics at work. No one would be surprised by those allegations. Your being charged with murder will hurt his chances more."

"What did you do after Sherri heard you on the phone?" Rod asked.

"I confronted her, tried to reason with her, but Sherri was idealistic about right and wrong, especially after she joined Cornerstone Church. She ran to her suite and locked the door." He shrugged. "I thought she'd cool down and I could try again in the morning. I went on to my suite. Within a couple of minutes, I heard a car crank. I looked out my window and saw Sherri driving away in a great hurry."

He sipped more water. "I ran to my car and followed her. She drove straight to the trail. I circled around to the far side of the trail and parked. I waited in the bushes near the entrance to the park. When she came back to her car, I begged her to reconsider. She refused." Drake hung his head. "I panicked and shot her."

"What about Megan?"

"I didn't know she was at the trail until after I killed Sherri. I was afraid she had seen me. I was going to shoot her, too, but a car drove up the street and I didn't want to be seen. I shoved her into the stone entrance and ran."

"You were behind the attempts on Meg's life?" Ethan asked.

Drake nodded. "I was afraid her memory would return and she would identify me."

"What did you do to her cars?" Rod asked.

He licked his lips. "I didn't do anything. I hired someone else to do it for me."

"Who?" Ethan asked.

"I don't know his name or what he looks like. I only talked to him on the phone."

"Then who was your contact?"

Drake remained silent.

"What do you know about Sherri's mother's death?" Rod asked.

"I shot her, too."

"Quite a killing spree for a man who doesn't even have parking tickets on his record. Why did you kill Mrs. King?"

"She called. Said Sherri had told her everything before she died, even told her she was afraid I would hurt her or Ty to keep the blackmail scheme quiet." A wry smile graced his lips. "Claimed to have evidence proving my guilt. She offered to sell her silence."

"And you didn't want to pay?"

"She would have been a leech, bleeding me dry even after I retired from public service."

"Why did she resort to blackmail?" Ethan asked.

Drake frowned. "How should I know? Maybe she wanted to go on a cruise. I didn't ask her how she was going to spend my money."

"How much money did she want?" Rod asked.

"Fifty thousand."

Rod studied the old man's drawn face. Fifty thousand dollars wouldn't cause much more than a ripple in the Drake account. Bank records showed his balance at well over $10 million.

"So how did you do it, Drake?" Ethan folded his arms across his chest.

"He's lying, Ethan." Rod scowled at the Senator's back as an officer escorted him to the holding cell. "Somebody shoved Meg from behind before he shot Sherri, not after."

"Protecting one of his sons."

"Yeah, but which one? They both had motives." He dragged his hand over the night's beard growth, exhaustion washing through him. "What should we do about Meg?"

"Escort her out of town before the sun rises. I'll hold Drake as long as I can without charging him." Ethan slanted a look at him. "Have a change of clothes handy?"

"In the car. Why?"

"Why don't you shower and change in the locker room while I make a few calls. I'll drive you to Meg's. You can leave your car in the lot."

Rod returned to Ethan's office, feeling marginally better. At least more alert for a short time. From past experience with all-nighters, he guessed he had about two hours before exhaustion would force him to sleep for a while.

Ethan hung up the phone and pulled out his keys. "Let's go."

They walked into the pre-dawn darkness in silence. Inside Ethan's SUV, Rod said, "What's the plan?"

"Check out Meg's angle on Ty and the adoption. I'll work on Kyle. Maybe we'll uncover something new."

Rod stiffened as Ethan turned the corner to Meg's street. A red Camaro occupied the space behind Josh's cruiser.

"Recognize it?" Ethan asked.

"No." Rod scanned the sleeping neighborhood, alert for changes, but detected none. Josh hadn't called in with a problem. Neither had any other patrol officer.

"Jot down the license plate and we'll check the house." Ethan parked on the street.

Rod handed him the information and climbed from the SUV. He approached the house, his hand sliding to his side and unsnapping his holster. Behind him, he heard Ethan draw his weapon.

The front door swung open and light spilled onto the porch, framing Meg in the doorway. "Hey, guys. Like my new wheels?"

Rod relaxed a fraction and stepped onto the porch. "You promised not to ditch Josh."

"I took him with me."

He speared the rookie with a glare. "And you didn't call it in?"

"Didn't see a need." Josh shrugged. "You told me to stay with her, not keep her in a cage."

Ethan shut the door. "She's a protected witness."

"I can protect her as well as you can."

Irritation welled in Rod. "Not if you're outgunned and outmanned, Cahill." He glanced at the gym bag by the door. "Is that all your luggage, Meg?"

"Except for my laptop." Her blue eyes studied his face. "No arrest during the night?"

"No. We need to get out of here before sunrise."

"Sounds like a bad western." Muttering under her breath at his abrupt response, she hurried down the hall.

"What happened?" Josh asked

"Senator Drake's in the holding pen," Ethan said, fastening the snap on his holster. "Confessed to both murders."

Josh's gaze shifted from Ethan to Rod and back. "You don't believe him."

Rod paced to the living room window and parted the emerald curtain. "He's protecting one of his sons."

"Do you know which one?"

"Not yet, but we will." Rod turned away from scanning the street as Meg re-entered the room, computer in hand. "Ready?"

"There's no other way?"

"You took other options out of our hands when you put that editorial in the paper," Ethan said. "Check in every two hours, Rod. Miss one call by so much as a minute, and I'll have cops from every berg within a hundred miles on your tail."

Rod grinned, not doubting Ethan's sincerity for a minute. "Yes, sir." He grabbed the gym bag straps and strode to the door.

Josh swept Meg into a hug. "Watch your six, sweetheart."

The Watcher hurled the mug across the room. The clay slammed against the wall and shattered, coffee dripping from the logs onto the wood floor.

Megan Cahill had gone too far. She was challenging him. Daring him. An act of defiance that would climax with her death. And if Rod Kelter got in the way, the Watcher would gladly send him to his wife and daughter.

He grabbed the phone and punched in a number. "I have a job for you."

CHAPTER EIGHTEEN

Outside, Meg pulled the Camaro keys from her pocket and dangled them in front of Rod's face. "Want to drive?"

"Nope." He opened the passenger door and tossed his bag in the back alongside hers. "I need to recharge for a couple of hours."

Meg sank into the leather driver's seat and cranked the engine, a sigh of satisfaction escaping. The leather seat molded perfectly to her body, the rumbling engine a pleasure to her ear. The machine under her hands went a long way toward soothing the irritation at running from her problem.

She glanced at the man beside her, his face illuminated for a few seconds as they passed under a streetlight at the edge of town. A scowl still wrinkled his forehead. She wanted to ask what happened overnight, but figured she'd eventually get the information she needed.

Meg swung her attention to the black and yellow ribbon unreeling in front of her. All in good time. Maybe if she let Rod sleep until they arrived in Kingsport, then plied him with breakfast and coffee, the information might slip out during casual conversation. Her lip curled. Right. None of the cops she knew told anything without careful deliberation.

She merged onto Highway 18 and pressed on the accelerator. The little sports car lunged forward, sending a shot of adrenaline through Meg's body. If Rod weren't with her, she would roll down the windows and let the morning breeze blow through the car.

"Speed limit's 55 on this road."

Meg narrowed her eyes and glared at her passenger. Rod's eyes remained closed, but one corner of his mouth twitched. "You think I'm speeding?"

Rod snorted, slouching further into the seat. "You're driving, aren't you?"

Scowling, she eased off the accelerator until the speedometer hovered closer to 55 than 75. She sighed. Plow horse speed for a thoroughbred racing machine.

When she merged onto Interstate 40, the first spear of sunlight pierced the gloom. She pressed the accelerator until the car reached the new speed limit. After a peek at her companion, confirming his sound sleep, Meg urged the speedometer a few more ticks past the posted speed limit.

Meg shifted her focus to the upcoming interview with the lawyer's secretary. Would she remember all the details about an adoption thirty years in the past? Arnie Castlebaum must have handled many adoptions over the years. She hoped Senator Drake's name attached to the adoption might spark the secretary's memory.

An hour later, Meg cruised Interstate 40 through Knoxville and formulated questions to ask the older woman. When Maeve called last night, she'd indicated the woman had medical tests scheduled for this morning, but could see her and Rod later in the afternoon.

Squinting at the sunlight streaming through the windshield, Meg dug her sunglasses from her bag and slid them on. None of this made any sense. Why kill Sherri? What could she know worth killing over? Something about the Senator? Was the phone call Sherri overheard the key or just a coincidence in a string of horrific events?

If only she'd had more time to talk to Sherri. Meg's vision blurred. Tears slipped down her cheeks. She didn't deserve to die. Could Meg have thwarted the killer's plans if she had done something different? Miles of blacktop disappeared in the rearview mirror as Meg contemplated Sherri's last few minutes of life.

She shifted in her seat and dug in her pocket for a tissue, sniffing.

"What's wrong?"

Meg stiffened at the sound of Rod's sleep-deepened voice. "I'm sorry. I didn't mean to wake you."

Rod scooted up in the seat. "Do you need to pull over? Are you sick?"

"Sick at heart."

"Sherri?"

She nodded.

He sat in silence a moment. "Losing someone you love hurts."

Meg darted a glance at him. His gaze was locked on her face. Her heart flipped in her chest, knowing he'd experienced a loss so deep she didn't see how he would recover. Would his heart ever mend enough to include her in his life? Another question weighing on her mind sprang to her lips. "Do you still hurt?"

"Every day." He laid his hand on her knee. "But it's no longer the first thing I think of when I wake each morning. When I first lost Erin and Kayla, I thought I would lose my mind. Grief ate me alive." His voice grew rough. "I didn't know a person could hurt so much and still live."

Fresh moisture welled in Meg's eyes. "How did you stand the pain?"

"Booze."

Rod's curt reply drew a startled breath from her. Meg had heard rumors, but never confirmed them despite her earlier hurtful remark.

"I worked as many hours as possible, hoping to exhaust myself enough to sleep without the nightmares."

One hand dropped from the wheel to cover his. "Nightmares?"

"Guess I had a hard time accepting that I wasn't with them in the car. If I had been, maybe I could have saved them. In the dreams, I'd see Kayla in her car seat, hands reaching out to me. Screaming for me to help her and Erin."

Rod turned his hand over and laced his fingers with hers. "If I couldn't work long enough hours to fall asleep from exhaustion, I downed a few beers, just enough to dull the memories. Then Ethan came."

Meg frowned. She remembered Serena mentioning he and Ethan had some kind of problem in the spring, but she'd always been vague on the details no matter how hard Meg pressed. "What happened?"

"Ethan made me go home."

"What's wrong with that?"

"The house was empty, Meg, except for memories that gutted me as soon as I walked in the door. I had nothing but work to occupy my thoughts. When Ethan forced me to go home, the only thing waiting for me was a case or two of beer. One night, when a six-pack wasn't enough to drown the pain, I drank a second six-pack. I was off duty at the time, but we were in the middle of the Muehller case. I knew better, that I was taking a chance. Ethan called me to process Serena's house."

"That was the night Serena's house was broken into?"

He squeezed her hand. "Yeah. Somehow, I drove to the crime scene in one piece, but Ethan knew as soon as he looked me in the face that I was drunk."

Meg bit her lip, thinking about her brother-in-law's probable reaction. "What did he do?"

"Drove me home, tossed me in the bed and ordered me to show up at the station the next morning, sober." Rod shook his head. "I thought my career was over. The next morning, though, he told me he needed a partner he could trust. He gave me one more chance, didn't even put the incident on record."

Meg scowled at him. "How come you got another chance at redemption and all I get from him is grief?"

"I didn't get off without any repercussions. I've been on probation since May that includes visits with Marcus Lang every week."

"Is it working?"

Rod chuckled. "Between Marcus and Ethan, I haven't touched any alcohol in seven months. Ethan didn't mince words. Told me if I showed up drunk on the job again, he'd fire me on the spot."

Meg could imagine the expression on Ethan's face when he said that, too. Probably looked just like he had last night when he read her editorial. She shuddered. "You hungry yet?"

"If I remember right, there's a pancake place at the next exit."

Her mouth watered at the prospect of blueberry pancakes with a side order of bacon accompanied by hot coffee. "Perfect."

Rod sipped his coffee and watched Meg work her way through the last of her pancakes. He smiled, amused at her enthusiasm. "Do you need another stack?"

She shook her head. "Hey, I was up all night, too, Kelter. I need fuel to replenish the engine."

The coffee cup paused halfway to his mouth. "But the *Gazette* went to press last night." If he'd known that, he would have insisted on driving. Rod studied her face, noting the shadows under her tear-reddened eyes.

"And I have another deadline in three days. Plus, I took a few hours off to nab the Camaro."

Rod caught the waitress's eye and motioned for the check. "Where did you get it?"

"Friend of mine in Knoxville owns a car lot. I called him after the Corvette blew up and asked him to look around for me." She grinned. "He found a real gem."

"Does he pay speeding tickets for his clients?" Rod asked, his tone mild.

Meg scowled at him. "I don't always speed."

"Want me to pull your driving record?"

Face flushing, she laid her fork beside her plate and slid out of the booth. "Maybe I should rethink dating a cop." She strode from the dining room.

He stood, laughing as she exited the restaurant. It felt good to laugh. Not much to laugh about in the last couple of years. Rod presented the check at the register and paid their tab. Pocketing the change, he wondered at the feelings sweeping through him. Contentment, joy, pleasure at being alive and with Megan.

He hadn't felt like this since Erin. He paused, his hand on the outside door, swallowing hard. Was it possible? Could he have fallen in love with Megan? Get a grip, Kelter. You can't focus on that right now. Too much is at stake. He drew in a breath and stepped into the mid-morning sunshine.

Rod opened the driver's side door of the idling Camaro. "I'll drive. It's your turn for a nap." He held out his hand as she started to protest. "No arguments, Cahill. Besides, you're not the only one who likes fast cars."

She climbed out to stand beside him, a smug smile forming on her lips. "Speed limit's 55 on this road, Kelter." She sauntered to the passenger side and slid into the seat.

Rod grinned. He'd have to watch his speed now or face hours of good-natured ragging. After adjusting the seat for his leg length, he drove to the highway and headed toward Kingsport.

He didn't want to know what Meg paid for the vehicle, but he had to admit the car handled like a well-oiled racing machine. Smooth ride, leashed power under the hood, quick response. He sighed. A pleasure to drive.

"What do you think?"

Rod grinned at her. "Great, except for one thing."

Meg stiffened, as if he'd insulted her. "What's that?"

"Wrong color. It clashes with my hair."

Meg's laughter filled the car.

"Meg, wake up. We're here."

She opened her eyes and jerked upright. Meg pushed her hair away from her flaming face. "Sorry. I didn't mean to use your arm as a pillow."

"I didn't mind."

His tone brought her gaze up to his. Something about it told her he meant more than he said, but what? A hint of warmth in his eyes, a softness that hadn't been there earlier.

Uncomfortable with her own rioting emotions, she turned to study their surroundings. Her jaw dropped. A six-room motel? Calling it a motel might be a generous description. A sign in the yard identified the place as the Three Tree Inn.

Meg unlatched the seatbelt and twisted in her seat, craning her neck. Sure enough, three pine trees stood in the yard along with some kind of bush. While she studied the scene, a black and red rooster strolled from the bush and strutted around the grass.

She glanced at Rod, eyes wide. "Where are we?"

"About 30 miles beyond Kingsport, in Virginia."

"What are we doing here?"

"We need some sleep. Neither of us will make it on a two-hour nap and I can't put you in a hotel on the main highway."

Oh, man. Her stomach knotted. She hadn't thought to check for a tail while driving. "You think someone followed us?"

"I don't know, but it's better to play it safe for now." He nodded toward the peach wooden structure. "I'll see if they have adjoining rooms."

"And if they don't?"

"We look elsewhere off the main drag." He leveled a serious look at her. "I need instant access to your room if there's a problem. Otherwise, you can trust me to stay on my side of the dividing line."

She waved her hand at him, as if brushing off his suggestion of impropriety. "I know I can trust you. That's never been a question."

"Remember that, if circumstances cave in on us, Cahill."

While Rod asked for two rooms with a connecting door at the motel office, Meg wandered around the yard, camera in hand. The rooster kept a wary eye on her, but otherwise ignored the human in his territory. She maneuvered herself into a good position and started snapping photos on her digital camera. Proof for her sisters at their next Cahill girls' night out.

If she didn't know better, she'd suspect the bird of posing. He paraded around the yard and, after checking that she still watched, stretched his neck and crowed. The bird repeated his performance every few feet.

After obtaining several good shots, she turned her attention to the surrounding area. She frowned. Few businesses or other dwellings occupied the area near the motel. A natural medicine shop, a quilt place. No restaurants, except for an ice cream stand.

A black pickup cruised by the motel. The bearded man driving the truck stared at her long enough to send a shiver through her body. Had trouble trailed them to the middle of nowhere in Virginia?

Meg started toward the motel office when Rod exited with two room keys in hand.

"We're in luck?"

"Rooms 5 and 6." He tossed her one key. "Your palace awaits, my lady."

"Promise to slay the dragons in my room? The brown ones with feelers?"

"As long as they don't have eight legs, I'm your man."

"Terrific. My knight quakes at the sight of spiders." Ignoring his laughter, Meg shot a glance over her shoulder, scanning the street. No truck in sight, but she couldn't shake the feeling someone watched them from a distance.

"Problem?"

Aside from the fear of waking with a cockroach as a bed buddy? "I guess not." Her fear was unreasonable. Who could have followed them? They snuck out of town before daylight and she'd taken the long way around town to avoid attracting attention from anyone who might be strolling through Otter Creek's streets before dawn this morning.

Meg squelched her uneasiness and headed for the gray-colored door bearing the number six. "Let's check out the accommodations, Kelter." She slanted a smile at him. "You're on deck for roach patrol. Think you're up to the challenge?"

She slid the key into the lock and turned. A gust of stale air from the room wafted across her face. Meg stepped inside and wrinkled her nose. The room smelled like the bottom of an ashtray. She walked to the air unit and flipped the switch. After a cursory inspection of the room and beds, she turned on the bathroom light. Torn linoleum and cracked tiles. She sighed. A stop at the store for disinfectant topped the to-do list.

"I don't see any extra guests." Rod leaned against the door jam, watching her. "I know it's not the Ritz, but can you deal with it for a day or two?"

Meg stared at the faded checked comforter, distaste growing by the minute. She desperately needed more sleep. The two-hour nap in the car left her sluggish. But the thought of sliding into the sheets on that bed sent a shiver down her spine. Guess that meant she'd be sleeping in her clothes on top of the comforter. She smiled at Rod. "It will be fine." She would make it work.

Relief crossed his face. "Great." Rod unlocked the door connecting to his room, and swung it open.

Meg glanced inside. His room was a mirror image of hers, except his spread was a solid green. "So what's the game plan?"

"I'll bring in our luggage." He glanced at his watch. "It's lunchtime, but I'm not hungry. You need anything?"

Meg shook her head. "Sleep first, then lunch."

Rod tilted his head, a smile curving his mouth. "Should I have coffee available when you wake?"

She yawned. "Might be wise."

Rod waited until he was positive Meg slept before calling Ethan. "Anything new?"

"The Senator's sticking to his story."

Not surprising. If he believed one of his sons killed the women, Drake would cover for them, especially now that he had been diagnosed with terminal cancer. Rod settled back against the bed's headboard. "What about Ty and Kyle?"

"Can't shake Candy's statement. She insists Ty was with her during the hours we're interested in."

Ty had been with Candy the night after Sherri was killed? "Cold. Can the neighbors confirm that?"

"Two noticed his car in the slot next to hers."

"What about Kyle?"

A squeak from Ethan's chair told him that his boss was leaning back, probably with his feet elevated. "Maid says he came in from the Pond restaurant around 12:00. After that, she went to bed. Her room is at the back of the house, off the kitchen. She says she didn't hear anything until I woke her ringing the doorbell."

So no one could confirm the Senator's alibi or Kyle's. Rod rubbed his jaw. Stalemate.

"How's Meg?"

"Hanging in like a trooper. I stuffed her with a huge breakfast and she just drifted off to sleep. Figured we both need to sleep a few hours after being up all night. We have an appointment with Mildred Barrett later this afternoon."

"Keep me posted. I'll expect to hear from you in two hours."

After ending the call, Rod checked on Meg. Satisfied she was safe, he slid off his shoes and lay on the bed, his gun within easy reach. He jammed the pillow under his neck and let his muscles go lax. Maybe they'd catch a break with the lawyer's secretary. He had a feeling they were going to need one.

Meg surfaced from a deep sleep to the crow of the rooster. She groaned and rolled over, squinting at her watch. She drew in a deep breath. Her nose twitched. Coffee?

Following the tantalizing scent, she located the steaming source on the nightstand. She sipped the hot liquid and closed her eyes. Not just coffee. Rod had brought her a mocha latte.

When she finished half the cup, Meg tapped on their adjoining door and stuck her head around the door jam. "Did you get any rest?"

Rod slid his arms into the sleeves of his jacket. "Some. Ethan says to stay out of trouble."

"Any progress?"

He shook his head. "Do you want to see Mildred or eat first?"

"Mildred. We can grab a bite after we find out if she knows anything that might help."

Rod held out his hand. "Keys?"

Meg scowled. "Hey, those are my wheels. Who said you could drive?"

"You're navigating."

"Maybe I can't read maps."

He laughed. "Get real, Cahill. You're not Madison."

"Why can't I drive?"

"Virginia police pay attention to speed. I'm not putting up with Ethan ragging on me for letting you get another ticket for speeding."

Grumbling, Meg dug her keys from her pocket and tossed them in his direction. "My choice on dinner, then, and you're paying."

He grinned. "It's got to be cheaper than paying a speeding fine."

An hour later, Meg dropped the map and surveyed the two-story brick facility at the edge of the parking lot. "She's on the second floor, room 231. We have to sign in at the front desk first."

Inside the building, the desk attendant glanced at their signatures. "Ms. Barrett is expecting you. Just go on up. Elevator's to your left, stairs to your right."

Opting for the stairs, they emerged onto a white-tiled corridor with eggshell-colored walls. Meg glanced in some of the rooms as she and Rod walked down the hall, searching for Mildred's room. In many rooms, televisions flickered, the sound of movies and game shows drifting into the hall. In others, residents slept or visited with family or other residents.

About half-way down the long corridor, Rod pointed out Mildred's door. Meg knocked briskly on the open door.

"Come in, my dear."

The cheerful room was decorated with many different kinds of quilts with one in progress on a round quilting hoop. The colors and patterns dazzled her eyes after seeing so much dreariness in the assisted living facility.

"Wow." Meg moved closer to examine one quilt in different shades of purple and green. "This is gorgeous. Did you make these, Ms. Barrett?"

"Keeps my hands busy. You must be Megan Cahill."

Meg dragged her attention from the quilt and focused on the object of her visit. "Yes, ma'am. Thank you for seeing us this afternoon. This is my friend, Rod Kelter."

Rod shook her hand. "You're quite the artist, Ms. Barrett."

The elderly lady laughed. "And you're a flatterer, Mr. Kelter. Please, both of you, have a seat." She motioned to the two chairs by her window. "I had one of the nurses bring them for you. Now, how can I help you?" She turned to Rod. "Maeve mentioned that you work for the police."

"Yes, ma'am. We'd like to ask you about an old adoption case your employer handled."

Mildred's brow furrowed. "We handled a lot of adoptions. They're all a blur now. I don't know if I'll remember any specific case."

"This one involved Senator Warren Drake," Meg said.

The old lady laughed. "You'll have to be more specific than that, dear. Senator Drake involved himself in a lot of adoptions over the years."

Rod sat forward on his chair. "What do you mean?"

"Didn't you know? The Senator orchestrated hundreds of adoptions."

"How?"

"Well, I don't know all the specifics, but it had something to do with his travels abroad for the Senate."

She shrugged. "When he returned from overseas trips, he brought another list of children available for adoption by parents here in the States."

"Your office kept records of these adoptions?" Meg asked.

"Of course, but the adoption records are sealed, you know. Arnie's son has them. Is there one adoption in particular you were interested in?"

"Drake's son, Ty."

Mildred nodded. "Ah, yes. The first adoption. You know, that one was the only adoption of a child born in the US."

Rod reached for Mildred's hand. "Ms. Barrett, I'm investigating the murder of Sherri Drake, Ty's wife. Some questions have arisen regarding Ty's adoption. Is there any way you can help me get the information I need?"

She sat in silence a moment. "I don't have access to official records."

"What about unofficial ones?" Meg asked. "Appointment books, maybe."

"Oh, yes." Mildred smiled. "I kept all Arnie's calendars and appointment books. Willis was going to throw all of it away after his father died." She shook her head. "I couldn't let him do that. It just didn't seem right. I boxed them up and brought them home for safe keeping. Filled three boxes."

Meg glanced around the room. Almost no closet space. She figured the boxes weren't here. Were they with her daughter? "Where are they, Ms. Barrett?"

"I left them with my daughter." She waved her hand. "As you can see, I don't have much room here for anything but my quilting."

"Would it be possible for us to look at those appointment books, Ms. Barrett?" Rod asked.

"I suppose that will be fine. No one's asked for them in years." She looked at Meg. "My cell phone's behind you on the table, dear. Would you mind handing it to me?"

Meg turned and grasped the black cell phone. Her eyebrow rose. "Nice phone."

Mildred laughed. "My grandson, Robbie, provides it for me. He insisted I have a phone in case of emergencies." She dialed her daughter's number and arranged for them to have access to the garage.

Rod stood. "Thanks for your help, Ms. Barrett." He leaned over and kissed her cheek.

She blushed. "I'm glad I could help." She smiled at Meg. "Pick out one of the quilts and take it with you, dear."

Meg's eyes widened. "Oh, Ms. Barrett, I couldn't do that. I'm sure your family must want these."

Mildred shook her head, eyes twinkling. "They all have two or more of my quilts. They would be quite happy for someone else to inherit some of my handiwork. Go ahead, dear. Choose your favorite and take it with you."

Meg studied each for a minute, but finally walked to the purple and green quilt that caught her attention when she first entered the room. "May I take this one?"

"Of course. Wonderful choice, dear. When are you getting married?"

Meg laid the quilt over her arm and turned. "Married?"

"That's a double ring pattern, usually given to newlyweds."

She grinned. "I guess I'll have to save it for later."

Mildred cast a speculative glance at Rod, who shifted uncomfortably from one foot to the other. "Maybe not too much later. Send me an invitation to the wedding. I'll begin work on something just for you."

She gave the older woman a hug. "You are an amazing lady. I'm so glad I met you. Will you let me come back and interview you for the paper?"

"Interview me? Whatever for?"

"Your quilts. Otter Creek's a small town. We have several folk artists in our community who would love to read about your designs and quilt patterns. I'll bring a camera and we can do a photo spread. Are you game?"

Mildred smiled, pleasure shining in her eyes. "Sounds like fun."

"Great." Meg pulled out her cell phone. "Give me your cell number. I'll call next week and set up a time with you." After Meg entered the number in her phone list, she and Rod said good-bye and left.

In the car, Rod said, "Want to stop for a bite to eat before we drive to the Westerman home?"

"Sure. Let's see if we can find someplace with wireless Internet connection. I'd like to check my e-mail."

Minutes later, Meg powered up her laptop in a coffee house and bit into her chicken sandwich. She wrinkled her nose. "Not as good as Serena's."

Rod chuckled. "I don't know of anyone's cooking that is as good as your sister's."

"You need to come to Mom and Dad's for dinner when they return from Hawaii. Mom's the only cook I know who comes close."

"I'd like that."

Meg opened her e-mail program and scrolled through the list of messages. "Hey, here's one from Serena." She clicked on the message and scanned it. "She says Kyle dropped by the newspaper office this morning."

Rod frowned. "How does she know about that?"

Meg scanned further, her appetite dwindling as she read. "She worked in my office today." She glanced up. "Serena wanted people to think I was still in town, working."

"I can't believe Ethan let her do that."

"According to this, he didn't know about it until late this afternoon. He was furious with her, but understood why she did it. She says there was no point in keeping up the pretense after Kyle barged into my office and realized it was Serena, not me."

"Did he tell Serena what he wanted?"

Meg refocused on the screen. "He wanted to know if I had given any thought to his proposal."

Rod's fork clattered to the table. "Excuse me?"

The stillness in his face made Meg think back on her choice of words. Her lips twitched. "The press secretary job."

"I see."

A full-blown smile curved her mouth for a moment until the danger Serena placed herself in came back to mind. "We don't have much time, do we?" Had she set a killer on her sisters' trail? All she wanted to do was draw the danger away from them. Instead, she feared she had dragged them into the killer's crosshairs.

CHAPTER NINETEEN

Sara Westerman flipped on the garage light. "Mother is quite a packrat. You may have to go through 40 or 50 boxes before you find what you're looking for."

Rod stared at the neatly stacked boxes which filled about half of the garage. Good grief. This could take hours, hours he wasn't sure they had. "Did she label them?"

A flush stained Sara's cheeks. "I'm the one who packed them and I did it in a hurry. Mother had been hospitalized at the time and when she was well enough to leave there, she went directly to the assisted living facility. I brought her the things she asked for, but everything else I threw into boxes so I could sort them later. I haven't had time."

He raised his brow, but said nothing. She hadn't had any time to sort through the boxes in five years? "I appreciate you letting us search. Do you want a receipt if we find what we need?"

She laughed. "If Mother said you could have something, that's good enough for me." She glanced at her watch. "Look, I've got an errand to run before the stores close, but my oldest son's in the house. Will you be all right if I leave you?"

"Sure." Meg smiled. "Tell him to come rescue us if he hears a loud crash."

"Will do." Sara waved as she walked back into the house.

Meg whirled to face him. "What are we going to do? This could take all night."

He strode to the nearest three-deep stack of boxes, lifted one to his shoulders, and placed it in front of her. "Divide and conquer, Cahill. I'll take the next one and we'll restack them after we determine the contents."

They worked steadily for a couple of hours, sifting through boxes. He moved the last two in front of Meg.

She wiped her hands on her jeans. "What if Sara threw them away, thinking they were trash?"

Rod loosened the tape holding the box lid together. "Then we'll think of something else. There's always a way to find what you need." He opened the flaps and peered at the contents of the box. Satisfaction bloomed in his gut. "I think this is it." He reached into the box and withdrew a handful of date books. "Here's 1977, 78 and 79."

Meg knelt beside her. "Let's start with 1977. I bet the paper trail would start then."

He handed her the books. "Here, you start scanning through them while I reposition some of these boxes." Rod worked in silence for a few minutes. When he'd placed the last box in the right spot, he returned to Meg's side.

"I don't believe this."

He glanced at her face. His eyes widened. Anger glittered in her eyes. "What's wrong?"

Red flared in her cheeks. "Take a look at this." She pointed to a jotted note on December 15, 1977.

Rod scanned the entry. Warren Drake. $50,000 deposit. Remaining $50,000 due on delivery. Delivery of what? "Is there more?"

"Oh, yeah." She flipped the pages to March 23, 1978. "Read this one."

Drake paid in full. Delivery complete. Deposit Julie Nelson's money after obtaining signature.

Rod sat on the concrete floor, book still in his hand. His gut twisted. "He bought Ty?"

"Well, it's sure not to pay for the hospital. Baby deliveries didn't cost that much money in the 70's. And March 23 is Ty's birthday."

He shook his head, still having a hard time believing the man he'd respected would sink so low. "Why?"

"Drake's wife couldn't have any more kids."

"I remember she had several miscarriages."

"Enough that the doctor told the Drakes they couldn't try any more."

"So? Adopt. I thought that's what they did with Ty."

Meg dragged the remaining box closer. "The Senator gave me the impression that his wife was desperate for another baby. And I think he would do anything for her." She glanced at him. "What I want to know is if this had something to do with Sherri's murder. She was looking into Ty's birth parents, trying to find the information for him."

"A crime more than thirty years old?" He rubbed his jaw. "I don't know. We've got no proof. He could accuse us of harassment. There's no statute of limitations, but, at this point, who would care? The baby's a grown man with problems of his own and the Senator's political career is almost over. Not to mention the fact that he's dying. Why should he get up in arms over rumors?"

Meg sat in silence a moment. "Maybe he's not the one who's worried."

Rod quirked his brow. "Kyle?"

"Think about it. He's depending on his father's reputation and influence to help get him elected. What would it do to his election hopes if people found out the Senator bought a baby for his wife? Even being an adoption advocate can't make up for buying a child like a dog or a car. Other people wait in line for years to adopt a baby.

Some never realize their dream. Drake jumped out of line and bought a baby on the black market. It's human trafficking."

Rod thought through Meg's logic. Much as he hated to admit that his former roommate could be guilty, it fit. "Sherri's mother was helping her. Maybe she learned too much."

Rod's watch alarm beeped. "Time to check in with Ethan." He flipped open his cell phone and punched speed dial. "It's Rod. Anything happening at your end?"

"Kyle ditched the tail we had on him. We haven't been able to locate him." Disgust laced Ethan's tone. "And the feds are breathing down my neck about the Senator."

Rod frowned. He'd prefer to know where Kyle had disappeared to but at least the man didn't know where Rod had taken Meg. "What about Ty?"

"Splitting his time between the Drake place and Candy's. He doesn't have a clue where his brother is."

"Didn't waste much time grieving."

"Watch your back, Rod. I don't like Kyle disappearing."

He didn't either, but how could he have found out where they were? "I'll talk to you soon." Closing his cell phone, Rod stood and picked up one of the two boxes they needed to take with them. "Time to roll, Meg. Can you handle the other box?"

Meg waited until they were on the interstate before breaking the silence. "What's wrong, Rod?"

"Kyle's disappeared."

"Disappeared? How? Didn't Ethan have a tail on him?"

"They lost him."

Meg's gaze darted to the rearview mirror. Headlights streamed behind them, none standing out from the others. "Do we need to worry?"

"Just stay alert." Rod's expression gave away nothing.

Small comfort. "Do you think he knows where we are?"

Silence.

"Rod?"

He sighed. "I don't know, Meg. Ethan and Nick didn't tell your sisters where we were going. Josh has the mouth of a clam. Is it possible one of your people let the cat out of the bag?"

"I didn't tell them. Just gave them instructions to keep in touch by cell and e-mail."

"So who else knew?"

Meg sat there a minute before the answer finally popped in her mind. She groaned.

"What?"

"Maeve."

"The mouth of the south."

"But how would Kyle get that information from her? He doesn't darken the doorstep of the beauty salon."

"Call her and find out if she's had any contact with him today."

Meg glanced at the clock. Maeve closed early on Saturdays. She pulled out her cell phone and punched in the hair stylist's home number. "Hi, Maeve. It's Meg."

"Meg! I was going to call you later, but I heard you were out of town. Did you find Mildred okay?"

"Yeah, Ms. Barrett is an amazing woman. I'm thinking about doing an article with her next week. She's quite a quilter. Listen, did you happen to talk to Kyle Drake today?"

"He was in town today, but didn't stop in. Why?"

"Did you tell anyone about me seeing Mildred this weekend?"

"Only Zoe."

A chill rushed over Meg's body. "Zoe? When did you talk to her?"

"I called your office while I had a slow spot. Sometime after lunch. Meg, did I do something wrong?"

"No, Maeve. Don't worry. I'm only tracking information."

"Well, if you're sure. You didn't tell me it was a secret. I'm sorry if I messed up a story."

"Don't worry about it. I'll talk to you later."

She ended the call and punched her speed dial. After three rings, Zoe picked up. "Zoe, it's Meg."

"Boss! How are you?"

"Do you remember what time Maeve called the office today?"

"Right after lunch."

"Was Kyle Drake there when you answered her phone call?"

"As a matter of fact, he was. He walked straight into your office, and, seeing Serena, came to my desk to ask me about you. Maeve's call came in while he was standing in front of my desk."

"Did you happen to mention Kingsport in your conversation?"

Silence. "I might have. Boss, what's going on?"

"It's probably nothing, Zoe. I'll talk to you tomorrow."

"Kyle knows where we are." Rod's voice sounded grim.

He pulled out his cell and punched in Ethan's number. "It's Rod. Kyle knows we're near Kingsport."

"Get back here. You need more fire power than you have."

"Hold on, Ethan. Kyle can't know exactly where we are. I registered us at the motel with fake names and paid for the rooms with cash. Let me try to track down Ty's birth mother. Her name's Julie Nelson."

"You can run it from the station."

"We're already here, Ethan. If you'll run her name for me, I think we can get the proof we need to nail the Senator on human trafficking charges."

"You serious?"

"Looks like he bought his wife a baby a little over thirty years ago."

"Ty."

"Sherri was trying to give her husband a special Christmas present, the name of his birth mother. She said in her diary that her mother was helping her in the search."

"But would the Senator think that secret worth killing for?"

"He might if he thought it would damage Kyle's chances for being elected to the Senate in his place. He has high plans for his son. Can't get any bigger than planning for your boy to be President of the United States."

Ethan was silent a moment. "There's no way Senator Drake could have run after Meg and Sherri, but it's possible he could have capped Mrs. King."

"The Senator couldn't have run, that's true. My money's on Kyle for that. What if Kyle chased Meg and Sherri down, but the Senator waited for them near the parking lot?"

"The Senator pulled the trigger?"

"The only prints we found on the gun were the Senator's. We found his button with his finger prints. I'm betting the lab finds Sherri's blood on his coat. It all fits, Ethan."

"So how do you want to play this?"

"Give me twenty-four hours to wrap this up. I'll have Meg back in Otter Creek by this time tomorrow night."

"All right. But if anything happens to either one of you, I'll personally see to your demotion and Meg's house arrest for the next fifty years."

"Yes, sir."

"I'll run the name and call when I have a report."

After he ended the call, Meg said, "Well?"

"We have to be back in Otter Creek by tomorrow night, whether we find the proof we need or not. Ethan thinks it's too dangerous to wait any longer."

"Do you agree with his assessment?"

"Yeah." He reached for her hand. "I'll take care of you. I promise." He just hoped Ethan hurried with the information. Rod's gut told him they might not have until tomorrow night.

At the motel, Megan threw open the door and stepped back. More stale air rushed out. She wrinkled her nose. Everything she owned would smell like cigarette smoke.

"Potent," Rod murmured. "Let me check the rooms."

"Where would he hide?"

He ignored her comment and brushed past her into the room. "Stay here."

Meg surveyed the surrounding area, what she could see. Night was dark here. She swallowed hard. Really dark. The mountains that entranced her earlier had disappeared in the blackness. Few streetlights peppered the black ribbon in front of the motel.

She shivered, wishing Rod would finish his search. After what seemed like another lifetime, he motioned her inside. "All clear."

Meg forced a smile to her lips. "Except for the air."

He secured her door. "You okay?"

"Why wouldn't I be?"

"Someone we thought was a friend is hunting us. It's okay to be worried."

"Worried?" Meg gave a weak laugh. "Try scared to death."

"Yet you put your head in the noose by writing that editorial."

"I had to draw his attention back to me. I couldn't take the chance he would hurt one of my sisters." She rubbed her arms. "It's one of the drawbacks of being an identical triplet."

He pulled her into his arms. "Ethan and Nick won't let anything happen to them." Rod tilted her head up. "And I won't let anyone hurt you. You're growing on me, Cahill. I don't want to lose you now."

Listening to the steady beat of his heart failed to calm the erratic beating of hers. She had a feeling they were headed for trouble.

The next morning, Rod rapped on the adjoining door. "Meg, we need to get moving." An irritated growl answered his summons. He grinned as he lifted the lid from a steaming cup of coffee and set the drink inside her door.

Within a couple minutes, a moan of appreciation drifted through the doorway.

He chuckled. Chocolate and caffeine moderated the tiger's roar. Returning to the Kingsport area map, he hunted for Julie Nelson's street. His finger traced the grid until he located his target on the far side of the city. His eyebrows rose. Unless the area had changed since his college days, Ms. Nelson lived in an upper-class suburb. How much cooperation could he expect from her? Drake's conviction implicated her in human trafficking as well. FBI Agent Craig Jordan might offer immunity if she testified against Drake. But would she go for it and at what cost to her present life?

"Ethan found Julie's address?"

Rod swung around. Meg stood just inside the doorway, dressed in jeans, tennis shoes and a navy Dallas Cowboys sweatshirt, holding her coffee. His heart squeezed in his chest at the sight of her cloud of blonde hair and sleepy blue eyes. "She lives in a ritzy suburb of Kingsport."

She sipped. "How long have you been awake?"

"Long enough to know you didn't sleep much last night."

"Did I keep you awake?"

She had, but not for the reasons she supposed. Kyle's disappearance worried him enough for Rod to keep watch through the night. "How soon can you get packed?"

"Two minutes if you bribe me with breakfast."

"Deal."

An hour later, Rod and Meg parked in front of a three-story Victorian-style white house. Leafless tree limbs and bushes shuddered under the onslaught of cold wind. Light glowed through the first-floor windows.

"Looks like we're in luck." Meg unbuckled her seat belt and opened the door. "How do we play this?"

"With great tact. I don't have jurisdiction here. Eventually, we'll have to call in the feds." He rang the doorbell and glanced around the area. Julie Nelson had done well for herself. A lot of classy old homes with large lawns, fountains, gardens, porch swings, all the signs of old wealth.

Locks snicked on the other side of the white door with a large brass knocker. The door opened. A tall, elegant woman stared at them. Rod's gaze locked on her eyes. Ty's eyes. Same shade of brown with green flecks. "Julie Nelson?"

She looked from him to Megan and back. "It's Simms now. Do I know you?"

"No, ma'am." Rod flipped open his badge. "My name is Rod Kelter. I'm a detective with the police. And this is Megan Cahill."

Julie Simms face blanched. "I'm late for church, Detective. Can't this wait?"

"I don't think this will take long."

"I suppose another five minutes won't make any difference." She stepped back.

Rod didn't bother correcting her timetable.

Julie showed them into the living room and sank onto the brown leather loveseat, her feet together, flat on the oak hardwood floor. "What is this about?"

"Your son."

Relief flooded her face. "You must have the wrong Julie Nelson. I have two daughters, both married." She smiled, more confident now. "I'll be a grandmother any day."

Rod leaned forward. "Mrs. Simms, I'm talking about the son you gave up for adoption over thirty years ago."

Her smile faded. "That was a closed adoption. Even my husband doesn't know. How you did find out?"

"Do you remember Arnie Castlebaum?"

"My parents hired him to handle the adoption." Her gaze darted to Meg and returned to Rod's face. "Why are you here? I didn't do anything wrong except have a baby out of wedlock."

"How old were you, Mrs. Simms?" Meg asked.

"Fifteen." She shook her head. "Old enough to know better, but naïve enough to believe once wouldn't hurt me."

But not old enough to sign the papers. Her parents must have been involved. "Does $100,000 sound familiar to you?"

"No. Detective, I don't understand what's going on. Why are you asking all these questions?" Her voice quivered.

"Mrs. Simms, I have evidence that your parents sold your baby for $100,000."

"Are you insane? My parents would never do something that despicable." Her eyes flashed. "Mom and Dad were honest, hard-working people."

"Did they need money for you, your brother or sister, for food?"

"I didn't have siblings."

So what happened to the money? "Mrs. Simms, I'll need to talk to your parents."

"Good luck with that. Mom died in October and Dad's in a nursing home a few miles down the road. He's in the last stage of Alzheimer's. He doesn't recognize me anymore."

"What about the adoption papers? Would your parents have kept the documents?"

"Don't you need a search warrant or something?"

"I can get one, but I hope that won't be necessary."

"Why should I help you?" Julie clenched her fists. "Why does it matter after all these years?"

"Your son's wife was murdered and I believe the man who bought him is involved."

Julie's face paled. "Murdered? Why?"

"We believe she was looking into the adoption. Will you help your son, Mrs. Simms?"

"I've got something." Meg stood, brushing dust and cobwebs from her jeans. She handed the bank book and papers to Rod.

"What is it?" Julie Simms hurried to Rod's side and peered at the papers in his hand.

Rod unfolded the document and scanned it. "The adoption paperwork." He handed it to Julie and turned his attention to the bank book. James Nelson had deposited $50,000 on December 15, 1977 and another $50,000 on March 23, 1978. He stared at the series of withdrawals over the next four years. "Did you go to college, Mrs. Simms?"

She glanced up. "I graduated from a Christian college. That's where I met my husband."

"How did you pay for tuition?"

"I worked in the library on campus. My parents paid the rest plus sprang for an apartment."

"Private college tuition is expensive. Ever wonder how they swung the payments?"

Julie's gaze dropped to the bank book. "No. Oh, no." Tears slipped down her dusty cheeks. "Excuse me, please."

Hand pressed to her lips, she dashed down the stairs. A moment later, a door slammed and the sound of muffled retching reached their ears.

Tough way to learn the truth. And it wouldn't get any easier. The case against Drake was bound to attract hordes of media attention since it involved a senator. No secrets would remain buried after the trial. Rod stuffed the papers and bank book in the pocket of his jeans and returned boxes to their original position.

"What's next?" Meg asked.

"Turn the evidence over to the feds."

"What about Sherri's murder?"

"That will be part of the indictment if we can find enough evidence." He motioned for her to precede him from the attic. "A confession would wrap everything up nicely."

As they reached the first floor, a phone rang. Julie threw open the bathroom door and stumbled to the living room. She sank onto the leather recliner and snatched the instrument on the third ring. "I'm sorry, sweetheart, but I don't think I'm going to make it to church this morning. I'm not feeling well right now." She leaned her head against the back of the chair. "No, I don't need anyone to sit with me. I'm going to make some tea. Maybe that will help. I'll see you after the service, love."

Julie ended the call and dropped her head into her hands. "Do you know what this will do to my husband?"

"He doesn't know about the child?" Meg asked.

She shook her head. "When our relationship turned serious, I told him my teen years were rough, that I had done some things I regretted. Ian didn't ask for details."

"How long have you been married, Mrs. Simms?" Rod asked.

"Twenty-eight years."

"Sounds like you have a strong marriage. Do you think he would love you any less for something that happened so many years ago?"

Her haunted gaze latched onto his. "Ian's not the one I'm worried about. He's the pastor of Grace Christian Church. What will our congregation say?"

Meg reached over and patted her hand. "If your church members read their Bibles, they'll say they love you."

"Will I have to go to jail?" Her voice trembled.

"No, ma'am. You were a minor at the time. Your parents are partly responsible, but I doubt anyone would be interested in pressing charges against your father considering the circumstances." Rod leaned forward, his arms resting on his thighs. "You will have to testify in court, though."

Julie flinched. "What about my son? Will he be at the trial?"

"Probably."

"I don't want him to think I sold him like a sack of potatoes and profited from it. I was just a fifteen-year-old kid. I tried to do the best I could for his well-being."

"Don't worry, Mrs. Simms. I'll make sure he knows the truth."

Outside, Rod tossed Megan the keys to the Camaro. "You drive." He settled into the passenger seat and closed his eyes.

Her eyebrows rose. "Are you sick?"

"I need to sleep a few minutes."

Dismay swept through her. "You really did stay up all night, didn't you?" She backed out of the Simms' driveway. "I could have kept watch part of the night."

"Wake me in an hour." He reclined the seat back. "If you notice anything odd or think someone's following us, let me know."

Megan cruised at the speed limit, hoping for a boring drive so Rod would sleep as long as possible. On the interstate, traffic started to build as she drove toward Knoxville. After a few miles following a double tractor trailer, she changed lanes and darted past the rig. Glancing in the rearview mirror before shifting lanes again, she noticed a black truck hanging back.

Meg frowned. The vehicle looked familiar, but she couldn't place it. She debated on waking Rod, finally deciding to wait until she was positive they had a tail. Periodically, she checked the mirrors. The truck remained about twelve car lengths behind them. As she weaved through traffic, the vehicle kept pace with her.

Her stomach tightening, Meg touched Rod's shoulder. "Rod."

"Company?"

Meg envied his ability to wake up, fully alert. She couldn't string coherent sentences together before downing a cup of coffee. "Black pickup. He changes lanes with me."

"He? You saw the driver?"

"Sun glares off the windshield most of the time, but I think I saw a beard on the driver."

"Did you recognize him?"

She hesitated. "I don't think so, but something about the truck is familiar."

Rod sat up and shifted his gun to within easy reach. "Take the next exit. Let's see if our tail follows. We need to fill your gas tank anyway."

"Would you mind operating the nozzle?"

"Don't want your hands dirty, Cahill?"

"Nope." Megan grinned. "Maybe we can snap a picture with the camera on my cell phone."

"I like the way you think."

She flipped on the blinker and, after exiting the interstate, piloted into a gas station. She shut off the engine and grabbed her phone.

"You up to a little stealth?" Rod asked.

"Sure."

"Come around to the gas tank." Rod took his time unscrewing the gas cap and inserting the nozzle. As he chose the gasoline grade, the black pickup cruised slowly to a stop near the air pump. "Just where I wanted him," he murmured. "Come here, Meg."

Rod set the pump. "Ready?"

For what?

He drew her into his arms and clasped his hands in a loose grip around her back.

"What are you doing, Kelter?"

"Sleight of hand, babe. Keep the camera between us. I'll turn slowly. Let me know when you have him in sight." He dipped his head close to her ear and proceeded to nibble on her lobe.

His warm breath tickled her ear and she shivered. Maybe this wasn't such a good idea. The man was a serious distraction. She forced herself to focus. Come on, come on. Just a little bit more. There. "Stop." She froze. She had seen him before, but where? "Got him." She adjusted the angle of the camera to catch the passenger side. "He's got a friend."

"Recognize either of them?" His lips brushed her neck, sending a cascade of warmth through her.

"Driver. Can't remember where with you doing that." She felt his smile against her skin as she snapped the second man's photo. "Got the friend's picture, too." Meg closed the camera app and slipped her phone into her pocket.

Rod freed his hand, tilted her chin up and kissed her mouth. "Nice work."

"Thanks." His approval shot streaks of warmth through her. And that bothered her more than she wanted to admit. Since when did she need his approval for her actions? Had the handsome detective come to mean more to her than she realized? "Where to now?"

"Home, Sherlock. Time to report in before Ethan sends out a posse." He held out his hand. "Keys, ma'am. My turn to watch for the bearded man if you want to catch a nap. It might be your last chance to rest for a while. I have a feeling events will shift into high gear once we reach Otter Creek."

CHAPTER TWENTY

Rod swung the Camaro into the police station parking lot. "Ethan's waiting for us in his office." A sense of anticipation tightened his gut. They had enough now to pressure Warren Drake for a confession. Still not enough to pin Kyle for murder and attempted murder.

"I hope he brought lunch. I'm starving." Meg retrieved her laptop and handbag from the backseat. "My bodyguard let down on his job."

He stopped so abruptly Meg ran into his back. "Why didn't you tell me?" How could he have forgotten something as simple as food? Just like always, he got so caught up in his work he forgot to eat. Erin used to remind him about meals. When she and Kayla died, he lost his appetite. At least he had until Meg. "I'm sorry."

"I was just teasing you a little, Rod." She squeezed his hand. "I'm a big girl. I know how to complain about hunger."

"Yeah, but I get wrapped up in work and forget about food."

"You're not the only one. If Serena didn't keep me supplied, I probably wouldn't eat more than one meal a day." Meg shrugged. "Too busy to stop. Deadlines wait for no one. They come whether I'm ready or not."

"I'll take care of lunch if Ethan hasn't already beaten me to it."

They walked into the nearly deserted police station. The desk sergeant nodded at Rod, speculation in his gaze. "I see your pretty lady is walking under her own power this time. Must be losing your touch, Kelter."

Rod's hand slid to Meg's back. If it had been another cop, Rod would have laughed at the possessive gesture. Humor didn't enter into the equation, though, as he stared at the desk sergeant, a notorious ladies man. "Ethan ready for us?"

The sergeant's eyebrow rose. "Go on back. He's got a fed with him."

Rod figured the feds were pressuring Ethan about Drake. He cupped Meg's elbow, urging her toward the squad room and Ethan's office.

"Who's the fed?"

"I bet it's Craig Jordan."

Meg's step quickened. "This might turn out to be an interesting afternoon."

A smile curved his lips. Seeing Meg maneuver information from Jordan ought to be something all right. Rod knocked on the door jamb and ushered Meg inside. Special Agent Craig Jordan stood.

Ethan came around his desk and swept Meg into a hug. "Glad you're back, Meg. Serena and Madison have really missed you." He inclined his head toward the agent. "This is Craig Jordan, FBI. Jordan, my sister-in-law, Megan Cahill. My detective, Rod Kelter, you already know."

Jordan nodded his direction. "Kelter."

"Nice of you to drop in, Jordan. Saved me a phone call." Rod nudged Meg to the remaining chair.

"Find anything?" Ethan asked.

"The adoption papers, receipt for the money and a bank book showing a final deposit the day of the adoption."

"Did Julie know about the money?"

Rod shook his head. "She was fifteen. Her parents convinced her to give up the baby. They took care of everything else. The family was poor, Ethan. They saved the money and added what little they could for Julie's college education."

"Do we have enough evidence to prosecute the parents?" Jordan asked.

"The mother's dead and the father's in the last stages of Alzheimer's. I'd focus my efforts on Warren Drake."

"What's the point?" Meg asked. "Drake's dying. I'm not sure he'll make it through the trial much less serve time."

"You want us to smack his hands and let him off?"

Meg scowled. "Of course not. It just seems like a colossal waste of taxpayer money to go through the motions with a man already living under a death sentence."

"Maybe the notoriety will convince someone else the penalty for human trafficking is too high."

She eyed him a moment. "Do you really believe that?"

"I have to." Jordan turned to Rod. "Where's the evidence?"

"Here." Meg unzipped the computer case, removed the papers and handed them to the agent.

"When will you move on Drake?" Ethan asked.

"After my team and I review the evidence. Tomorrow morning at the latest."

Rod leaned against Ethan's desk, his hands curled around the edge. "I want to talk to Drake one more time, see if we can get him to roll on Kyle."

The agent stilled. "You think the son's involved in the murder?"

"Up to his eyeballs, but we don't have any proof."

After a moment, Jordan nodded. "Fine. I'll let my agents know in case the Senator decides to run."

Not likely, Rod thought. He was more worried about Kyle than himself. The Senator didn't seem to care about anything but his sons. His eyes narrowed. That might work in their favor.

With a nod, Jordan left, evidence in hand. Ethan sat in the chair the agent vacated. "Any problems on the way back?"

"Picked up a tail." Rod handed him the license plate number. "Meg took pictures with her phone."

"I've seen the driver before, but I can't remember where." She gave her phone to Ethan.

He studied the pictures. "I don't know either of them." Ethan punched a few buttons on her phone and returned it to her. "I sent the images to my computer. Good work."

To Rod, he said, "How long did the tail stay with you?"

"Until we reached the town limits. They kept going on Highway 18."

"So whoever sent them knows you're back in town." Ethan's hand rubbed the back of his neck. "I'll have to pull Josh off patrol."

"Why?" Meg stiffened.

"You're still a target," Rod said.

"So I need a babysitter?" She scowled. "I don't think so. I'm going to the office for a while. After that, I'm headed home. I'll barricade myself in both places and won't open the door unless it's one of you. Someone can stay with me tonight. Okay?"

He glanced at Ethan, who shrugged. "I'll walk with you to the *Gazette* office." Rod lifted her computer case and pulled Meg to her feet.

Meg stood by Zoe's desk and listened to Rod's footsteps echo in the empty building. A shiver raced over her body. She never realized how creepy her beloved newspaper office became with people gone, the press and phones silent.

Rod's steps drew near. "It's clear. All doors and windows are locked." He stopped beside her. "Make sure they stay that way."

"Don't worry. I have a deadline barking at my door. I probably won't look up from the keyboard for a few hours."

He ran a finger down her cheek. "Call me when you're ready to leave. If I'm not close, I'll have another cop follow you home."

"Rod," she began.

He interrupted her with a soft kiss. "Please."

Her protest died on her lips. Did the man have to be so aggravating and sneaky? If he'd issued an order, she would have bucked. How could she refuse a gentle request? She sighed. "All right."

He smiled. "How about dinner later?"

"Sounds great."

The office seemed even more empty after he left. With a last cursory glance around the darkened interior, Meg barricaded herself in her office and sank into her leather chair. She dug the notes from Julie's interview from her bag and powered up her laptop. Waiting for it to boot, she jotted an outline for the article. She longed to lean back in the chair and prop her feet on the desk for a nap, but she needed to write down the emotions from this morning's interview before they faded.

She opened the word processing program and wrote. The words trickled at first, then faster as the current of thought and emotion swelled. The hurt and horror she sensed from Julie poured onto the paper as Meg wrestled with the logistics of keeping the identities of the innocents involved concealed.

Two hours later, she saved the file and shut down her computer. She stood and stretched, groaning as knotted muscles released. Probably the result of a boulder-filled mattress. She could use a Coke. Maybe Zoe stocked the refrigerator before she left Saturday.

Meg unlocked her door, peered into the gloom and listened. No unusual noises. She padded to the break room and opened the white refrigerator. A shelf full of 20-ounce Cokes gleamed in the light. She grabbed the closest bottle, unscrewed the top and guzzled half the contents.

On the return trip to her office, she slowed near the trashcan, her nose wrinkling. The pungent scent of tuna and overripe bananas grew stronger with each step. Somebody forgot to take out the trash before closing the office yesterday.

Coke in one hand, Meg tugged the trash bag loose and headed to her office. The Dumpster was a few feet from the back door. It should be safe enough. She left the drink on her desk and unlocked the steel door.

Shadows filled the dimly lit alley. Fear settled low in her gut. Maybe this wasn't such a good idea. A sharp wind cut through her clothes, sending a shiver cascading over her body. Well, she already had the door open. Might as well go on to the Dumpster.

A couple of steps from the steel bin, a hand clamped over her mouth. A rock-hard arm jerked Meg off her feet.

CHAPTER TWENTY-ONE

"What do you want?" Ty Drake surged to his feet, his glass thudding on the library desk. Light from the chandelier reflected on the windows, concealing the darkness outside.

Rod steeled his heart against the anger and betrayal on his friend's face. He had a job to do. "I need to speak to the Senator. The butler told me to wait in here."

"Haven't you done enough damage to my family?"

Rod controlled the flinch. "Your family destroyed themselves. My job is to clean up the mess, keep it from spreading."

"Yeah?" Ty's bark of laughter cracked the quiet of the room. "Well, you failed, man. Thanks to you, I'm unemployed. Again."

Regret swelled inside his chest. The gossip about Otter Creek Community College's new president not tolerating scandal appeared accurate. "I'm sorry."

Ty picked up his tumbler, finished the contents in one swallow and stumbled to the sidebar. He poured the rest of the contents of an open bottle into his glass.

"How much have you had, Ty?"

"Not enough." He raised the glass to his lips. "I'm still standing and conscious."

Rod sat on the edge of the desk, watching his friend, remembering his own battle with the darkness. "The booze is only a temporary fix."

Ty hurled the empty glass against the brick hearth. Glass fragments littered the floor. "How else am I supposed to live with the pain?"

Rod searched for the right words and realized there weren't any. "Talk to Marcus Lang. He helped me."

"Just how much stock should I put in the advice of a fellow lush?"

Heat burned Rod's cheeks. "Former fellow lush," he said, his tone mild. "I haven't touched any alcohol since last spring."

Ty dropped into the leather armchair. "Why not? Don't you still miss Erin and Kayla?"

"Every day." The familiar ache throbbed in his chest. "I had to quit drinking, Ty. I almost lost my job last spring. Showed up drunk at a crime scene." Acid churned in his stomach at the memory. "Ethan had to drive me home. He gave me one more chance and kept the incident off my record."

Ty's lip curled. "How decent of him. Too bad he won't extend the same courtesy to my family."

Rod ignored the last remark. "I drank to forget, but the relief was only temporary. When I woke up the next morning, all of it came back in spades along with a hangover. Lang helped me realize destroying my career and drinking myself into the grave wouldn't bring back my family."

Footsteps echoed on the hardwood floor. Rod stood and faced the doorway. Warren Drake entered the room looking more haggard than Rod had ever seen him. He appeared 20 years older than he had two days ago.

Drake frowned at his son and Rod. "What's going on?"

"More questions, Senator Drake."

Ty struggled to his feet. "I'll call the attorney, Dad. Don't say anything until he comes." He walked to the hall, throwing his hand out for balance as he passed through the doorway.

Drake caught his son's arm. "After you make the call, get some coffee."

Ty stared at the Senator for a moment, then flicked Rod a glance and left.

"You might want to shut the door, Senator," Rod said softly.

Drake closed the door, waved Rod to one of the leather armchairs and collapsed into the other one. "Are you here as a family friend or a cop?" A wry smile appeared on his lips. "If you still claim us as family. Might not be too healthy for your career, though."

"I'm here as both friend and cop." Rod leaned his forearms on his knees, his hands clasped. "Senator, I found Ty's birth mother."

Drake's eyes closed, his head dropped back against the leather. "For more than thirty years, I've kept this secret buried, yet you managed to uncover the truth in a matter of days."

"I had some help."

"Our intrepid *Gazette* editor, Megan Cahill, no doubt."

"And Sherri."

Drake's eyes popped open. "Sherri?" He dragged a shaking hand over his face. "Yes, of course. I should have realized."

Alarm bells rang in Rod's head. The Senator didn't know about Sherri looking into Ty's birth? Rod knew the chances of Drake killing Sherri over the blackmail were about zero. Reporters flashed headlines about good-old-boy politics almost daily. It was old news within fifteen minutes any more. Yet the Senator didn't know about Sherri poking into Ty's birth. So what did that leave? His and Ethan's conclusion must be right. Drake was covering for one of his sons, but which one? "Ty doesn't know, does he?"

Drake licked his lips. "He knows a lot of things, Rod. He knows he's adopted and that his mother and I loved him dearly. We would do anything for our sons. Anything. What greater love can a parent have?"

Rod ruthlessly controlled the fury swelling in his gut. "How about showing your children an example of integrity and honor? To accept responsibility for your own actions and take the consequences like a man? They're not kids anymore, Senator. Kyle and Ty are grown men." He leaned closer. "Look, I know you love them, but you aren't doing your constituents a favor by allowing your son to get away with murder. Don't do this. Don't take the murder rap for him."

"You don't believe I killed Sherri and her mother?" His voice sounded hoarse.

Rod shook his head. "I can make a case for it, but I don't think you did it. I saw how you treated her, especially after the rape. Her own father couldn't have loved her more than you did."

An odd mixture of guilt and pain crossed Drake's face. Rod frowned. Was the crackling fire casting weird shadows on the Senator's face, making him see things that weren't there? "This may be your last chance, Senator," he pressed. "Come clean about your role in Sherri's death. I will uncover the truth with or without your help. But when I prove you had nothing to do with the murders, I'll charge you with obstruction if you don't tell me the truth now. You'll spend the remaining months of your life in a prison hospital as a guest of the government."

The Senator's gaze drifted to the fire. He remained silent a few moments. The grandfather clock in the corner ticked away time as Rod waited for Drake's decision. Finally, Drake turned to face him and Rod knew from the set look on his face that the Senator would rather die in jail than betray either of his sons.

"I love them." Drake stood. "I appreciate what you're trying to do, Rod. I won't forget it."

Rod's hand rested on the back of the chair as he looked back at the old politician. "I have to pursue this to its final conclusion."

Drake nodded. "I wouldn't expect anything less from you. You're a fine man, Rod, one I would have been proud to call my son."

Those words, though sweet to hear, left a bitter taste in his mouth. Rod shook his head and opened the door. Ty hovered nearby in the hallway. Rod turned. Drake hadn't moved. "If you want to break the news yourself, Senator, do it now. The newsies will plaster the airwaves with it in a matter of hours."

Rod slammed the front door behind him.

Fear hammered through Megan. She strained to see anything in darkness thick enough to suffocate in. Her lungs constricted, felt like a two-ton Chevy sat on her chest. Panic flared. She dragged in a wheezing breath. Maybe the trunk didn't catch when that goon threw her in. She beat on the trunk lid, but it didn't budge.

The car took a curve too sharp, tossing her around the trunk as if she were a rag doll in a dryer. She tried to wedge herself into a corner, at least keep the bruises to a minimum. Lot of good that would do. She had a feeling her luck avoiding the killer had just run out. A grim smile curved her mouth. Wouldn't matter much if she had a few less bruises for her funeral. If she only had a flashlight or something that gave off even the tiniest bit of light. Right now, the blanket of darkness terrorized her more than facing a murderer.

Another curve threw her to the other side of the trunk, banging her hip against the far wall. She growled and reached back to rub the spot. Her hand brushed against something hard, rectangular in her pocket. Her heart leaped. Cell phone. But would she have a signal?

Meg dug out the phone and punched the button at the bottom. Yes! A signal and a little light. Immediately the fear receded enough to catch a few breaths and the strangle hold on her chest eased. Hands shaking, she hit her speed dial and prayed.

Rod thumped the steering wheel in frustration. He stomped on the gas, his tires squawking on the Drake driveway. The SUV barely cleared the brick columns at the entrance to the drive as he skidded into the street.

He'd hoped for a more successful conclusion to his fishing expedition. Acid churning in his stomach at the futile gamble, Rod gritted his teeth. Meg would have to remain in protective custody until he found proof enough to arrest either Kyle or Ty. Knowing her, he was in for a fight, but she would lose. He didn't intend to lose another woman who meant the world to him.

He rubbed his bristly chin. Might as well face the truth. He loved that little spitfire writer and he would do anything to keep her safe. He shuddered. If anything happened to her, Rod didn't know if he could face the loss, not again. He had to protect her. He couldn't lose her now.

His cell phone chirped. "Kelter."

"Rod, help me!"

He slammed on his brakes, guiding the vehicle to the side of the road, his department-issued SUV fishtailing on the deserted road. He jammed the transmission into park. "What's wrong, Meg?" He struggled to keep his voice calm despite the firestorm of fear billowing inside. The rookie he left watching the newspaper office hadn't called. Could someone have snuck into the back of the building? But all the doors had been locked.

"Two goons grabbed me and stuffed me in the trunk of a car."

"Did you see their faces? Is it the same guys who followed us earlier?"

"I don't know. Maybe." A loud thump sounded, followed by a cry of pain.

"Meg, talk to me." Keeping the cell phone pressed against his ear, Rod grabbed the radio. "Dispatch, this is unit two. Patch me in to Blackhawk."

"The mayor's in his office. Want to try back later?"

Rod scowled. "Negative. This is code 1." He switched his attention to the phone. "Meg! Come on, baby. Talk to me."

The radio crackled to life again. "Blackhawk."

"Ethan, go to the secure channel." Rod flipped his radio to the appropriate setting and waited for Ethan's signal. When he received it, Rod said, "Meg's been kidnapped. Two men stuffed her in the trunk of a car. She called me on her cell, but she's not responding right now."

"I'll start the process for pinging her phone. Where are you?"

"About ten miles from the Drake place. The Senator and Ty were there, but I didn't see Kyle."

"Any one of them could have recruited help to snatch her." Anger made his words clipped, his tone sharp. "I thought we put a man on her. What happened?"

"I don't know yet. Send Santana to Meg's office to check on Jenkins."

"Roger that."

Rod dropped his radio handset and focused on his connection to Meg. All he heard was road noise, the occasional squeal of tires on pavement as if the driver had turned too quickly. After what seemed like a lifetime, he heard Meg's shallow breaths. "Meg?"

"Yeah."

Rod drew in a deep breath, relief rolling through him at tidal wave speed. If she could talk to him, they had a chance to figure this out before something irreversible happened.

She fumbled with the phone a second. "Sorry about that. I think I'm wedged in here better. I've been rolling around like a bowling ball."

His eyes narrowed. A big trunk indicated a large car. "Are you all right?"

"I would be a lot better if I had a night light." Her voice was pitched unnaturally high.

Oh, man. He'd forgotten her fear of the dark. "Doesn't the cell phone give off a little light?"

"For a few seconds. I'm back to wishing I had night vision goggles. You wouldn't happen to have any handy, would you?"

He forced a chuckle while his heart squeezed in sympathy. "I'll see about adding that to our standard equipment list. Help me find you, Meg."

"I'll try."

"That's my girl." Rod froze. He hadn't meant to let that slip.

"Am I really?"

He caught the wonder in her tone. His hand tightened around the phone, wishing he could hold her instead of a piece of plastic. "Yeah, Cahill, you are. Now, how about helping me locate you so we can talk about it in person?"

"Sounds like a good plan."

"Did you get a look at the car?"

"Just the tail lights. It's a Lincoln Town Car. Maybe dark blue or black. I couldn't tell in the alley light."

That's why Jenkins hadn't called in a problem. He didn't see the car or the goons took him out before they snatched Meg.

"Did they say anything to you?"

"Does, 'Scream and you die' count?"

"Yeah." His voice roughened. "Did they say what they wanted?"

"Not to me, but I overheard them talk about my laptop and flash drive."

He relayed the information to Ethan. They were after her computer? Rod's brow furrowed. Why? Then his head dropped against the head rest. The editorial. Someone feared she had written her eyewitness account of Sherri's murder for the newspaper, this time pointing fingers and giving names. Which one of the three Drakes was desperate enough to kill Megan Cahill to keep his identity a secret?

"Which direction did they turn when they left the alley?"

She gave a wry chuckle. "The first bruise is on the back of my head. They turned right."

Rod snapped on his overhead light and jerked open the glove compartment. He shook open his map of Dunlap County and Otter Creek. "You're doing great, baby. What else can you tell me?"

"This car needs new shocks."

His lips twitched. "Stay on task, Cahill. What about the road, the turns, anything like that?"

"We stopped for the traffic light at Main and Third, then hung a left. That's the bruise on my hip."

His finger traced the car's movement. Heading out of town, but from this route they could have taken Highway 18 or one of the back roads out of the county. "Did they ever leave the blacktop?"

"Not so far."

He heard her breathing harder, faster. "Meg, stay with me. You can do this." He willed her to beat back the fear.

"I'm trying. It's just so dark."

"Close your eyes."

"It's dark there, too, Kelter."

"Yeah, but it's supposed to be dark when you close your eyes. Come on, Meg. Trust me. Close your eyes and focus on my voice."

"Okay."

He could almost see her scrunch her eyes. "You've driven all over Dunlap County. You know these roads. Think back. Do you remember anything familiar, like a huge pothole or gravel?"

"No, nothing. I lost track of the turns." She paused.

"Meg? What is it?"

"We're slowing down."

Rod waited in the ensuing silence, muscles taut, jaw clenched, praying he could figure out where those men were taking Meg before they killed her. He feared he didn't have much time left.

"Ow. Somebody needs to pave this cow path. We've turned onto a dirt road. I hear gravel hitting the car's underbelly."

Rod flattened the folded portion of the map with his hand as he scrutinized the area south of town. Several unpaved roads split off from Route 37. He snapped off his light and shoved the car in gear. Which one had the men taken? Where were they heading?

A beeping noise broke into the silence. "What's that?"

"A warning that my battery is dying."

Rod stomped the gas. His SUV leaped forward. "You need to end the call, baby. Ethan's pinging your cell signal."

"I really don't want to do that." Meg's voice shook.

Rod's gut clenched into a knot. The call had been a lifeline and he was going to yank it out of her hands. "I will find you. Believe that and hold on."

"Rod, it feels like we're riding on a washboard."

Washboard. Planks. Hope surged. "A bridge?" Silence greeted his question. "Meg?"

Nothing.

He glanced at his cell phone. No signal. He'd lost her. Rod closed his phone and grabbed the radio. "Ethan?"

"Go ahead."

"Meg's cell battery is low. I lost her. Not sure if I hit a dead zone or if her battery quit."

"Yeah, well, I'm not doing much better. I'm on hold, waiting for the shift supervisor's approval. Did she say anything to help us figure out where they're taking her?"

"Sounds like they went south from the newspaper office. Just before the signal cut out, she said they had turned onto a dirt road and crossed a planked bridge." He heard Ethan's footsteps as he crossed to his map of Dunlap County.

"There are three possible bridges. I'm dispatching all available units to that area, but that's a lot of territory to cover, especially at night. I'll call the Sheriff's department, see if they can provide more manpower." Static crackled over the air. "Rod, we need to narrow the search grid. Any gut feelings about where they could be heading?"

Rod weaved through an s-curve before replying. "I feel like there's something I'm missing, something I ought to know but can't remember." The speedometer inched closer to one hundred. "Read the names of roads branching off Route 37."

"Hold on a minute. The shift supervisor's on the line now."

Moonlight speared the darkness, shooting rays of light on the black ribbon of road laid out in front of his vehicle. He didn't dare push his speed any faster. The trees already passed in a blur outside the windows. His brow wrinkled. Something hovered just at the far reaches of his memory.

"Rod, the service provider is initiating a trace. Ready for the road names?"

"Shoot." He tapped the brakes enough to negotiate the turn onto Kermit Road, which would dead end into Route 37. Rod listened to Ethan's litany of road names, testing each one against the ghost of memory lurking at the back of his conscious thought.

"Edge Lane, King's Ridge, Canterfield Place, Horse Branch Road."

"Hold it." Rod's grip on the steering wheel tightened. "Canterfield Place. That's it. The Drakes have a cabin near there." He dug deep, searching for the thin wisp of memory. He'd been a kid then, maybe eight or nine, spending a long weekend with Ty and Kyle while his mother and father had gone away for a few days.

He grimaced. After they returned, nothing had been the same. His father moved out and the stable home life he'd always known ended in divorce. "Sarasota Ridge. It's a three-story structure, well-lit area, hard to sneak up on. That has to be where they're headed. I'd stake my life on it."

"You willing to stake Meg's life on it?"

The question sent the knife edge of fear racing down his spine. What if he was wrong? He had to be right, couldn't even think about the alternative. The thugs could have knocked Meg out and stolen her laptop and flash drives without taking her hostage. That meant those bozos were given orders to snatch her, too. He didn't doubt they would kill her after they had destroyed the incriminating information.

The speedometer needle crowded 110. Time was running out.

CHAPTER TWENTY-TWO

Meg stumbled into the cabin's living room, blinking, squinting at the light blinding her after the extended ride in the trunk. Rustic leather and log furniture greeted her gaze, along with wood floors, throw rugs and glistening windows which reflected the lamplight.

A hand on her back shoved her toward the stairs. She caught herself on the stair rail and glared at the offender over her shoulder. "Didn't your mother ever teach you to ask politely when you want something?"

Beard man bared his teeth. "Shut up and get moving."

"All right, all right." Meg held onto the railing, not wanting to show the lingering weakness in her legs after the dark ride. "Hey, Beard man, aren't you a long way from home? Surely you have a wife and some kids who miss you."

"Yeah, so?"

Words were her life. Maybe she could talk her way out of this. "So, how about letting me go and I'll forget I ever saw you."

A bark of laughter sounded behind her. "Forget it, blondie. Even a pretty little thing like you ain't worth a bullet in my kid's head. You just should have stayed out of something that wasn't your business."

Meg reached the second floor and paused. Another shove.

"Keep going. Next floor."

She licked her lips, a cold sweat beading on her back. "Did I ever tell you I don't like heights? That's why God made me so low to the ground, you know."

"Quit yakking and climb." A beefy hand on her arm propelled her toward the stairs. "And if you even think about doing anything funny, just remember those sisters of yours won't be so pretty after I get through with them."

Fury swept through Meg. She yanked her arm away from Beard man. "You mess with my sisters and you're a dead man." Ethan and Nick would scour the earth until they had hunted him down.

An ugly grin bared his yellow teeth at her. "Why should you care? You aren't going to be around."

Meg hoped Beard man was just mouthing off to scare her. Doing a good job of it, too, she admitted to herself as she climbed the last few steps. "Where are you taking me?"

He propelled her toward an open doorway at the top of the stairs. "Boss told me to keep you on ice for a while."

"Who's the boss?"

He shoved her toward the bed. "Face down."

Nausea boiled in her stomach. She stiffened and lurched away from the plaid-covered mattress. "What? Why?"

"Boss man wants you contained and quiet." Beard man grabbed a length of rope and duct tape from the nightstand. "Figured this had to be better than staying in the trunk until he's ready to talk."

She agreed with that. A soft bed trumped a pitch-black trunk any day. "Until who's ready to talk? Who is your boss?"

He spun her around to face the bed, yanked her arms behind her back and proceeded to tie them. "You ask too many questions, blondie."

Meg gritted her teeth against the pain from already bruised shoulders being forced into an uncomfortable position. "Take it easy. Since you bozos didn't put any padding in the trunk, I already feel like a punching bag after a day at the gym."

Beard man turned her to face him, an unpleasant grin on his face. "Shut up." He ripped off a small strip of duct tape and slapped it on her mouth, then tossed her on the bed. After tearing a longer length of tape, he wrapped it around her ankles. "If I hear a peep out of you, you'll go back in the trunk. Understand?"

A shudder wracked Meg's body. If she spent too much more time in that trunk, she would lose her sanity. She also had a better chance of getting free from ropes than the trunk. She nodded.

Beard man turned and walked out the door. A key scraped in the lock. Then there was silence.

Meg glared at the closed door. Great. Trussed up like a Thanksgiving turkey and locked in a bedroom on the third floor of the Boss man's cabin. She wiggled her wrists. Good, there was a little play in the ropes. Provided she got free, how would she get off the third floor without those two goons seeing her?

One thing at a time. First, get free of these blasted ropes. Then, she would check her cell phone and try once more to reach Rod. The last time she checked, her cell didn't have a signal.

Meg twisted her wrists harder, trying to create more play in the knot. So, what if she didn't have a signal? What about a land line? Could she use that? She glanced at the nightstand. No phone. Maybe on the other nightstand. Meg swung her legs around and rolled her body onto her right side. Nothing on this table either.

She growled, disappointment slamming through her. Okay. No phone, so calling for help on the cabin phone was out. That left getting off the third floor without being seen and run like a rabbit for the road.

Good plan except for one thing. Knots of frustration gathered in her stomach. She didn't know where this cabin was located and had no idea in which direction to run to the road. It was dark in the woods surrounding the cabin. If she wandered too far off track, she could be lost for days. Keeping wild animals company didn't hold much appeal.

On the other hand, staying too close to the cabin meant the bozos would find her and drag her back to the Boss, whoever that was. Where was a superhero when you needed one?

The ropes slipped a little lower on her hands. Meg smiled behind the duct tape despite the painful skin scraped raw by the ropes. Beard man might be in for a surprise when he came back into her prison loft.

Rod steered his SUV behind some dense bushes off Sarasota Ridge and picked up his radio. "Ethan, I'm about a half mile from the Drake cabin. I'll scout around and let you know if I find Meg."

"Roger that. No hot-dogging, Rod. If you find her, call for back up."

Only if he had that option. "Out." He slipped an extra clip for his weapon into his pocket, grabbed his flashlight and set off on foot for the Drake cabin. He didn't bother turning on the flashlight. No need in announcing his approach if someone happened to glance out the window. Besides, he spent hours every summer for years in these woods playing hide and seek with Ty. He could almost navigate these woods blindfolded.

He climbed to the top of the rise and pressed his back against a cedar tree. Light shone from nearly every room in the cabin and spilled onto the surrounding landscape. Rod scanned the area around the three-story structure. Same security lights. No foot patrol.

Keeping to the shadows, Rod moved forward, watching for movement in the rooms or outside activity to indicate he'd been spotted. He reached the edge of the clearing and a light in the third-floor bedroom winked out. Rod paused. That was the bedroom he'd used when he stayed with Ty.

A noise reached his ears, one he recognized. The window rose on the third-floor bedroom. A jean-clad leg slid over the sill and a sneaker-clad foot searched for a place to brace. Rod's heart skipped a beat when Megan climbed out on the roof and shut the window.

Megan breathed deep, leaning her head for a moment against the glass pane. Her palms sweated despite the frigid night air. The plan sounded good when she rehearsed it in her head. Reality was a different beast. Third floors were high and she hadn't been lying when she told Beard man she hated heights.

Her hands clung to the sill in a death grip. She had to get off this roof and that meant looking for a lower level. Meg glanced around. Did Boss man have a garage around back? A garage would have a lower roofline.

Meg forced herself to let go of the sill and hugged the roof as her feet found secure footing. Lungs aching from the cold air, she crawled across the shingles, looking toward the drop-off to her right. Ten feet. Five feet. Two feet. By the time she reached the edge, her muscles trembled as though she had just finished a race. She braced herself and peeked over the side.

A lower level of shingles shimmered in the security lights. Maybe five feet lower, but the closest rise of the roof lay in shadow and skewed her depth perception. She rolled onto her back a moment and stared up at the cloudy night sky.

She thought about the drop a moment and sighed, her breath rising in a white mist. Meg considered the odds of the drop being more than five feet and knew she didn't have much time. Beard man was bound to check the room before long. If she stayed out here on the roof, they would eventually see her in the bright lights. She shivered. If the temperature kept dropping and the predicted rain and sleet mix hit, she would slide off the roof anyway provided she didn't freeze to death first.

Meg gathered her ragged courage, peered over the edge and studied the slope again. She would have to lower herself over the side, drop into the shadows and, if she was lucky, find a foothold before sliding off to another level or the ground. All without making too much racket. No problem.

She grabbed to the edge, scrambled over the side and extended to her full length. Her feet dangled in the air. Praying for safety, she let go.

She dropped about a foot and slid close to the edge of the new level before gaining another foothold. Meg remained motionless except for her heaving chest. One level down, but how many more to go? A shudder rolled through her body. She didn't know how many more of those blind drops she could take.

She wiped the sweat beading across her forehead and forced herself to sit up. She could almost hear the clock ticking minutes of her life away. Time to get off the roof. Meg crawled toward the nearest ledge and peeked over the side. A smile curved her mouth. The next level looked about two or three feet down and it was an oblong shape, like a garage.

Meg eased over the edge, forestalling a slide by jamming her foot against a heat vent. She glanced back at her third-floor prison. Still no sign of discovery yet, but that wouldn't last long. On all fours, she crawled to the end of the roof. She gritted her teeth. A ten-foot drop between Beard man and freedom.

Not allowing herself to dwell on the possibility of broken ankles and arms, Meg hugged the shingles and slithered to the lowest point on the garage roof. She peered over and drew a deep breath. An eight-foot drop was better than ten feet and if she hung over the side again, only a three-foot drop. If her estimate was correct.

A shout coming from her prison made the decision for her. If Beard man looked out the window and saw her on the roof, she was toast. One of the men would catch her before she could make it to the woods.

Meg grasped the edge and slid her weight over until her hands were the only things visible. At least the ground was covered with grass, not concrete. She released her hold on the roof. She rolled with the landing, ending up on her side.

More shouts and curses emanated from the house. Meg stood on shaky legs and began to run toward the tree line nearest the house.

Beard man shouted, "She's outside."

Adrenaline poured through her system. She gave an extra burst of speed and plunged into the darkness of the trees. Running from the lighted yard into the forest gloom didn't give her vision enough time to adjust to the change and forced her to slow down. She needed a path or a place to hide. She paused beside some thick bushes and rejected them as a possible hiding place. Too close and not dense enough. She would have to risk injury and push on into the forest.

She turned to run again, but for the second time that night, one hand clamped over her mouth and another clamped around her waist.

Rod hauled Meg back against his chest, controlling her frantic attempts to get away. "It's Rod, Meg."

As soon as she heard his voice, Meg sagged against him. Rod released his hand on her mouth, turned her into his arms and pulled her deeper into the shadows. "We've got to get you out of here. My car is close. Can you run?"

She lifted her face sporting a grim smile and nodded.

He grabbed her hand and took off, retracing his steps, listening for sounds of distress from Meg or noise from their pursuers. Rod helped her down the steep ravine and urged her back into a full-out run on the other side. They had only gone a few hundred feet when he spotted something moving off to the right. Had to be one of the goons who kidnapped Meg.

Rod veered to his left, dragging Meg with him. He slowed their pace and drew his weapon. He figured they were about one quarter of a mile from his SUV with at least one hunter between them and safety.

He signaled Meg to go deeper into the trees. When he spotted a large fallen log, he motioned her to the ground and rolled her into the shadow between the log and the ground. Rod pressed his lips against her ear. "Don't move. No matter what happens."

She grabbed his head with both hands and kissed him. Rod drew back after a moment and grinned. He had to hand it to her. She was one spunky woman. He positioned himself behind a large tree nearby and listened to the sounds in the forest, waiting for a direction to start hunting.

Heavy gray clouds boiled overhead, the breeze kicking up a notch to a bone-chilling wind, whispering of the storm to come. Rod's gaze scoured the surroundings, lingering on the deeper shadows. What he wouldn't give for a pair of night vision goggles right now.

A faint noise off to his right drew his attention. He frowned. Didn't seem to make any attempt to hide his presence. A moment later, a dog trotted into his line of vision.

Rod's jaw dropped. Ty's dog? The Irish setter spotted Megan and raced toward her. Meg's eyes widened, a grin curving her mouth.

He waited another minute, watching for further movement from the forest before approaching the dog. Could it be Savannah? Grasping the dog's collar, he turned the tag over. Dallas. His old friend still named pets after cities. A finger of uneasiness raked down his spine. Did Ty still train search dogs?

A shrill whistle sounded a short distance away. Dallas immediately started barking. Guess that answered his question. Rod jerked Meg to her feet. "Run!"

They darted through the gloom, batting aside low-hanging branches, sliding on muddy patches of bare earth, Dallas all the while keeping pace with them and baying out their position.

He pulled Meg faster. If he could get enough distance between them and the goons, get Meg close enough to the SUV, he would send her ahead and try to hold them off. But he didn't hold out much hope of that while Dallas did what he was trained to do.

The noises of their trackers drew nearer. The dog howled louder. He contemplated killing the dog, saw no other option and stopped running. He aimed his weapon at the dog.

"No." Meg yanked on his other hand. "You can't. Please."

"He's leading them right to us."

"Please."

Rod hesitated a couple seconds, stared at her white, pleading face, then, against his better judgment, threw the dog a disgusted look and urged Meg into a run. He just hoped his concession to her didn't get them killed.

Meg's feet slipped on wet leaves as she scrambled up yet another rise. How much further was his SUV? Her breath came in wheezing gasps now, the cold air biting deep into her lungs. She fell face forward only to be hauled upright by Rod and practically carried up the ridge. Muffled curses sounded behind them.

Rod shoved her ahead of him. "Faster, Meg. Don't look back."

If she weren't so exhausted, she would have laughed at the irony. This whole mess started with the nighttime forest run and it looked like it would end that way as well. She poured on another spurt of energy and crested the rise at a dead run. Rod's SUV sat five hundred yards ahead.

A shot rang out in the night, followed by a thud. Meg gasped and skidded to a halt, expecting to feel a bullet tearing through her body. Nothing. How close were they? She whirled to ask Rod, but he still had not appeared over the rise. Fear stabbed her heart. Where was he? He'd been right behind her all the way up the hill.

She ran back to the crest and peered over. No Rod. Where could he be?

A voice called out, "I got your friend, blondie."

She stilled. Beard man. Was it a trick to get her out in the open and pick off Rod or was Beard man telling the truth?

"The next bullet goes in his head."

CHAPTER TWENTY-THREE

The next bullet? Her mind replayed the shot and thud. Beard man shot Rod? She didn't want to believe, but feared it was the truth. Rod would have found a way to warn her by now.

Meg couldn't leave him. She took one step down the rise toward Beard man. Two steps. Three.

Beard man stepped into view, a rifle pointed at her chest, Dallas jumping around his legs. A gun poked out of his belt in the front. Something in her gut told Meg the gleaming weapon was Rod's. He would never give up his gun voluntarily.

"Where is he?" Meg slid the final few feet to the bottom of the hill.

He motioned to his left with his head. "No more tricks, blondie, or he's a dead man."

She dropped to her knees beside a white-faced, unmoving Rod. Blood soaked his right side near his waist. When she touched his face, he moaned. At least he was still alive. She had to get him to a hospital.

"Don't let him die. Please." She turned her face toward Beard man. "I'll do whatever you want."

"Meg."

Her gaze swung back to Rod's blue eyes, glazed with pain. She leaned close. "Rod."

"Leave me," he whispered. "Get help."

"Shut up, Kelter," she whispered back, her tone fierce. "We run or stay together."

His eyes flickered behind her. Meg knew without turning Beard man had the gun at her back.

"Get him on his feet or we leave him behind." Beard man poked her in the back with the tip of the rifle. "Move."

She helped Rod sit up, noting the sweat breaking out on his forehead, evidence of the strain. He struggled to his feet and swayed where he stood until Meg maneuvered under his left arm and circled his waist with her arm.

They made slow progress toward the cabin. The further they walked, the more Rod leaned on her. "Meg," he murmured, "if I go down, you have to run."

She glared up at him. "If you go down, I'll find a way to get both of us out of there. I'm not leaving you."

"Shut up and walk," Beard man said.

"Yeah, yeah, we're going." Meg tightened her grip on Rod's hand. Her legs trembled with fatigue from her earlier run and now from Rod's added weight. No matter what, she wouldn't leave him behind. He couldn't walk out of here on his own. At least if he was with her, she had a chance of protecting him. She tossed a glare over her shoulder at the lumbering mountain man trudging behind them. She didn't doubt Beard man would leave Rod out here to die in the cold.

By the time they reached the stairs at the front of the cabin, Rod was breathing heavy. His foot didn't clear the first step and he sprawled on the stairs, taking Meg down with him. Her knee took the brunt of the hit. She breathed through clenched teeth, waiting for waves of pain to subside before trying to move again.

"Come on, move." The rifle jabbed into her shoulder. "It's cold out here."

She glanced at Rod's pasty expression and sensed he needed another minute to gather his strength. The porch light illuminated his pallor. "Why didn't you leave us out there? You could have told the Boss we got away and warmed yourself by the fire. It's not too late for that. Turn away and we'll be out of sight before you count to twenty."

Beard man aimed the rifle at Rod. "Get up." The dog barked as if emphasizing the suggestion.

Rod squeezed Meg's arm and gave a slight nod. She helped him to his feet and up the stairs. The door knob turned easily under her hand. The warmth inside the cabin was a welcome relief from winter's chill bite. She felt Rod shivering and hoped the reaction came from the sudden temperature change, not blood loss.

Once inside, Beard man shut the door and pointed to the hallway. "Straight back. The Boss is waiting."

Meg scanned the photos lining the hallway. Her stomach churned. This cabin belonged to the Drakes. Pictures of Kyle and Ty grinning with their latest catch, waving from the family canoe, one of the boys standing at the dock, silhouetted in the sunset. A younger Rod grinned at her from a few of the pictures.

She paused at the threshold, earning herself another jab in the back. "Okay, already." Rod tucked her tighter against his side. Meg acknowledged the gesture of support with a quick smile. No matter who or what waited for them inside, they would face it together.

Meg stiffened her spine and propelled them forward. At the far end of the room, Kyle Drake turned, a gun in his hand.

Rod kept his hold on Megan, fighting to stay on his feet and keep his focus. Blood trickled down his leg and seeped into his sock. "You don't want to do this, Kyle."

"You're right." Kyle's eyes glittered. "I don't want to, but I have no choice."

"We always have choices," Meg said. "And with those choices come consequences."

Kyle laughed, bitterness leaching into his tone. "Sometimes those consequences are unintended and lead to things no one imagined." He glanced at Beard man. "Thanks, Joe. Consider your debt paid in full. You have the new I.D. and money?"

"Yes, sir."

"Take your cousin and get out of here."

A moment of silence. "You sure you can handle them alone?"

Rod deliberately swayed.

A smirk appeared on Kyle's face. "No problem."

After Joe left, the weapon's barrel shifted to Meg. "Where are they, Meg?"

"What are you talking about?"

Kyle gestured toward her laptop, sitting on the desk. "Where are the editorial and the manuscript?"

"Which one?"

"Don't play with me. The editorial naming Sherri's killer." Kyle's voice took on a sharp edge.

Rod pressed his fingers tighter around Meg's shoulder in silent warning. He knew that tone. He'd been around Kyle enough in college to recognize his step closer to losing control.

"Why did you kill Sherri?" she countered.

Kyle scowled and sighted his weapon.

"No." Rod shoved Meg behind him. The world around him spun. He bit his tongue and used the pain to focus. "Enough people have died already." Reaching one hand back, Rod pulled Meg right up against his back. When she would have withdrawn her hand, he squeezed hard. She drew in a sharp breath, but quit trying to wriggle free of his hand. "Tell him where it is, baby."

"Are you sure?" she whispered.

He nodded, praying for strength to stay on his feet. He shifted them toward the chair on his right.

"Don't move." Kyle took a step closer, eyeing them in turn.

"Chill." Rod leaned his hip against the heavy leather recliner. "You want the editorial, don't you? You kill either one of us, you won't get it."

Kyle's eyes narrowed. "Why not? What's to keep me from killing both of you? All I have to do is erase the hard drive on the laptop and wipe the thumb drives clean."

Rod forced himself to smile. "Because that's not where she left the editorial." As he talked, he guided Meg's hand to his right hip pocket and pressed hard against the phone. When Meg wiggled her fingers, he released her hand, but kept his arm in the same position.

"You know where it is?"

"Sure."

Meg withdrew the cell phone from his pocket.

"What's the catch? You wouldn't hand me your only bargaining chip." Kyle moved another step closer. "Meg, step away from him so I can see you."

"Your man did a number on him. I'm holding Rod up." She slipped the phone back in his pocket.

"Move or I'll shoot him where he stands."

Rod stilled, preparing to leap toward Kyle. If he moved fast enough, took Kyle down, Meg could get away.

Meg stepped to the side, her arm brushing Rod's. "You want that editorial, don't you? If you kill either one of us, you won't get it."

"Why not?"

"It's on my computer at home and the file is password protected. Both of us put in half the password. Neither of us knows what the other used." Meg smiled. "But, I'm sure one of Ethan's computer geek friends at the FBI will figure out the password in a matter of minutes with one of those programs that crack codes."

"Give it up, Kyle." Rod grasped the back of the recliner for support and infused harshness in his tone. "You can't win this."

"You think you're so clever." Kyle sneered. "All I have to do is destroy Meg's computer. Two for one deal. I'll bet that's where the manuscript is, too."

"Why did you kill Sherri?" Rod asked. "None of this makes any sense. Was it because of Ty's adoption?"

"Ty's adoption has nothing to do with why Sherri had to die."

"Did you kill her to protect your father?" Meg asked.

"You must be joking." Kyle snorted. "Dear old Dad's going to die in a few months. Why would I bother to protect him?"

"Wouldn't a senator buying a child hurt your chances of being elected President?"

"Nobody cares about the President's relatives anymore."

At that moment, the pieces of the puzzle sifted into place in Rod's mind. "The manuscript. This is about the book Meg's writing, isn't it?"

Kyle gave a mocking smile. "Took you long enough, Sherlock. And here I thought you were the golden boy of Otter Creek's cops."

"But that's crazy," Meg said. "The only person with something to fear is . . ." She stopped, the color in her face draining.

"Go ahead." Kyle motioned at her with the nine-millimeter Ruger semi-automatic. "Finish the statement."

Meg remained silent.

"The only person with something to fear is Sherri's rapist." His face hardened into a mask of hatred. "But she lied. It wasn't rape. I loved her."

"You make me sick." Her voice cracked.

Rod captured Meg's clenched fist. "I saw the police reports, the pictures of her injuries. You're lying to yourself, man."

"I didn't want to hurt her, but she didn't give me a choice."

Meg tried to jerk her fist out of Rod's clasp, but he tightened his grip. He'd let her take a swing at Kyle if the man didn't have a gun in his hand and if she let Rod have the first punch.

"She was in the hospital a week because of the injuries you inflicted. She was never the same," Meg said, fury infusing her tone. "She became a prisoner in her own house after dark."

"She threatened to go to the cops."

"I thought you loved Ty. How could you hurt him that way?"

"He didn't deserve Sherri. Ty resumed his skirt chasing habit a few months after the wedding. I would never have done that to her."

"Nobody would use you as the poster child for sexual purity."

Rod controlled a flinch at Meg's acid tone. Kyle didn't need much to push him over the edge and Meg's diatribe might shove him into a freefall.

"I would have been faithful to her when we married."

"She was already married to your brother."

Kyle scowled. "He's no blood relation to me." He aimed the Ruger at Rod. "Enough talk, Meg. Tell me where the manuscript is or I'll finish my old friend off right now."

Rod stared at Kyle and knew the last grain of sand was sliding closer to the hour glass funnel. "What happened that night, Kyle?" He didn't have to specify which night.

"She was home alone. Again. Crying because of Ty." He said the name almost as a curse. "I took her for a walk around the grounds. I was so careful with her, gentle. I wanted her to know how different I was from Ty, that she could depend on me. I would always be there for her. I held her while she cried for a man who didn't appreciate her."

He frowned. "I just wanted to show her how much I loved her. When I kissed her, she tried to tear herself from my arms, but I couldn't let her go. She said it was wrong, that God wouldn't approve. I told her how much I loved her and begged her to marry me, join me as the First Lady. Sherri broke away and started to run."

The clock chimes tolled the hour. Eleven o'clock.

"I caught her and tried to show Sherri how much I loved her." Kyle's voice dropped to a near whisper. "Things just got out of hand."

"Why didn't she turn you in to the cops?" Rod asked. "Why the lies about not knowing her attacker's identity?"

Kyle's face hardened though his lips remained closed.

"You threatened her, didn't you?" Meg said. "You threatened to tell Ty yourself, but with your own spin on the story. Ty idolized you, counted himself lucky to have such a prince of a brother. She wouldn't have wanted to destroy the only family Ty had and you used that against her."

"She promised to keep my name a secret if I stayed away from her."

Rod shook his head. "That's why you and the Senator were on the road all the time."

A tear slipped down Meg's cheek. "And then she found out the Senator bought Ty. She only wanted to give Ty his best Christmas present ever, the information about his birth mother."

"You followed her to the walking trail, didn't you?" Rod said. "Why?"

"She overheard me talking to one of Dad's contacts on the phone about brokering a baby deal for her and Ty. I tried to reason with her, but she was hysterical." He blinked, seeming to bring himself back to the present. "I brought the gun to get her attention, let her know I was serious about her staying silent. She went crazy at the parking lot and tried to take the gun from me. It went off by accident."

"An accident? Right. That's why the bullet struck Sherri in the back." Kyle said earlier he didn't care anything about his father's actions in buying Ty. Was he lying or was there some other reason Sherri would have run out of the house and straight to Meg? Rod's eyes narrowed. It was at night, a time when normally Sherri would have been locked inside her suite at the Drake mansion. Instead she braved her fear and chose a secret place to meet, one not well lighted, one not populated. A meeting with only Meg.

Heat burned in Rod's cheeks. The truth had been staring him in the face for days. "She overheard you talking about your plans for Megan, didn't she? What was your plan? Hire Meg for campaign PR, then White House press secretary with a courtship on the side? Vetting candidates for a wife, Kyle?" A harsh laugh escaped. "Would have been the social event of your Presidency, provided a newsie like Meg didn't expose your serpent personality during the campaign."

Kyle shrugged one shoulder. "My fault, really. I should have made sure the study door was locked."

"Sherri died because of me." Meg's voice quivered.

"No, Meg," Rod said, his tone quiet. "Sherri died because Kyle tried to cover his tracks." He turned to Kyle. "You killed Sherri so she wouldn't tell Meg about you. You knew if Meg learned you raped Sherri, she would make sure the assault made headlines and squash your White House hopes."

"No sex offenders in the White House," Kyle said.

"Why the attempts on my life if you had plans for me?" Meg asked.

"I thought you were smarter than that." Kyle looked disgusted. "I wanted you distracted enough to stop any progress on the book. I knew if you kept digging, you would find out the truth about that night. I was just trying to scare you. The explosive in your 'Vette was triggered by my cell phone. I made sure you weren't in the car."

Meg's eyes narrowed. "And that makes it okay? You blew up my car, you little creep."

Kyle leveled the Ruger at her. "I should have blown you up with the car. You are nothing but trouble. Because of you, I have to relocate a couple of good friends and set them up for life in a foreign country. You and your boyfriend messed up everything."

"So you're going to kill us?" Rod asked. "This isn't going to work, man. Ethan knows I'm out here. We can't just disappear. He'll never give up searching for his sister-in-law and his partner." His lips curled. "Blackhawk will piece it together and toss you in jail to rot beside your father."

An unpleasant smile curved Kyle's mouth. "You don't have proof I killed Sherri or I'd be sitting in jail right now. Blackhawk can't charge me with your deaths if there are no bodies. Even if he does find proof, what's two more? The state can only hook me to liquid death once."

A noise in the hallway had all of them turning toward the door. Kyle cursed softly and stepped toward the entrance. "Not a word from either of you."

Rod's eyes narrowed. Was it Ethan or someone else working with Kyle? He slowly tugged Meg closer to his side, gaze fixed on the doorway. His eyes widened as a tall, thin figure appeared in the doorway.

Ty. Rod pushed Meg behind him, watching, calculating the new odds. Not good. Even injured, he probably could take Kyle down. If he was by himself. If Ty was in on this with his brother, his and Meg's chances for surviving the next ten minutes just plunged below sea level.

He couldn't imagine Ty working with Kyle in all of this. Was he an accessory in Sherri's death? Rod thought back through the interviews with Ty. Nothing that indicated he was less than a heartbroken though two-timing husband. Could his friend be that good an actor?

"What's going on?" Ty stared at Meg and Rod, pausing as he noticed Rod's bloody shirt. His eyes widened. "You're bleeding!" He started forward, but halted when he noticed the gun in Kyle's hand. "What's with the gun, bro?"

"Get out of here, Ty." Kyle kept his focus on Rod. "You don't want to be part of this."

Ty stepped closer to Rod, examining the bloodstain. He drew in a sharp breath. "You shot him?" Ty's voice rose. "Are you crazy? He's a cop. This isn't the way to help Dad."

"I know what I'm doing, okay? It's all going to work out fine if you'll trust me."

"Give me the gun, Kyle," Ty said. "We'll get the best lawyer in the country. He'll get you off."

"Listen to him, Kyle," Rod said. "You won't get away with this. Too many people know the facts. It won't take long for someone else to put the puzzle together."

Kyle swung the gun toward him. "Shut up, Rod."

Ty held out his hand toward his brother. "Give me the gun."

"Ty, you don't know what's at stake. You don't know what's going on. Just leave before you destroy everything."

Studying the brothers, Rod didn't see any sign Ty knew the truth about Kyle. He thought Kyle had gone off the deep end to protect the Senator. What would happen if Ty learned the truth? Would he turn against Kyle or join ranks with his adoptive brother? He had to divide their loyalties if he and Meg stood any chance of survival. "Ty, ask Kyle why he's planning to kill me and Megan."

Pure rage crossed Kyle's face.

Ty's gaze shifted from Rod to Kyle. "What's he talking about?"

"Nothing. He's just wasting time in an attempt to save his worthless life."

"He's lying, Ty." Rod kept his attention on Kyle. Just one instant of distraction was all he needed to get to the .38 in his ankle holster. He offered Kyle a wry grin. "Tell your brother the truth about the night Sherri was attacked two years ago."

Ty took one step closer to his brother, his face a mask of confusion. "What? Do you know something you didn't tell the cops?"

"Of course not." Kyle's gaze pinned Rod, a promise of retribution shining in his eyes.

"If you know something, you have to tell the cops. The scum who raped Sherri deserves to rot in jail."

"I'm telling you, I don't know anything." Beads of sweat formed on Kyle's flushed face. "Get out, Ty. Go home. You can't testify to something you don't know about."

"Didn't you ever wonder why Kyle claimed to have heard nothing the night Sherri was raped? He was at home, in the library, Ty." Rod shifted his weight to the balls of his feet. "Sherri screamed for help. The attack happened where Sherri planted her garden. Right outside the library's French doors."

Ty dragged in a ragged breath. "I don't understand. What are you saying?"

"Shut up, Kelter or I swear I'll shoot you now," Kyle said.

"Kyle raped Sherri."

"No!" Ty's face reddened with rage.

Rod pivoted and shoved Meg to the floor just as Kyle fired the Ruger. His right leg buckled. Pain exploded in his thigh and he collapsed on top of Meg.

CHAPTER TWENTY-FOUR

Meg tried to scramble to her feet.

"No." Rod covered her head with his hand. "Stay down."

Sounds of scuffling reached her ears. She pushed Rod's hand away and raised her head. Ty and Kyle rolled on the floor, fighting for possession of the gun. The weapon discharged again, shattering the window. The curtains billowed with the rush of cold air filling the room. Ty knocked the gun from Kyle's hand, sending it skittering toward the fireplace.

Meg pulled away from Rod's weak grip and stood. Sirens screamed from the police cars speeding up the driveway. Kyle pounded his brother with a right uppercut to the jaw, then shook his head, wiped his bleeding mouth and rolled off him, looking for the gun.

If Kyle got his hands on that gun one more time, he would kill Rod before Ethan and the rest found them. She leaped to her feet and ran across the room as Kyle reached for the weapon. Meg stomped on his hand. He roared with pain and swept her feet from under her with a blur of his arm.

Meg landed on her back. In an instant, Kyle dove on top of her, hands around her throat. His grip tightened, face a dark red, eyes glittering. Her hands clawed at his, raking deep gouges in his skin, her body bucking without success against his considerable weight. His expression hardened and the vice of his hands closed more.

"Let her go, Kyle, or I will kill you," Rod shouted.

Kyle froze and glanced over his shoulder. He released her. Meg grabbed a series of deep breaths and the black dots clouding her vision faded. She turned her head to see Rod on his stomach, arms extended, face grim, a gun pointed at Kyle.

"Get away from him, Meg." Rod's voice carried a hint of urgency.

She noticed his hands shaking and the sweat pouring down his face. Still perched above her, Kyle's body tensed, like a snake coiling to strike at prey. The rotating blue and white bar lights from the cruisers lit the room. So close but Meg feared not close enough. Rod was at the end of his strength. She knew from the look on Kyle's face he'd seen the same thing.

Kyle crawled off her and rose to a squatting position, balanced on the balls of his feet, readying himself to spring. Meg drew her legs against her chest and, using both feet, kicked Kyle in the side, shoving him headfirst into the desk. His head hit the back of the desk with a loud thud. He slumped to the floor, unmoving.

Afraid her legs wouldn't hold her weight, Meg crawled to Rod's side. He kept his weapon trained on Kyle.

From the hall came a cry. "Police!"

"Down the hall, Ethan," Rod called. "Situation is secure."

Ethan slipped into the room, weapon drawn, followed by an armed Nick. He scanned the room and motioned Nick to the gun Kyle had dropped. "You okay, Meg?"

"I'm fine. You've got to help Rod."

When Ethan cuffed Kyle, Rod relaxed his grip and laid down his gun, leaning his head against his still extended arm. "Thought you'd never get here."

"Doesn't look like you needed us at all," Nick said, securing the weapon. He pulled out his handcuffs and shackled Ty's wrists. "Took down the bad guys with no help."

"No," Meg said to Nick. "Ty tried to help us."

Rod coughed. "They'll work it out, baby. Let them do their jobs."

"How bad are you hit?" Ethan left the still unconscious Kyle and knelt by Rod's side.

"Took a bullet in the side. In and out. Another in the leg."

"We need to get you to the hospital." Ethan reached for his radio.

Meg stayed his hand. "He can't wait. Give me the keys to one of your cruisers. He's lost a lot of blood."

"Take mine," Nick said. "Keys are in the ignition." He motioned another officer over and knelt beside Rod. "Was it Kyle?"

"Yeah." With Nick's help, Rod got to his feet and limped out to the SUV. The pain in his side was so fierce he could hardly breathe and his leg felt like it was on fire. The cold air slapping his face revived him enough to climb into the car under his own steam, shivers racking his body. "Watch Ty," he said, teeth chattering hard enough for his sympathetic friend to hear. "Kyle is the one who raped Sherri."

Nick whistled softly as he strapped Rod into the seat. He looked at Meg. "Be careful, sugar. There are a few slick patches going down this ridge." He grinned. "Turn on the bar lights. At least this time, you won't get a ticket for speeding."

Meg turned on the engine. "Thanks for the warning."

Nick shut the door and stepped away from the SUV.

Rod could feel himself sinking into blackness. "Never thought I'd say this to you, baby, but you better step on it." The tires squawked as the SUV leaped forward. And the blackness descended.

"Where is that doctor?" Meg limped around the waiting room, darting glances toward the hallway, wishing the surgeon would appear. Yet another glance at her watch showed the time five minutes later than the last time she checked. And an hour beyond the time expected for the surgery to last.

The early reports showed nothing vital hit. No major organs involved. Were the injuries worse than the preliminary report had showed? If the doctor didn't show soon, Meg would slip past the old harridan guarding the desk and blackmail a nurse or intern into ferreting information from the surgical suite.

"Shall I storm the operating room?" Josh stood, one shoulder against the wall near the doorway, watching Meg pace.

She rounded on him, her teeth bared. "Don't tempt me. They should have been finished an hour ago."

"Meg, you need to sit down and put the ice pack back on your knee." Madison tugged on her hand. "Otherwise, Rod might mistake me for you and try to kiss me."

Meg threw herself into the chair beside her sister with a snort. "Nick would pound Rod's face in the dirt. Then I would have to kill Nick and he's sort of growing on me."

Josh grinned. "Well if you want to keep Kelter's ugly mug untarnished, sit down and chill."

She threw another sullen glance at her brother, but remained still as Madison repositioned the ice pack. She didn't know how much longer she could wait. The tension made her skin feel too tight and her lungs refused to fully inflate.

She fumed over the loss of her laptop. What she wouldn't give right now for access to her word processing program. She needed to write the evening's events down for Ethan and the *Gazette* and fill in the manuscript's holes with the pieces Kyle had provided.

An overwhelming sadness blanketed her. So much pain for Ty, such a senseless assault on Sherri, then her murder and her mother's death. Her head feeling too heavy to hold up any longer, Meg leaned against the back of the lounge couch, eyes closed. Mountains of heartache because of Kyle's push for power and the Senator's ruthless pursuit of a child for his wife. An entire family destroyed by selfishness and greed.

A renewed determination surged within Meg. Sherri's book begged to be finished. Her hopes and dreams, her fight to survive and recover could inspire other assault victims. Her voice deserved to be heard. The *Gazette* deadlines, however, were relentless. She wondered if she could persuade Ruth to stay on for another month, just long enough for Meg to finish the rough draft.

"Meg." Madison nudged her. "I think that's the surgeon who worked on Rod."

She sat up, her gaze focusing on the scrub-clad silver-haired man listening to an animated discourse by the desk battleaxe. Her beady eyes speared Meg with poisoned glances.

Meg's lips curled. Battleaxe did not want to get into it with her about desk-side manners right now. She wasn't in the mood to play nice.

Josh straightened away from the wall, his gaze fixed on her. "Keep a lid on it, Meg. Don't make me have to do something we'll both regret."

"So stay out of my way."

He took a step toward her. "I'm serious, Megan." His voice dropped to a growl. "Don't put me or yourself in a situation we'll have to deal with in an official capacity.

You won't do Kelter any good if you're barred from the hospital."

Meg slid her foot from the chair. The ice pack landed on the floor with a soft thud as she stood. The surgeon burst into laughter and turned toward the waiting room. The battleaxe scowled at his retreating back.

The surgeon's gaze zeroed in on Meg, his smile broad. "You must be the infamous Cahill woman."

She shrugged. "I'm Megan Cahill."

"I'm Ben Chase. I operated on your friend. Why don't you come with me, Ms. Cahill. Detective Kelter left instructions for me to update you after the surgery."

Butterflies tumbled in a chaotic frenzy in her stomach as she followed the doctor from the waiting room. Battleaxe sniffed in disdain as they passed the desk. Meg supposed she ought to be grateful the woman didn't work on Rod's floor or Josh might have to keep her penned in the room.

The doctor led Meg to a room with a small couch and two chairs. He motioned her to one of the chairs and sat in the other. "Detective Kelter is in recovery. I'll have an aide take you to him in a few minutes." He grinned. "Someone other than the Battleaxe."

Heat suffused her cheeks. "She told you that, huh?"

Chase chuckled. "I've worked with her for twenty years and never seen her that incensed."

"She wouldn't tell me anything and didn't bother to check with anyone when I asked for updates."

"Asked?"

"Okay. Maybe I demanded information, but I tried to be nice the first few times."

Chase laughed as he patted her hand. "Congratulations, Ms. Cahill. You're the first person to ever rattle the Battleaxe. And, yes, we call her that too. Now about your young man. Our first assessment of Detective Kelter was right on the money. No major organs hit. He needed a couple pints of blood, but his counts are good now. His blood pressure has stabilized. He'll be limping for a few weeks until that leg heals, but he should recover with no residual effects from either of his wounds."

"That's great news." The tension in Meg's body dissipated, leaving her weak, almost dizzy.

"Would you like to see him now?"

She smiled so hard her face hurt. "Please."

"Remember, the anesthesia might make him say some interesting things. It hits some people harder than others. I'll send the aide out to the waiting room to get you in a couple of minutes. In the meantime, you can update the rest of the folks waiting for word on him."

Meg limped along the tile floor after the perky aide who guided her down the large aisle dividing the recovery room. She wondered about all the different medical equipment. Long, dense material curtains divided each area to provide a sense of privacy for patients and their families. Nurses moved with efficiency, monitoring the vitals of the six patients currently occupying the recovery room. Their quiet conversations with family members and patients gave Meg a sense of calm, a soothing change from the tension of the last few hours.

The aide showed Meg to the last bay. Rod lay with the head of his bed slightly raised, hooked to various machines, an IV in his hand. She drew in a deep breath. Though pale and utterly still, he looked so good to her. She blinked away tears stinging her eyes and moved to his side.

She picked up his hand and held it between both of hers.

He drew in a deep breath, opened his eyes. "Meg." Relief burned in his gaze. "You okay?" His voice, though weak, sent warmth zinging through her veins.

"I'm supposed to ask you that, Kelter. You're the one lying down on the job." Tears misted her vision and spilled down her cheeks, despite the smile curving her mouth.

"Don't, baby." His hand squeezed hers. "Come here." He tugged her toward him.

She moved closer, though a little reluctant. All the wires and meds intimidated her. "I don't want to hurt you."

He gave a small smile. "Can't. Drugged up too much. Better take advantage while you have the chance."

Meg laid her cheek alongside his for a moment and thought about what could have happened. The ride down the ridge and into town seemed to take hours though the clock showed twenty minutes. The sirens and lights shortened the journey, but she'd never been more afraid than when she couldn't rouse him. "If you ever scare me like that again, I'll shoot you myself."

He pressed her hand. "I hear you."

For the next couple of hours in recovery, Meg alternated between standing by Rod's side and sitting in a nearby chair while nurses checked vital signs and administered pain medication.

One of the nurses noticed Meg limping to the chair. "Are you in pain?"

Rod's gaze, almost clear of the effects of anesthesia, zeroed in on hers. "Meg? Did he hurt you?" His heart monitor registered a faster beat.

"Settle down over there, hot shot. My knee hurts from hitting the stairs. I had an ice pack on it before I came to you."

"The doctor checked you?"

"Yes. Just a few bruises."

"Hmm." The nurse checked Rod's IV. "Sounds like you have a story."

"Two goons kidnapped me. Super Cop got shot rescuing me."

The nurse's eyes widened. "You're Megan Cahill, the newspaper lady. I heard the local radio station talking about the search for you. I'm glad you're all right."

"Me, too," Rod said softly.

A quiet tap sounded on the open door. Rod glanced at Meg, sprawled in the chair next to his bed, sleeping. She didn't stir. Good. "Come in," he said in a subdued tone. The door swung inward.

Serena Blackhawk peeked around the edge and smiled at him. Her gaze fell on her sister. Her expression softened. "How long has she been asleep?"

"About two hours."

Serena came further into the room, carrying a laptop computer and a gym bag. "Ethan said he was finished with Meg's computer. I thought she might like to have it."

"What's in the gym bag?"

She set the computer and bag on the floor near the window. "Clothes for you and Meg. Ethan stopped by your house on the way to the station and picked up a few things for you."

"Knew it was a good idea to give him a key to my house." Rod nodded at Meg. "Think you can convince her to go home and rest?"

Serena shook her head. "Why waste my breath? You should know by now she won't go home until she's ready." A tiny smile curved her lips. "I don't blame her. If it were Ethan in that bed, I wouldn't leave him either."

"Talking about me behind my back, love?" Ethan's tall frame filled the doorway, his warm gaze focused on his wife.

Even in profile, Rod couldn't miss the love-filled expression on Serena's face. He grinned at his boss. Ethan Blackhawk was one lucky man. Rod's gaze drifted across to Meg's beautiful face, the mirror image of Serena's. His heart squeezed. After he lost Erin, he never thought he would feel that same kind of love for another woman. But Megan Cahill had surprised him. The prickly, take-no-prisoners newspaper editor had stormed her way into his heart and captured it. Did she know?

Serena's soft laughter drew Rod's attention. She slipped into the shelter of her husband's arms, her face beaming.

Rod rolled his eyes. Those two should have taken a longer honeymoon. "Should I limp out of the room?"

Ethan chuckled and approached Rod's bedside, Serena still tucked next to his side. "You look pretty good for a guy who went two rounds with a Ruger and lost."

"Didn't move fast enough." His quiet laughter morphed into a groan as he pressed against the ache in his side.

Meg jerked awake with a gasp. "Rod? Are you okay?" She clutched his hand.

"I'm fine. Sorry, babe, but it hurts to laugh." He threaded his fingers through hers. "How do you feel?"

"Like I've spent some time in a car trunk." She pushed strands of hair away from her face and nodded at Ethan and Serena. "Hey, guys."

"You are an amazing woman, Megan Cahill," Ethan said, a broad grin forming on his face.

"Yeah? Why do you say that?"

"Know many hostages who get the best of their captors? Kyle has a concussion. The FBI picked up the two guys who kidnapped you. One man's eye is swollen shut and the other has a fat lip." He laughed. "I wouldn't want to meet you in a dark alley without full riot gear, honey."

Serena held out her hand to Meg. "Let me treat you to a Coke and something to eat, Meg. You haven't eaten anything since you arrived."

Meg's eyes narrowed. "I would kill for chocolate right now." She looked at Ethan. "You'll stay with him."

Rod's lips twitched, not missing her demand. Ethan intimidated a lot of people, but Meg wasn't one of them.

"Yes, ma'am." Ethan's eyes twinkled at Rod.

Meg loosened her grip, but Rod wouldn't let go. She turned to him, eyebrows high. "Problem?"

"Forgot something, didn't you?" At her quizzical look, he reached up and tugged her close. He pressed a gentle kiss to her lips before forcing himself to release her. Her scarlet cheeks and glare of promised retribution sent a zing of satisfaction down his spine. Yeah, loving this woman was going to be fun.

Meg cleared her throat and stepped back. "Later, Kelter."

After the two women left, Ethan dropped into the chair Meg had vacated. "Does she know?"

"Know what?"

"You're in love with her."

Rod swallowed hard. "Is it that obvious?"

Ethan grinned.

Great. Rod sighed. So much for trying to win her heart slowly. "I haven't told her yet."

The smile faded from his boss's face. "Kyle lawyered up as soon as he regained consciousness."

"Not surprising."

"Probably the wisest move. Won't matter, though. We've got him on the 9-1-1 tape confessing to Sherri's murder."

"What about her mother?"

"Funny thing about that." Ethan folded his arms across his chest. "Jordan called the Sheriff and offered rush service with the FBI lab. When their lab techs analyzed the mother's pillowcase, they found an unknown hair. Care to guess who left his DNA at the crime scene?"

Rod thought through the events of the previous night. He frowned. Kyle never admitted to killing Sherri's mother. Was it an omission on his part or the truth? "From your expression, I'd say it wasn't Kyle. So, who was it?"

"Senator Drake."

"Why did he kill her?"

"He found out she was going to give Ty his birth mother's name as a last gift from Sherri."

"How? Did she call and tell him?"

Ethan shook his head. "When I confronted him with the evidence, he finally admitted that he'd called Mrs. King to check on her. He was worried about how she was holding up after Sherri's death. She volunteered the information. The Senator said he did it to protect Ty."

Rod scowled. "He killed Mrs. King to protect himself and his secret."

"That's the way the FBI sees it."

"So the feds have jurisdiction now?"

"I doubt they'll get him to trial, but Jordan's welcome to the Senator. I wanted Sherri's killer. How long did the doctor say you would be out of commission?"

"He won't release me for duty until after the first of the year. I'll probably get out of here in a few more days, though. Maybe I can convince him to let me come back for half days or something if you need me."

"Don't push it, Rod. Nick and I will split the shift and cover it until you're back on your feet."

He grinned. "Serena might not like that."

"What won't I like?" Serena stepped into the room with Megan on her heels.

"Your new husband working overtime until after the end of the year."

Serena laughed, her gaze resting on Ethan's face. "Overtime? Ethan's job is 24/7 year-round. If I get too lonesome at night, I'll ride along with him on patrol or take a midnight snack to his office. I knew what I was getting into before I married him."

His gaze locked with Meg's. Would she be able to handle the potential dangers of his job? Erin had never said a word about his choice of career. He remembered, though, the heartfelt kisses and long looks as if she were committing his features to memory in case he didn't return. Would Meg be willing to risk her heart on a cop?

Megan Cahill's beautiful face covered a will of steel. He didn't doubt Meg could take the swing shifts and missed dinners. But would she be willing? Rod held out his hand. Meg sank into the chair next to his bed and clasped his hand in a tight grip.

Ethan stood and draped an arm around Serena's shoulders. "Need anything before we leave, Rod?"

"I'm good. Thanks, Ethan."

He nodded. "I'll check on you tomorrow. See you later, Meg."

Ethan and Serena's footsteps echoed in the hallway. Meg's soft breathing broke the silence that descended on his room. His heart rebelled at the thought of declaring his love for this special woman in as impersonal a setting as this hospital room, especially knowing any moment a nurse was scheduled to take his blood pressure or poke him with another needle.

He studied her face, marveling that just the sight of her sent his heart into an erratic rhythm. Rod noticed her eyeing the laptop case and smiled. "Ethan finished with your computer. You probably should check to make sure everything is on the hard drive."

Her eyes gleamed. "I think I will."

"Maybe you should take it home, babe. You need to rest and you won't get any with hordes of nurses checking me every fifteen minutes."

"It's not a horde. You have one nurse per shift."

He grimaced. "Yeah? You sure? Maybe somebody cloned her because I'm telling you she shows up every few minutes to keep me from sleeping."

Meg grinned. "You're grumpy, Kelter. Sounds like you need a nap."

"So do you. Meg, I know you're exhausted. I'm not going anywhere and all the bad guys are in jail. Go home and get some sleep." He grinned. "When you come back tomorrow morning, sneak some real food and Serena's coffee in here."

Meg shook her head. "No way am I leaving you here alone with the night nurse. She has a thing for red-haired super cops."

He frowned at her. "Meg."

Her grip tightened on his hand. "Get over it, Kelter. I'm staying. I'll go home when you leave this place."

He took a breath to argue with her and realized it would be a waste of air. He'd seen that determined, stubborn look often enough over the last few days to recognize the glint of steel in her eye. He'd be better off getting out of the hospital as soon as possible.

Right on schedule, the night nurse sailed in and checked his vitals again. "Looks good, Detective Kelter. You'll be out of here before you know it." She handed him a small white paper cup with a couple of pills in it. "Pain meds." After he swallowed them, the nurse took the empty cup and tossed it in the trash. She grabbed her cart and headed for the door. "Call me if you need anything."

Meg retrieved her laptop and scooted her chair closer to the bed. While the laptop booted, she glanced at him. "Go to sleep. I have work to do." She smiled. "Don't worry. I'll protect you from the overzealous night crew."

Rod snorted, but closed his eyes and let the medicine take him under to the sound of her clicking keyboard. Periodically throughout the night, he would wake and scan the darkened room. Each time, sensing he was awake, she reached over, squeezed his hand and repeated the same thing. "Everything's okay, babe. Go back to sleep."

CHAPTER TWENTY-FIVE

Rod swam up through the murky darkness to consciousness and forced his eyelids open. Bars of sunlight streamed through the blinds, highlighting the gold glints of Megan's hair as she steadily typed on her laptop keyboard. "Hey."

Her blue gaze jumped from her screen to lock with his. A smile curved her mouth, color rising in her cheeks. "How are you?"

A tide of mischievousness swept through him. He struggled to keep his expression blank. "Not so good, Cahill." Worry shadowed her face and Rod smothered the guilt that he'd caused her more pain. He planned to fix it.

Meg rose, placed the laptop on the seat she'd vacated and moved to his side. "What's wrong? Do I need to call the nurse?"

He smiled, his hand cupping the nape of her neck, and urged her closer. "Depends. Should I call her to kiss me?"

She frowned. "Not if she wants to stay out of the ER as a patient."

"You don't play well with others?" Rod teased.

"I never learned to share."

"Me either," he whispered.

The touch of her lips sent all other thoughts from his head until a knock sounded on his door. Rod reluctantly allowed her to move away though he retained possession of her hand and turned his attention to the doctor grinning at him from the doorway.

"You're looking much better than the last time I checked on you, Detective." Chase paused at his bedside. "The night nurse tells me you had excellent care all night." He smiled at Megan. "I take it you didn't sleep at all last night, young lady."

A rosy blush stained her cheeks. "No, sir."

"You know, we do have an excellent nursing staff, aside from the Battleaxe. You need to let the nurses earn their wages."

Rod's gaze swung from his doctor to Meg. "Who's the Battleaxe?"

Meg's cheeks flushed an even deeper scarlet. "I'll explain later."

"Your young man is out of danger, Ms. Cahill. The best thing you can do for him right now is take care of yourself. So, as his physician, I'm telling you to go home and get some rest."

"Need a ride, Meg?" Nick Santana eased into the room, Madison's hand clasped in his.

"What are you doing here?" Meg asked, shutting down her computer.

"Ethan sent us over to keep tabs on Rod."

She froze. "Is he still in danger?"

Nick snorted. "Ethan wants to make sure he doesn't check himself out of this joint before he's mended."

"Hey," Rod said, irritation coloring his tone. "I'm still conscious here." Under normal circumstances, he didn't like people keeping tabs on him, but he'd make an exception for Meg. And despite Nick's assertion about keeping him in the hospital to heal, he knew with a glance that his co-worker was armed and the gun wasn't to keep him in his bed.

"You'll stay with her, won't you, Madison?" Rod asked.

"Sure." She pulled out her car keys.

"But what about the knitting store, Maddie?" Meg asked. "You need to open the store in a few hours."

Madison shrugged. "Del can handle it for a few hours. We're usually pretty slow on Mondays." She took the laptop from Meg. "I can use a few hours of downtime myself. I bought a new pattern I want to try."

"And you just happen to have it with you."

She patted the bag on her shoulder. "Knitting is a great way to pass the time in a hospital."

"I should have known." Shaking her head, Meg turned to Rod, leaned down and brushed her lips against his. "Rest. No parties, no sneaking out." She turned to Nick. "If he has so much as one new scratch on him when I return, you will answer to me."

Her brother-in-law grinned at her. "I'll take care of him, Meg."

Satisfaction bloomed in Rod's gut. Meg had kissed him in front of her family without any prompting from his direction. Maybe, just maybe, this beautiful woman felt at least something for him. "Same goes, Cahill. Rest. No parties, no sneaking out."

She grinned, waved and was gone.

"Well," Chase said with evident satisfaction. "I know how to clear out a room." He eyed Nick. "You here for the duration?"

He nodded. "Orders from the police chief."

"How soon can I get out of here, Doc?" Rod asked.

Chase chuckled. "Your boss, Blackhawk, warned me you wouldn't be a good patient. Maybe a couple more days, Detective, if you rest, let your body heal. I'll check in on you later."

Rod speared Nick with a knowing glance as the door closed behind the doctor. "Okay, spill it, Santana. Why do I need an armed guard in my room?"

"Precaution." Nick moved the chair Meg had been occupying to the end of Rod's bed. "Ethan released Ty a few minutes ago."

Rod noted Nick positioning himself so he could see the door and intercept any threat coming from the hallway. He couldn't imagine Ty trying to take him out now. He knew his friend was angry and hurting, but the tide of emotions should have centered on his brother and father.

Or Meg. His eyes narrowed. Meg's friendship with Sherri and her research into the book led to the series of events culminating in Sherri's murder. Even flat on his back, Rod could protect himself if he had his firearm. Meg couldn't. "You should be with Meg. I can take care of myself." His heart hammered against the wall of his chest. Had he sent her home into renewed danger, unprotected?

Nick shook his head, humor sparkling in his eyes. "Ethan's orders are for me to ride herd on you. Josh gets the unenviable job of keeping an eye on my intrepid sister-in-law." He slipped off his jacket, leaving his shoulder holster visible and his 40-caliber pistol within easy access.

Rod relaxed. Good. No one would get to Meg without going through Josh first, and that Army soldier was one formidable obstacle. "Tell me what's been happening around town while I've been laid up."

"You've only been out of circulation 24 hours, Rod. No heists or kidnappings other than yours and Meg's. In fact, it's been almost boring." He settled back in the chair, his attention focused on the door. "I arrested the dude who held up Hank's."

"Yeah? Who was it?"

"Dean Simmons."

Rod frowned. "Name doesn't sound familiar. He been in trouble with the law somewhere else?"

"Nope. He's never even had a ticket in his life."

"What's his story?"

"Got laid off from the car plant a few months ago. Can't find another job and his wife refused to move so he could look for work. She wouldn't leave her mother and grandmother. One of the kids ended up in the hospital with appendicitis and they don't have medical insurance any more. The bills rose too high. He got desperate."

"Oh, man. Was he armed?"

"Black water pistol. Ethan's talking to the prosecutor, trying to get him and his family some help."

A knock and the door swung open. Ty Drake stood in the doorway. Exhaustion hung on his body like a second skin. "May I come in?"

Nick surged to his feet, placing his body squarely between Rod and the doorway. Eyes on the newcomer, he said, "Your call, Rod."

"It's okay, Nick. Come on in, Ty." He studied his friend's demeanor as he trudged into the hospital room. He still looked dazed, as if he couldn't quite grasp the revelations that had shattered his world in the last two days.

Rod waved Ty to the chair sitting at the foot of his bed. "How are you holding up?"

He sank onto the edge of the seat. "Do you really care?"

"I wouldn't ask if I didn't."

Ty turned his head and stared pointedly at Nick. "Can't you step outside?"

Nick shook his head. "Not going to happen."

A stunned expression dawned on his face. "You think I would hurt him?"

"What do you want, Ty?" Rod turned Ty's attention back to him and steeled himself for a diatribe of anger and bitterness, railing that if he'd left well enough alone, Ty wouldn't have lost everything and everyone in his life.

Ty dragged his gaze away from the other detective and focused his shadowed gaze on Rod. "I wanted you to know I appreciate your determination to find Sherri's rapist. She deserved better treatment than either he or I gave her." He swallowed visibly. "I know I didn't make your job easy." His gaze speared Rod's. "I had no idea about Kyle or the Senator. I think I would have done the right thing and turned them in if I had known."

Rod noted the change in Ty's naming of Drake. No longer his father, but the Senator. Yet another sign of his shattered world.

"I don't blame you for what happened, Rod. You were the best kind of friend, one who didn't turn aside when things got ugly. You did your job no matter what the obstacles, and I realize now you did the right thing."

"What's next for you, Ty?"

"I want to get away from here, from the memories."

Rod understood the need to run. He'd wanted to sell the house after he lost Erin and Kayla, but couldn't let go of memories or them. "You'll have to stick around for the trial."

"I know, but after that, I want to move away from here. Get a fresh start."

Rod didn't know how receptive Ty was at the moment, but he had to try. "You can't run from yourself. I know. I tried it." His lips curled. "Even at the bottom of a bottle, I was still there. The change has to start with you. Otherwise, you'll end up doing the same things the same way and getting the same result. You."

Ty watched him, his brows knitting. "You've really changed, haven't you?

"I'm a work in progress."

"It's Meg, isn't it? She's changing you." He frowned. "Sherri tried to change me, too. It didn't work. I guess I didn't want it to work. Maybe I didn't love her enough."

"The difference in me isn't because of Meg." Not totally, anyway. "I had to make the changes for myself, Ty."

Nick leaned one shoulder against the wall, his arms across his chest. "We've all been where you are."

"You have a family closet full of murderers and human traffickers?" Bitterness echoed in his tone. "A career teetering on the edge of nonexistence?"

"I'm not talking about your family. This is about you and the choices you face. Do you still want to be known as the guy whose adoptive family made some big mistakes, the one whose wife was raped and murdered?"

"No, of course not."

"Then quit wallowing in the past, in other people's mistakes, in your own mistakes."

On the rolling table, Rod's cell phone rang, breaking the silence. Nick reached over and handed him the phone. "Kelter."

"Detective Kelter, this is Julie Simms. You said I could call if I needed anything."

His hand tightened on the phone. "Are you all right? Your family's okay?"

"We're fine, detective, thank you. I told my husband and daughters about the baby."

Rod's gaze shot to the "baby's" face. "Okay."

"We've all prayed about it and we feel it would be better to meet him in person before the trial begins."

"There may not be one." Not if the Senator's lawyer stalled long enough. He'd most likely die before a trial could begin.

"But we won't escape the media coverage, regardless. Isn't that right?"

Even though Meg had worked hard to avoid revealing Julie's identity, the chance of the other media extending the same courtesy was next to nil. "Yes, ma'am."

"I want to meet my son without the media as witnesses. Can you arrange that?"

"If he's willing. Let me see what I can work out. Call me back in a few minutes."

"Thank you, Detective Kelter. Please tell him how much we'd love to meet him."

Kelter ended the call, his gaze still on Ty's face. Would he be willing to meet his birth mother after all the disappointment with his adoptive family? "Ethan told you about the circumstances of your adoption?"

Ty's face twisted. "Yeah. My birth mother thought she gave me up for adoption and knew nothing about the money."

"She knows now. She's asking to meet you. Are you willing?"

Ty leaned forward, his gaze intent. "You're serious? She wants to meet me?"

Rod indicated his phone. "She's the one who called me to set this up."

"How do you know about my birth mother?"

"I interviewed her a few days ago, tracking down some leads on your, uh, the Senator."

"Why didn't she try to find me before now?"

"It's better if you ask her. But I will tell you that her husband only found out about you in the last few days. She had you when she was very young, before she met her husband."

"And he's okay with this?" Ty looked skeptical.

"The whole family wants to meet you."

"Family?" He sat up. "I have brothers or sisters?"

Rod grinned. "Sisters, one with a child on the way. You're going to be an uncle soon."

A small smile appeared on Ty's lips as he rose from the chair. "An uncle."

"Are you willing to meet with them?"

"Yeah. Why not? I think Sherri would have liked me to meet them. How will you arrange the meeting?"

Rod considered the options and settled for the most logical choice. "Your birth mother is supposed to call in a few minutes. Would you like to talk to her and arrange the details yourself?"

He shrugged, but Rod noted the interest growing in his friend's eyes.

Rod's cell phone rang again. He glanced at the caller ID, smiled and pressed the talk button. "Hello, Mrs. Simms. Your son, Ty, is standing about two feet away from me. Would you like to talk to him?" He pulled the phone away from his ear and extended his hand to his friend. "Your mother, Julie Simms, is very anxious to talk to you."

A short time later, Ty left Rod's room, a smile on his face and a spring in his step for the first time since Sherri's murder.

"Are they good people?" Nick asked.

"The stepfather pastors a church in Knoxville, but I didn't get a chance to meet him. Julie's a fine woman, strong, compassionate. After her initial concern about her husband and church, she focused on Ty and what he'd been through."

"I think Sherri would have been pleased to know that."

CHAPTER TWENTY-SIX

The End. Meg stared at the final words of Sherri's story, a wealth of emotion roiling through her. She saved the document, an overwhelming sense of relief flooding her, followed by sadness and loss. In a sense, she had delayed grieving too much over Sherri's death by plunging into the manuscript. In the pages of typed text, Sherri still lived. After many days spent reminiscing and making sense of Sherri's tragic loss, reality loomed. A reality of missed holidays, birthdays and phone calls because of the death of her friend.

Meg closed the word processing program and shut down her computer with a sense of finality. Oh, she still needed to edit the 80,000-word document, but that skill required a different part of her brain. The creative side, the side where she spent so much of her time in the two weeks since her abduction and rescue, was no longer needed. Now the analytical part of her brain would rake through every word, discarding passive verbs, infusing life with active verbs.

Car doors slammed outside. Meg glanced at the clock on her kitchen wall. 6:30. She smiled. She had to hand it to the handsome detective. He was always prompt, now that he was on medical leave from the police department.

She opened the door before the Big Ben chimes finished ringing. Meg stared at the bookcase sitting on her front porch. Ethan and Josh climbed the stairs with another bookcase balanced between them. "What's this?"

"We're just the delivery men. Where do you want them?" Ethan asked.

"Uh, I guess the living room."

"Have you culled through your book collection since last week?" Josh scowled. "You'll need to clear a path if you haven't. I'm not about to spend my first Christmas at home in years laid up in a hospital with a broken bone."

Heat flamed in Meg's cheeks. "Give me a minute." She hurried into the living room, grabbed stacks of books and carried them to the kitchen table. She cleared enough room for the men to maneuver and waved them inside.

By the time they finished, four floor-to-ceiling bookcases stood tall as sentinels against her walls. "Wow." Meg fought to keep her mouth from hanging open. "Who bought these for me? They're a perfect fit. They even match the furniture."

"You'll have to ask our third man." Ethan nodded toward the open door.

Rod leaned against the doorjamb, arms crossed over his chest. "Do you like them?"

"On that note, I'm out of here. Come on, Ethan." Both men eased past Rod into the cold night.

He shut the door and turned to face her. "Do you like them, Meg?"

Something in his voice told Meg the answer meant a lot to him. "They're beautiful, perfect. Where did you get them?"

"Rod's workshop."

"You made them? For me?" Her eyes narrowed. "When? You were supposed to be resting."

"I started on the bookcases after I came to your house the first time." He held his hand up. "And before you decide I'm criticizing your housekeeping skills, I realize someone with your job needs a lot of research material. I thought you could locate information easier with a place to organize the resources." He grinned. "Besides, I was climbing the walls with so much silence and enforced rest. I worked on all the pieces separately, then asked Ethan to help me put them together in the final form."

Meg crossed the room and stepped into his open arms. "Thank you, Rod. I appreciate the practicality of your gift, but the fact that you made those bookcases means even more. So, is this my Christmas gift?" She pulled back to smile up at him.

"Part of it." He shifted his weight off his injured leg, as if uncomfortable.

Meg flushed. "I'm sorry, Rod. I wasn't thinking. Please, come sit down."

He sank onto the denim-colored couch beside her and enfolded her hand between his. "I'm not very good at expressing myself sometimes, Meg. Not like you are. So I probably won't do this right."

Meg pushed a stray lock of red hair from his forehead. He'd allowed it to grow longer than his usual military cut while off duty. She liked the extra length and her fingers itched to run through the red strands. "Just talk to me, Kelter."

"After I lost Erin and Kayla, I didn't think I would ever be interested in another woman. I guess my heart has been frozen."

A cold knot formed in the pit of Meg's stomach. Was he going to end their relationship? Did he not care enough about her to try?

He cast a sidelong glance at her, his lips twitching. "At least, it was frozen until a smart-mouthed editor became a key witness in my case and torched all the barriers I built."

"Hey!" Meg scowled. "Smart-mouthed?" She wrinkled her nose and the scowl morphed into a grin. "All right. You got me. I resemble that characterization."

"I've gotten very attached to that editor." His blue eyes focused on her. "Somehow, she burrowed inside my heart so deep, I'll never get her out. I don't want to let her go because I've discovered in the last two weeks that I'm in love with her."

A broad smile blossomed across Meg's mouth. "I'm glad to hear you say that because the editor is madly in love with the detective who nearly died protecting her."

Rod reached into his pocket and pulled out a velvet-covered box. "I wasn't sure if you would toss me out on my ear because of the bookcases, so I spent the afternoon scouring the jewelry store for the perfect ring, something unique."

He slipped a gold ring out of the box and slid the ring on Meg's finger. Breath caught in her throat. Reflected firelight danced on the surface of the emerald solitaire.

"Marry me, Meg."

She threw her arms around his neck and hugged him close. "Yes. The sooner, the better."

He pulled back, a stunned expression on his face. "Are you serious?"

"About accepting your proposal or the timing?"

"The timing."

She traced his lips with her fingertip. "Dead serious. You don't exactly have the safest job in the world."

"But don't you want a big church wedding with all the trappings and publicity?"

Meg shuddered. What a nightmarish thought. "I had enough of the society wedding glitz with Serena and Ethan's extravaganza last month. I have no desire to replicate that hoopla. I want something simple, private. Definitely no media blitz."

His dark gaze searched hers. "What about my job? Can you live with my career?"

Meg held up her hand with his engagement ring. "I wouldn't have accepted this if I couldn't deal with your job. No one has a guarantee of tomorrow."

He dropped a brief kiss on her lips. "And I don't want to come home to an empty house anymore."

Meg tilted her head. "So what are we going to do about it?"

Twenty-four hours later, sweat dotted Rod's forehead despite the thirty-degree temperature at Aaron and Liz Cahill's back door. The small hand clasped in his gripped harder.

He turned to Meg, gaze slicing through the darkness, thoughts of escape foremost in his mind.

"Are you regretting what we did?"

"No, not for one minute."

"Then why do you look like you want to cut and run?"

A weak laugh escaped. "Maybe because that's exactly how I feel." He pulled her close, marveling at how right she felt in his arms, wondered if he would survive the next few minutes. "I'm counting the hours until we catch our flight." Rod rested his chin on the top of her head. "You have to admit, though, we're doing this backwards."

"Everything will be fine. Trust me."

He closed his eyes a moment. Meg didn't understand. He faced interrogation by four men inside the Cahill home. No matter that he counted two of them close friends. Her father was inside, waiting beside her brother. None of them knew. Would they understand or approve? If not, he had fences to mend. Not a great position when facing four formidable men. He wasn't sure whether to expect a blessing or a blasting.

A sense of doom forced words from his throat. "I love you, Megan."

She laughed softly, her breath misting in the night air. "Sounds like you expect a firing squad."

He hoped the next few minutes passed with a less painful end. "Might as well get this over with. My leg is stiffening up from the cold." Rod reached around Meg and opened the door into the dimly lit kitchen.

Meg breezed past him. "Hey, where is everybody?"

"In the living room, sugar." Liz Cahill's voice sounded muffled. "We're putting up the Christmas tree—an artificial one."

"I've brought someone I want you to meet." Meg threw him an impish grin.

He rolled his eyes, but remained silent. This was her show. Maybe, just maybe, if she did this right, he would get out of this house with his skin intact.

She threaded her fingers through his and drew him down the hallway to the living room. Seven pairs of eyes focused on him. Their expressions ranged from curious to puzzled. The only pair of eyes he focused on belonged to Aaron Cahill.

"What's going on, Meg?" Josh turned from the tree, topper in hand.

Meg grinned, beaming at her family. "I'd like you to meet Rodney Kelter, my husband."

Stunned silence greeted her announcement. Rod held his breath, waiting, sweating.

Serena broke the tension-filled quiet first. "Congratulations!" Smiling, she enveloped Meg in a hug, released her, and turned to Rod. "Welcome to the Cahill clan, Rod. We already felt like you were one of us. This makes it official."

"Thanks." Rod remained stiff in her embrace, eyeing the four men in turn as Madison kissed him on the cheek before enfolding Meg in a hug. Ethan looked stunned, but he detected no hostility. Nick's grin and wink made him feel he had at least one advocate to plead his case.

His gaze settled on Josh. Though the former soldier's lips were set, his thoughtful expression gave Rod some hope of eventual acceptance from that quarter as well. The knot in his stomach grew as he faced Meg's father and mother. Liz's silvery blond hair reflected the Christmas tree lights as she walked to him.

"This is quite a surprise." Liz took both of his hands in hers. "We've gotten to know you well these last few months, Rod. You're a man of integrity, one I respect." She squeezed his hands briefly and released them.

"I appreciate that, Mrs. Cahill."

"Please, it's Liz."

Aaron Cahill stepped up beside his wife and drew Meg into his arms. "You certainly caught us by surprise, sweetheart."

"I know, Dad. You're not mad?"

"No. I'm concerned, though." He shifted his gaze to Rod. "We love this young woman. God gave her and her sisters to us and we consider all three of our girls a gift from Him. I expect you to value my daughter and treat her with the respect and honor she deserves."

"I will, sir. You have my word on that."

Aaron's gaze grew intense. "Becoming a husband doesn't automatically wipe out whatever problems and baggage we come into the marriage with."

Rod's cheeks heated. "I'm aware of that, sir."

"Dad." Meg pulled away from her father. "I walked into this marriage with my eyes open." She slipped her hand into Rod's.

"It's okay, Meg. He has a right to ask." Rod nodded at Aaron. "You're right to be concerned, but I've been honest with Meg about the drinking. I haven't touched any alcohol in months and I've been in counseling for the addiction. Ethan can vouch for me as well as Pastor Lang. I know I'm asking a lot, for you to trust me with your daughter. I can't guarantee I won't mess up. All I can promise is I'll do my best to be the husband Meg needs and deserves."

A small smile appeared on his father-in-law's face. "That's all we can expect." He held out his hand. "Welcome to the family, son."

ABOUT THE AUTHOR

Rebecca Deel is a preacher's kid with a black belt in karate. She teaches business classes at a private four-year college in Nashville, Tennessee. She plays the piano at church, writes freelance articles, and runs interference for the family Westies. She's been married to her amazing husband for more than 20 years and is the proud mom of two grown sons. She delivers monthly devotions to the women's group at her church and conducts seminars in personal safety, money management, and writing. Her articles have been published in *ONE Magazine*, *Contact*, and *Co-Laborer*, and she was profiled in the June 2010 Williamson edition of *Nashville Christian Family* magazine. Rebecca completed her Doctor of Arts degree in Economics and wears her favorite Dallas Cowboys sweatshirt when life turns ugly.

For more information on Rebecca . . .
Sign up for Rebecca's newsletter: http://eepurl.com/_B6w9
Visit Rebecca's website: www.rebeccadeelbooks.com

Made in the USA
Middletown, DE
18 January 2019